CHASING before

Also by Lenore Appelhans

The Memory of After

The Best Things in Death (an e-short story)

CHASING before

Book 2 of the Memory Chronicles

Lenore Appelhans

SIMON & SCHUSTER BFYR
New York London Toronto Sydney New Delhi

SIMON & SCHUSTER BFYR
An imprint of Simon & Schuster Children's Publishing Division
1230 Avenue of the Americas, New York, New York 10020

For information about special discounts for bulk purchases, please contact Simon & Schuster Special Sales at 1-866-506-1949 or business@simonandschuster.com.
The Simon & Schuster Speakers Bureau can bring authors to your live event. For more information or to book an event, contact the Simon & Schuster Speakers Bureau at 1-866-248-3049 or visit our website at www.simonspeakers.com.
Also available in a SIMON & SCHUSTER BFYR hardcover edition
Book design by Lizzy Bromley
The text for this book is set in Janson Text LT Std.
Manufactured in the United States of America
First SIMON & SCHUSTER BFYR paperback edition August 2015
10 9 8 7 6 5 4 3 2 1
The Library of Congress has cataloged the hardcover edition as follows:
Appelhans, Lenore.
Chasing before : book 2 of the memory chronicles / Lenore Appelhans. — 1st edition.
pages cm — (The memory chronicles ; bk. 2)
Summary: Four months after Felicia saved Level 2 from the Morati, corrupted angels who trapped her and her boyfriend Neil in the afterlife, she learns some shocking truths about her life that make her question whether she should continue the fight on Level 3.
ISBN 978-1-4424-4188-0 (hardcover : alk. paper) — ISBN 978-1-4424-4190-3 (eBook)
[1. Future life—Fiction. 2. Death—Fiction. 3. Angels—Fiction.] I. Title.
PZ7.A6447Ch 2014
[Fic]—dc23
2013040677
ISBN 978-1-4424-4189-7 (pbk)

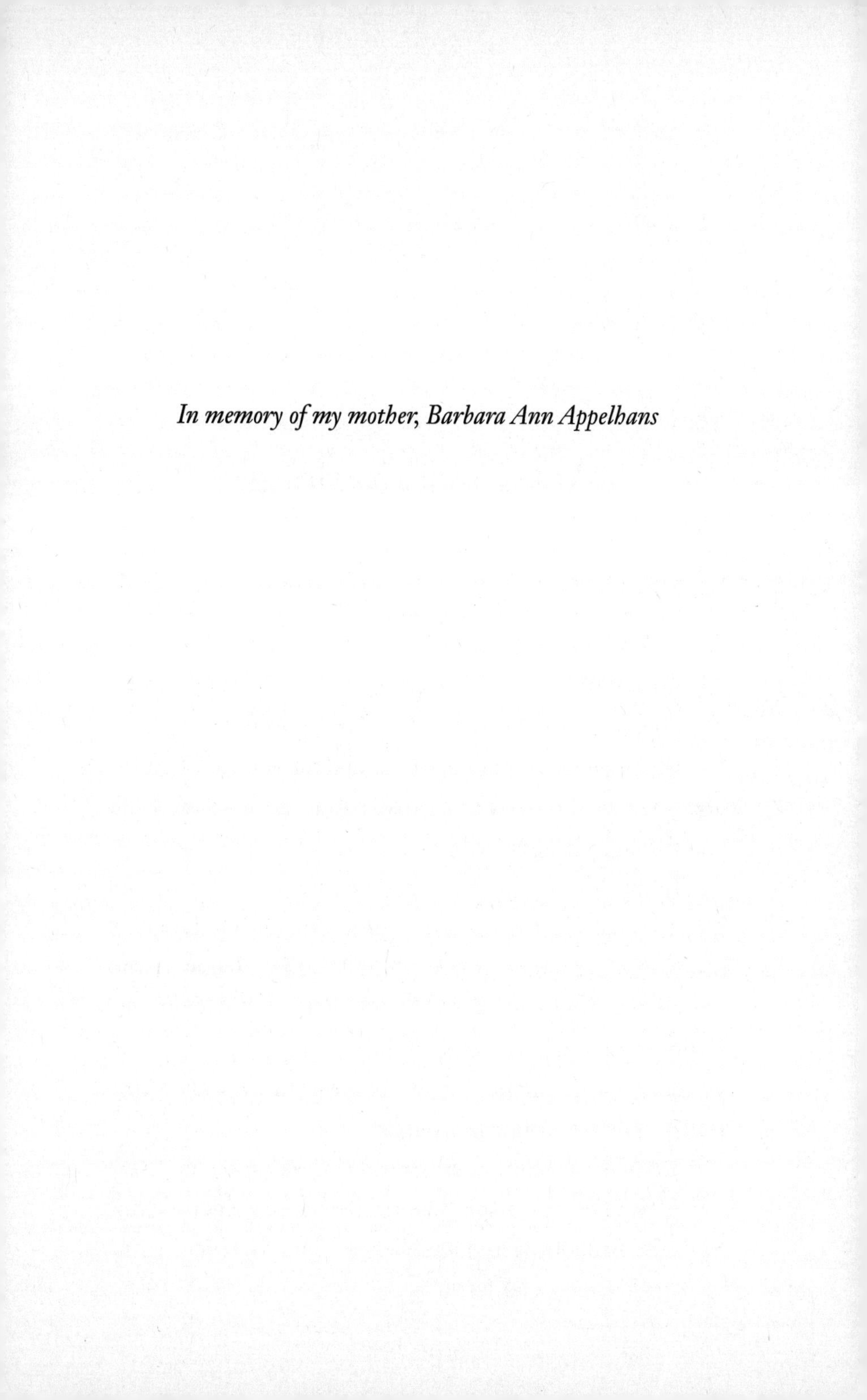

In memory of my mother, Barbara Ann Appelhans

Acknowledgments

CHASING BEFORE owes its existence to the support of a great many talented people. My eternal gratitude:

To my agent, Stephen Barbara, and the team at Foundry. Sorry for all the panicked e-mails and health scares I put you through this past year.

To my editor Christian Trimmer, for adopting me and the novel halfway through the process and raising the stakes in such brilliant ways. To my editor Alexandra Cooper, who shared my vision for the Memory Chronicles from the beginning and whose insight helped shape early drafts. And to Catherine Laudone, for the brainstorming session that led to some major breakthroughs.

To the entire Simon & Schuster team, especially Lizzy Bromley, Venessa Carson, Justin Chanda, Bernadette Cruz, Michelle Fadlalla, Katy Hershberger, Bara MacNeill, Anna

McKean, Jenica Nasworthy, Chrissy Noh, Anthony Parisi, and Angela Zurlo. To the team at Usborne in the UK (Amy Dobson, Rebecca Hill, and Becky Walker). To the team at Listening Library (Jenna Lamia, Fred Sanders, Janet Stark, and Rebecca Waugh), for the amazing audiobook production. And to my other foreign publishers for expanding the book's audience.

To Ann Bonwill (always my first and most enthusiastic reader), Nicole Bonia, Jenny Bragdon, (the brutally honest) Christina Franke, Kelly Jensen, and Lydia Kang, for providing feedback and much needed virtual cupcakes. And to Heather Anastasiu, for so generously beta reading into the wee hours during a tough deadline.

To my author support system: SCBWI Germany/Austria, the Apocalypsies, the Lucky 13s, and the League of Extraordinary Writers. And especially to those who went above and beyond while I was touring: Emily Hainsworth, Antony John, Lauren Morrill, Lauren Oliver, Lissa Price, Beth Revis, Megan Shepard, and Tamara Ireland Stone.

To friends, family, and readers all over the world. Shoutouts to Jamie Bennett, April Conant, Mitali Dave, Linda Joplin, Allison Lamphere, Candace Levy, Karin Perry, Tirzah Price, Beth Shaum, and Melody Simpson, for so fervently spreading the word.

To the indie bookstores that hosted me on tour: Watermark Books in Wichita, Kansas; Mysteryscape in Overland Park, Kansas; Books, Inc. in San Francisco; Malaprops in Asheville, North Carolina; Fountain Bookstore in Richmond, Virginia; Hooray for Books in Alexandria, Virginia; Little Shop of Stories in Decatur, Georgia; Blue Willow Bookshop in Houston; Anderson's Bookshop in Naperville, Illinois; Left Bank Books in Saint Louis; Fundamentals Bookstore in Delaware, Ohio; and Books of Wonder in New York City.

To the doctors, nurses, and staff at the Buergerhospital in Frankfurt, Germany, for saving my life (two days after my revisions were due!) and treating me so well during my hospital stays.

And finally, to Daniel, who understands and accepts that my creative process is best fueled by naps, showers, chocolate, extensive music playlists, and long walks in the park, and who enables me to continue doing what I love every day.

Prologue

I COULDN'T HELP MYSELF. What kind of excuse is that, anyway? It absolves you of personal responsibility. It's not your fault that in a moment of weakness you kissed the boy that your best friend liked. That you foolishly fled the scene of her murder. Or that you hacked your way into an airline's website to book yourself a free plane ticket. But in my case it's true.

It started the day before my thirteenth birthday. The day I almost died and my soul became inexorably linked to the Morati, the angel guardians of Level Two, who hated their assigned jobs as thankless caretakers of the afterlife waiting room, and vowed revenge. Something took root inside me that day. Something evil. And it's been growing ever since.

For the longest time I didn't know it was there. I thought I had control over myself. That my mistakes were my own. When I confessed my dark secrets to Neil, he helped me understand that I needed to forgive myself and move on.

Then on the day before my eighteenth birthday, I died. I ended up in Level Two, recruited for a mission to overthrow the Morati and free the people whose souls they were using as batteries to fuel their war against heaven. Because of my special connection to the Morati, they needed me to break into Level Three. They hooked me up to their mainframe, but instead of helping them, I played my part to bring them down. Or at least I thought I did.

But I now know the truth. Destroying the Morati's machines didn't cut off my link to them—it only made it stronger. I'm a ticking time bomb. And one day soon everything is going to explode.

one

STEPPING THROUGH THE PORTAL out of Level Two is like jumping from the high dive out at the swimming hole. There's a whoosh of air, the exhilarating and slightly terrifying sensation of flying, and then the freezing plunge into murky depths. Unlike when I used to hit the lake water, though, I keep my eyes open, fixed on the hand that Neil holds in a death grip as we spin through an inky blackness.

With a heavy, bone-jarring thud we land on a hard surface, dripping wet and disoriented, but whole. I look up from the white of my knuckles to Neil's face, just in time to see his mouth slacken in shock.

He expected to walk into the Christian vision of heaven—streets paved with gold and cherubs playing harps.

Maybe I did too. Instead twisted, blackened filing cabinets tower over us like angry sentinels. Their deformed bodies line both sides of a narrow passageway.

Already regretting our decision to move on from Level Two, I turn. Behind us is a brick wall, making it clear that there is no going back. In front of us, a few paces away, stands a lone woman, her spotless pale pink blazer and pencil skirt at odds with the soot-covered walls. She hasn't noticed us. She begins to flit about, pulling on the handles of warped steel drawers and kicking at all the burned-edged papers that flutter out and lap at her heels.

I run my free hand down the soggy skirt of my sundress and then bend down to scoop up a charred sheet that has flown in my direction. Though the edges flake off as soon as I touch them, it is obvious this was once a document of great importance. Fancy gold lettering unfurls across buttery-cream linen, like a wedding invitation, but it's not in any language I recognize.

Neil leans over to inspect it too. He shakes his head and mouths, "What happened here?"

I can't imagine it was anything good. I shrug and let the paper fall back to the ground. Neil steps forward, pulling me with him, and the crinkle and crunch under his foot finally alert the woman to our presence.

As she turns, she snaps her fingers. Intense bright light floods into our faces, momentarily blinding us.

"State your names, please," she says in a curt, high-pitched voice that sets me more on edge than I already am.

Once my eyes adjust to the light, the hallway and the woman come back into focus. She clutches a clipboard tight to her chest and peers over at us, her face pinched.

Neil pulls at the collar of his red polo and clears his throat. "Neil Corbet and Felicia Ward."

"Felicia Ward," she says thoughtfully. Her whole demeanor softens, making her look much younger than I thought at first. Though that doesn't mean much in the afterlife, since as far as I know, people are preserved at the age at which they died on Earth. This woman could be a thousand years old and still appear twenty. "I'm Libby." She steps toward me and bows. "It's good you've come. We've been expecting you."

The bowing throws me off. "What do you mean? How could you know I was coming?"

"Ordinarily I'd say it's because you're in our files." She taps her fist against the nearest hunk of metal. "They used to contain the name, birth date, and death date of every human ever born on Earth. When a person ascended from Level Two, his or her card would automatically appear in these cabinets. But the files haven't been useful to us since someone blew up this records room."

Wait a minute. People are blowing things up? Here? But how? I squint at her, overwhelmed. I don't know what to say.

She whistles loudly between two fingers. "Megan! Please turn off the welcome light."

The passage dims, bathing us in the warm, dusky glow of candles. A girl wearing a neon-orange T-shirt dress and kneesocks descends a ladder I didn't notice before. "Sorry," Megan says, showing a mouthful of braces. "But the bright light is absolutely *essential* to the experience." Her delivery is slightly mocking, like she's parroting a phrase she's heard one too many times.

Megan hands us fluffy orange towels, as if she expected us to arrive like drowned rats, and we accept them gratefully, wrapping them around our shoulders.

"Yes," Libby says. "We may have a mess, but we haven't abandoned all our matriculation procedures."

"Does everyone arrive soaked to the bone?" Neil works on drying his hair with the ends of his long towel.

"Every time you cross into a different level, you pass through the Styx River. It's the border between all dimensions." Libby has the polished monotone of a flight attendant.

She spins a desk so that it cuts us off from the rest of the hallway. With a grim smile she scoots the clipboard and a pen across it.

"These forms are our interim solution while we wait for a celestial custodian to deliver updated files. Fill these out, and then we'll take you down to get processed."

I'm too bewildered to ask questions. Libby's request is so simple, and while I get my bearings, I might as well go with the flow. I release Neil's hand reluctantly and pick up the pen to complete the form. It has only two lines: name and age. My name is easy, but my age is more difficult. I could write "seventeen," since that's how old I was when I died. Or I could write "one hundred million," because that's how old I feel after spending so much time in Level Two.

Libby extracts another clipboard from her desk and clamps a sheet of paper and a pen onto it. "There you are, Neil," she says a little too sweetly for my taste. Maybe his reputation as the always perfect, always friendly Boy Scout precedes him as well.

"How do you know who we are?" It comes out more harshly than I intended.

Libby materializes a pencil and uses it to secure her thick, curly reddish-blond hair into a bun. At least I'm familiar with materialization from my time in Level Two. If it works the same way here, all you have to do is call something up in your mind, and it appears, seemingly by magic. Of course, it's only a copy of what you had on Earth, not the real thing. "Everyone who's been arriving from Level Two has been talking about Felicia Ward," Libby says. "It had been years since anyone had come through, and now we get hundreds in every day. They keep telling us the Morati had been holding humans back, and you set things right."

I lift my clipboard to eye level, pretending to get a closer look. "I helped a little, I guess," I mumble.

"Oh, c'mon," Neil says, rubbing my shoulder. "She was so brave." I peek over and see his adoring smile.

"That's good to hear," Libby says. "You must summon that courage again, I'm afraid. The Morati must have slipped in with the crowds and destroyed our files so we wouldn't know they weren't human. Angels are the only ones capable of destroying such celestial creations. And you're the one who ruined their plans. They'll be looking for you."

Me? I shudder and drop the clipboard onto the desk. Of course it makes sense that they'd want revenge, but I honestly thought I was beyond their grasp for good now.

"And if they find you, who knows what they'll do?" Megan adds. Despite her earlier snark, her wide-eyed gaze and the hitch in her voice convey genuine concern in a way that Libby's businesslike tone cannot. "People who die here disappear. No one knows where they go."

If dying in Level Three is the end, I don't even want to contemplate it. Not after I finally found Neil again. Not when I've finally found a measure of happiness. "But I was told that Morati were trapped in Level Two. How could any of them get through?" My information didn't exactly come from the most reliable source. After all, Julian was Morati. He was a Morati aligned with the rebels, and he took my place in the machine to bring the system down, but he was a Morati nonetheless. I have to admit that since then I've thought about Julian's fate far more than I should, and each time it makes me ache. Against all reason, despite all the lies, I miss him. The way he stared at me before he disappeared—determined to protect me—I can't get it out of my head.

Libby shrugs. "I don't know. But the Morati are here."

And when she says it this time, it's like I'm punched in the stomach with the certainty that she's right. I feel them. Not as strongly as I did when I was plugged into their mainframe, but just enough to know that they are indeed somewhere on this level. I can't help hoping Julian is here too.

"How can you be so sure? What about other angels?" Neil asks as he slides his completed form across the desk. I glance at it. Since he has written "eighteen" for his age, I retrieve my form and hastily scrawl eighteen on it too, even if it's not technically true, before letting my clipboard clatter on top of Neil's.

Libby grimaces. "Angels were never assigned here. Humans administrate this level as we see fit. And we only very rarely get visits from celestial custodians. The last time was fifty years ago at least, and that was long before my time. We think the Morati destroyed our files so that we can't verify anyone's identity. We can't track them down."

Neil shuffles his feet. "So you saw fit to have all your records on material that could burn?" There's an annoyed, almost accusatory edge to his voice, but the girls don't seem offended.

"If you can believe it, they used to have rolls of papyrus." Megan rolls her eyes, making me warm to her even more. "Normally the files wouldn't burn. But angels can destroy what angels create."

Libby stands up straighter. In the way she holds her shoulders, rigid but slanted forward like too much responsibility is weighing upon her, Libby reminds me of my mother, someone I was never able to get along with, no matter how hard I tried. Libby retrieves our clipboards, dematerializes the desk, and motions for us to follow her. We pick our way through the long, dark hallway, with Megan trailing behind us. In the dim light the cabinets cast ominous shadows.

I drag my feet, dreading going any closer to Morati hell-bent on getting revenge. There must be some way to find them before they find me. "Couldn't we track them down by searching everyone's memories? That'd verify who they are, right?"

"In most cases, yes," Libby confirms. "But angels and the more powerful humans here can control their memories, showing only what they want to and concealing what they don't. That's why we haven't had any luck finding them yet."

"Careful!" Neil maneuvers me away from a drawer that juts out at a sharp angle, but my foot catches on something, and I trip into his arms, dropping my towel. He's thin, but strong—the steady presence in my life I was missing for most of my death. And for a minute I allow myself to rest on his chest and imagine we are far away from here, that his heart still beats, and that we're still alive.

"Yes, please watch your step." Libby looks back at me over her shoulder with a mixture of envy and pity, but she keeps walking. "The people of Level Three need you."

I pull away from Neil, startled, and hurry after her. "What? Why?" It's totally selfish, but I don't want to be needed—not by anyone other than Neil. I want to be able to figure out what I want, without any pressure. And time with Neil. That's what post-Morati Level Two offered me.

But we became restless, and the lack of privacy, as well as the promise of something exciting just beyond our reach, convinced us to move on. It might turn out to be the biggest mistake of my afterlife.

"You have a ton of potential, Felicia. You were able to bring down the Morati once, and maybe you can do it again. If you develop your skills further, we think you could be the one who can expose the Morati, by looking into their memories and seeing their true selves. And then we can neutralize their threat." We've reached a door, and Libby stops in front of it. "If you survive that long," she says, low enough that Neil doesn't seem to hear it, but I do. Despite my potential she's skeptical of my current value. And I can't say I disagree with her.

Libby turns the knob. "What I've told you is classified, known only to the security force and a few others. If people were aware of the Morati's presence, and that they can blend in with us, people could panic. It would only make our hunt for them more difficult. Please keep this to yourselves." When we nod our assent, Libby throws open the door. Now that we're both completely dry, Megan takes Neil's towel and dematerializes it.

We walk out into a small courtyard bordered on all sides by arched walkways, and with a fountain at its center. I look up and see blue sky. The whole scene is so Earthlike, so real, it makes me want to cry. I can almost imagine I'm home again, that the artificial white surroundings of Level Two were only a long nightmare and I've finally woken up.

Neil peers upward as well, and his eyes shine. He puts his arm around me and draws me close. I rest my head on his shoulder, and his curls brush against my forehead. If time could stand still in this moment, we would be perfectly happy, wrapped up in each other, regardless of what's going on in Level Three.

"Before you go through processing, you can get an idea of the layout of this section of Level Three." Libby waves us over to a sign that features the sort of map I remember from shopping malls, complete with a red dot proclaiming "You are here." "Megan, please do the honors."

Megan grins so widely that sunlight reflects off her braces. "I'd love to!" Her eagerness gives me the impression that Libby doesn't let her do much. "We're in Area Two, also known as the Training Center. Dorms are all between Western Avenue and Western Bridge, which leads to Area One. Oh, and then your classes will be in these buildings here to the east, past Eastern Avenue. The middle corridor includes this central administration building, where Libby's office is, and other important buildings such as the Muse Collection Library. It's all separated by courtyards or lawns until you get farther north." She taps a drawing of a hill. "This is where we have all our assemblies. And then beyond that we have our sports fields. Got it? Or do you have questions?"

I have so many questions, I don't even know where to begin. But Neil blurts, "Why do you still have braces?" It's a good question, if a little rude. We can materialize our appearance to the best version of ourselves, so it is unusual that Megan would keep unnecessary metal in her mouth.

Megan pulls her lips back, like she's at the dentist, revealing a gap between her top front teeth. "When I died, I'd had these on for a whole year. Back then I couldn't wait to get them off. But now they make me feel more like me, you know?"

I understand. I spent most of my time in Level Two in a plain white shift, and I love being able to wear my familiar clothes now.

"Libby says that once I've distanced myself enough from earthly things, I'll be ready to let my braces go, and pin them on the Forgetting Tree." Megan sneaks a glance at Libby. "Detachment is part of my training to be a muse, my chosen career."

"They'll hear about all that soon enough," Libby admonishes. "Give them a chance to settle in first."

"Wait until you see more of the campus." Megan changes the subject and ignores Libby's look of irritation. I appreciate it, because her chatter helps to lower my anxiety level. "We have everything a vocational training center needs. Well, except we don't have a cafeteria, of course. Or bathrooms."

While it would be heavenly to take a long hot shower, I'm not too bummed about the lack of a dining hall. In my book, in the competition for foods I miss the least, cafeteria offerings are up there with those cardboard-like pizza pockets they serve on international flights.

"So we're staying in dorms?" Neil asks. "Aren't there tons of people here? How do you find a place for everyone?"

"Enrollment has been down as a result of the Morati keeping everyone locked up in Level Two for so long," Libby answers. "And most of the trainees we had before that time have long moved on to their afterlife careers. It was mostly just us murder victims until about four months ago, when people were able to move up again."

"That was four months ago?" My head feels fuzzy when I think about time. It never mattered in Level Two, and there was no way to mark it, so I lost my sense for it.

"Yes. It was chaotic that first week, with all the changes we had to make," Libby says. "We have a larger security force now, but most of our population isn't aware what the destruction of the records room means. And like I said, we want to keep it that way."

We're walking again, turning a corner and arriving at a bank of three booths with turnstiles, much like the toll-gates on a major highway. This must be processing. "You go through the center one," Megan says. She explains that the booth on the left is to process children under twelve who return to Earth to be reincarnated, and the booth on the right is for those who died on Earth at age sixty-five or above. The elderly are allowed to take up residence in the senior center in Area Three until the next Ascension Day retirement ceremony, when they can move on to the next level. Both children and the elderly have caretakers until they leave Level Three.

Libby hands our clipboards to the attendant in the center booth, who scrutinizes us briefly and then returns our documents. It's like passport control, only we're entering a whole new world instead of a new country. When the attendant nods us through, Neil and I push forward, followed by Megan and Libby.

Megan steps ahead and leads us around another corner. When I look up, I gasp. Because leaning against a column is the last person I ever thought I'd see again. My former best friend, Autumn.

two

AUTUMN STARES STRAIGHT ahead, her expression blank. I take in her stiff pose, bile rising in my throat as images of her slashed and lifeless body on my bed burst through my skull.

I squeeze my eyes shut for a moment and lean against Neil. He is aware of my horrible betrayal of our friendship—that I caused a snowstorm of bitter feelings by sneaking around with Julian behind her back. He's never met Autumn, of course. She was murdered before I knew him. But he's seen her in my memories of happier times. I told him all about how I was forced to move from Germany to Ohio, mainly because of my poor decisions in the wake of her death.

I picture Autumn at her most alive—on the crest of a

roller coaster at Disneyland Paris, throwing her arms up, doubling over with laughter—and only then do I dare look at her again. She wears a simple black long-sleeved T-shirt and yoga pants. Her blond hair is pulled back into a severe ponytail, and her face is scrubbed clean of the makeup she never used to leave her house without. Her feet are also bare, toes overlapping the edge of the covered sidewalk and digging into the green grass of the lawn.

Megan goes and sits down next to her on the concrete, as if she's settling in for a long wait.

Libby makes a mark on one of the clipboards. "This is Autumn. She helps train promising candidates for the seraphim guard, and as the head of our security force, she screens new arrivals."

When Libby finishes her introduction, Autumn finally looks our way. Her eyes widen, and I brace myself for a boiling burst of condemnation. She rocks on her heels and then closes the distance between us in three bounding strides. Before I can move, she knocks into me, tearing me out of Neil's grasp.

I curl my shoulders in to protect myself from her blows. It takes a second for me to process that she's not sneering and jabbing at me. She's squealing and jumping and hugging me as if she's *excited* I've crawled back into her life, as if she's forgiven me when I haven't even been able to forgive myself. It's so unexpected, so undeserved, that the huge knot of shame in my chest comes undone and spills out of me in heaves and spurts.

"What's wrong?" Autumn asks, releasing me. "Aren't you happy to see me?"

In this moment I am happy. Even if I can't quite trust this dawning awareness that I might have the chance to win my oldest, dearest friend back. It seems too good to be true. I need to tell her how sorry I am. How much penance I've paid for the wrong I did her. "I'm sorry," I blubber. "For what . . . I did. With Julian." I stumble over the words, feel them collide in my mouth, like they're too big to fit in there all at once.

Autumn shakes her head, and her ponytail swishes back and forth. "Oh, Felicia, it's fine. It really is. The first thing you learn in Level Three is how to let go. Make peace with your past. I have."

Her eyes sparkle with sincerity and joy. Level Three has obviously been good to her. I'm overcome with gratitude that the unpredictability of the cosmos has arranged this in my favor. Even if my future is uncertain, even if the Morati lie in wait beyond this encounter, at least I can die again knowing that I'm forgiven. With Autumn and Neil by my side.

Libby clears her throat, and Autumn startles, as if just now realizing that we have an audience. "Who's this?" Autumn asks brightly. Neil laces his fingers through mine, and Autumn smiles. "Your boyfriend?"

I nod. "Neil. He's the sweetest guy I've ever met."

"And he's cute!" Autumn winks, making Neil duck his head and blush. We all trade bemused glances, and I start to think Level Three might be okay after all.

"We should probably begin," Autumn says with chipper enthusiasm. "Even though I know you, I still have to screen you."

"For what?" I ask.

"Autumn and a few of the other elite members of the security force greet new trainees to make sure they're mentally fit for service," Libby explains. "She'll read your memories via your palm. I assume you've both done memory transfers before."

We have. After the fall of the Morati's hive architecture and the memory chambers, touching palms was the only way to access memories. Neil and I dipped in and out of our lives on Earth with regularity in the months we spent together before coming here.

I pull away from Neil so I can lift my palm for Autumn. I hope she's not planning to show me her death memory. It's not that I don't wonder who killed her—that mystery was never solved—but I don't want to relive it with her.

Autumn leans forward and allows our palms and the pads of our fingers to connect. The instant they do, I'm sucked into a black hole. Murky images fly and scratch at me like ravens spooked from a fence. I can't hold on to anything long enough to process it. I twist away from her, breaking contact.

"I'm sorry!" Autumn winces. "I should have warned you that memory transfers with someone as practiced in mind blocking as I am can be unpleasant. In order to assess your mental strength, I put up defenses instead of openly showing you one of my memories. It wouldn't be fair to everyone else if I were to go easy on you because you're my best friend."

We all chuckle uncomfortably, even Megan, who twists blades of grass between her fingers, forming them into tiny animal figurines. So far two giraffes and a penguin stand at attention next to her on the sidewalk.

"Your turn," Autumn says to Neil. After my reaction to the screening, Neil is understandably hesitant. But he's never been one to question authority, so he dutifully lifts his palm and only flinches once while they're connected.

Autumn releases Neil, and he stumbles back to my side. "See? That wasn't so bad." The honey in her voice is sticky and leaves a slightly bitter aftertaste.

Libby poises her pencil above her clipboard. "Your verdict, please."

Autumn shrugs. "I'd say they're both suitable for something midlevel. Muse, maybe. Felicia is, like, a genius on the piano." She's casual about it, but I notice the extra emphasis she gives the "mid" in "midlevel." She always had a competitive streak, especially with me. She's obviously earned her high position, and I don't begrudge her for it.

Libby raises her eyebrows but makes another mark on her clipboard, while Megan jumps up and claps her hands, knocking her grass figurines over. "Muse? How cool! I can totally show you two around!"

"Great," Autumn says. "But don't you think someone should be at the records room in case any new arrivals come in?"

Megan looks over to Libby for instructions. "You will handle that this afternoon while I help these two get settled in," Libby says, addressing Autumn. Her hard tone suggests it's more an order than a request.

Autumn's mouth gapes open at this obvious deviation in protocol, and her nose wrinkles in irritation. "Of course." Then she pulls me into another quick hug. "I still can't believe you're really here—"

"So," Libby interrupts, "the fact that you two are friends works to your advantage, Felicia. Because Autumn is so well known as the head of security, the Morati will steer clear of her if they're smart. So far they've kept a low profile, so we don't anticipate a major attack. It gives us time to figure out what their end game is."

If Autumn is surprised that we've been briefed on the Morati's infiltration, she hides it well. "You're safe with me." She squeezes my shoulder. "I'll come by your room after my shift and check on you, okay?" The conviction in her voice helps to tamp down my panic about the Morati a few notches. If my powerful best friend is watching out for me, maybe I won't have to constantly look over my shoulder.

"You're the best," I say. She grins, gives me a thumbs-up sign, and sets off back the way we came.

As shell-shocked as I am by Level Three's revelations—that the Morati somehow slipped through, that Autumn is here and doesn't hate me, and that it appears we'll have to choose and train for some sort of afterlife career—I can't help but feel a tiny shiver of excitement for all the possibilities that await. And maybe that does make me courageous.

Neil bends down and retrieves Megan's discarded grass giraffes, cupping them carefully like he once handled a baby bird. "Can I keep these?" he asks her, inspecting them up close. "They're beautiful."

Megan nods excitedly. "Thank you. I was really into sculpture before."

"It shows," Neil says.

Libby sighs, indicating she's not nearly as impressed. She leads us through an archway and down another narrow walkway until we emerge onto a perfectly manicured lawn, bordered on all sides by impressive stone buildings.

There are small clusters of people milling about, lounging on benches, sitting cross-legged under trees. Oddly, the members of each group all wear the same color. Otherwise, the scene looks straight out of all the glossy college brochures I used to get before my scholastic achievement took a nosedive midway through my senior year. After my meltdown when Autumn died, my mother sent me to live with my paternal grandmother in Ohio. The Foreign Service revoked my diplomatic passport for abusing it, and my mother had to make a choice between her career and me. She didn't choose me. I was so upset, I didn't even bother to apply to any schools. Neil was all set to go to Ohio State, and I thought about joining him at the start of the spring semester. I'm now hit with another twinge of longing for my earthly life. I mourn the fact that I'll never know how things might have turned out if Neil and I had lived.

As we walk, Libby passes Neil and me each a brochure from her clipboard. "In Level Three you train for your afterlife careers. Like Megan said, she's training for the muse program."

I flip through the brochure. Careers are divided into sections based on where the work is performed. Under "Earth" I see headings for muses, demon hunters, spirit trappers, and guardian angels. Under "Level Three" are the healers and caretakers, and under "Level Four" is the seraphim guard. The careers are ranked by degree of difficulty, and muse is, indeed, considered midlevel. The most elite careers are with the demon hunters and the seraphim guard.

Neil points to one of the subheads on page two. "I think muse does sound perfect for us." He reads aloud from the brochure. "Muses inspire the arts and enrich people's lives. Prerequisites include: one, an excellent memory; two, a complete detachment from one's earthy life; and three, a natural talent in art, poetry, dance, music, comedy, or history."

I nod, Autumn's less-than-stellar recommendation still rankling a bit. "Yeah, we should do that."

"Really? You want to?" Megan asks. "I can't wait to introduce you to everyone in the program. I also played the tuba for years." She puffs out her cheeks and places her arms out in front of her like she's holding the large instrument. "You should've seen how much my lungs could hold back then."

She looks so comical, both Neil and I have to laugh.

"Well, you're still full of hot air," Libby teases. It's the first time she's loosened up the whole day.

On the building north of us, which is the Muse Collection Library, according to the map Megan showed us, a brick changes color from blue to orange. The facade is a mishmash of different styles, as if hundreds of architects had a hand in its construction. It's strange but beautiful.

"It is lovely here," Libby says. "Everything that wasn't already put in place by the celestial custodians is collectively materialized. There are subtle changes every day, when the mood strikes someone to update something." She points at a frowning gargoyle on the peak of one of the towers, and its expression morphs into an enigmatic, *Mona Lisa*–type smile.

We stand for a moment, taking everything in. A clique of students all wearing yellow jostles past us. One of them stops to give me a backhanded high five and shouts into my face, "Hunters are yellow!" When I don't respond, he mutters "Demons are blue" and rushes off to catch up with his friends.

"Uh, what was that?" I ask.

"Your dress is yellow," Megan says. "They thought you were a demon hunter."

"Here you show your affiliation to your career by wearing its color," Libby explains, pointing to the yellow background behind the demon hunter description in the brochure. Below it the healer text appears on a red background. Some healer might come by and spout off a motto to Neil now, all because of the color of his shirt. In any case, he looks as lost and confused as I feel.

"Don't worry if this all seems complicated at first. You'll learn the peculiarities of this place as you get settled in," Libby assures us. "We all have the goal to make the most out of our afterlife, but we go about it in different ways."

"Muses wear orange," Neil says, obviously deducing it from the color of Megan's dress. He scans the brochure. "But what is pink?" he asks, referring to Libby's suit.

"Pink is neutral." Libby materializes a big black binder stuffed with ragged-edged papers and dumps it into Megan's arms. These papers don't look like they've been burned, merely crinkled and haphazardly arranged. "I assume the two of you would like to room together."

"Yes," I say at the same time that Neil says, "No."

I spin and face him, confused. "What do you mean, no? Why not?" I don't want to leave his side for a second, let alone whatever time we're meant to spend in our dorm rooms. And with the Morati lurking, I'd feel safer with Neil around.

Neil flicks his gaze back and forth between me and Libby, biting his lip. "It's just . . . well, we shouldn't live together until we get married."

He stresses that last word so earnestly, it's all I can do not to laugh derisively. I can't believe he thinks being married or not matters in the afterlife. "You're not serious."

Neil reaches out and caresses my face, looking me straight in the eye. "Don't be mad. I *want* to room with you. It could very well be that nothing I was taught to believe is true, but I can't flip a switch, forget about my morals, and be a different person. I need time to adjust."

Maybe Neil thinks I'm immoral because I'd room with him without hesitation. Is Neil still too good for me, even in death? Back on Earth he was the worship leader at church, until he had to give it up because I wouldn't sign a purity pledge. People whispered behind our backs that I was corrupting him. But I never intended to. I only ever wanted us to be together. What's so bad about that? Still, I can see that I need to be patient. Neil was patient with me. When I couldn't open up to him about my shameful past, he never pressured me. Maybe he'll be more relaxed once we get used to it here, once he realizes his church group is not patrolling his every moral move. So I nod, letting him know I understand, even if I can't trust myself to speak right now.

"We'll put you in rooms across the hall for now, and if you want to move, you can tell me." Libby scrawls something on one of her tattered sheets and hands it to Megan. Then she shuts the binder and taps the cover with her pencil. "Megan, go ahead and show Neil to his room. I want to talk to Felicia for a moment."

Neil raises one eyebrow but gives me a peck on the cheek and follows Megan. "See you in a second."

Once they're out of earshot, Libby leads me to a bench and we sit down. "I think we need a second opinion regarding your mental fitness. You should go out for the seraphim guard. That's the best way to develop the kind of skills you'd need to expose the Morati."

"But Neil wants to be a muse. Couldn't I develop those skills another way?"

Libby pats my arm. "You don't have to share everything. I learned that the hard way."

"What do you mean?"

"I came here with someone as well. My fiancé." She pauses as if she's lost in thought. "Life on Earth is finite, so we make promises easily. When we say 'forever' there, we know that it will end sometime. In the afterlife 'forever' is a much bigger promise. And it's one that most of us are not capable of keeping."

My skin prickles. "But some people can."

I need to believe that this is true. Neil has saved me more than once already. I love him and I can't lose him.

She shrugs. "Maybe. But Jeremy and I couldn't. It was his idea to camp out on the side of Interstate 70. I found it too difficult not to blame him for us getting murdered."

"I'm sorry."

"It doesn't matter. Look, all I'm saying is that you should do what's best for you. You're a person first, and part of a couple second."

I stand up, and immediately feel light-headed. "Yeah. I'll keep it in mind." I don't care what Libby says. Neil and I will always be together. And I'd bet my afterlife on that.

three

LIBBY AND I WALK to the dorms in silence, ascend four flights of stairs, and then enter a wide hallway. With its red-and-gold-patterned carpet and white walls, it looks like a fancy hotel rather than a dorm. A bellboy pushing a luggage rack wouldn't be the least bit out of place.

Libby leads me to room 532 and opens the door. The room is completely bare except for beige wall-to-wall carpeting and a window. "This looks comfy," I say, unable to stop the biting edge to my words. Thanks to her unwanted relationship advice, Libby's not exactly my favorite person right now.

"It's up to you to materialize your own furniture."

When I respond only with a glare, she turns on her heel abruptly and walks off. "Neil's in 531," she calls. "Good luck."

Good riddance. I slam the door to my empty room, cross the hall, and raise my knuckles to knock on Neil's door. Finding that it's open a crack, I peek in. He's laughing with Megan. He has already changed into an orange T-shirt and set the grass giraffes on his old desk from home. His curtains are there too, drawn over the window above his bed and his guitar stand. The only item I don't recognize is a wooden kitchen chair. Megan sits on it with her hands tucked neatly under her thighs.

"I'm here." I push the door lightly and step in. "Libby left."

"Hey! Megan is ready to give us a tour. Isn't that cool?" Neil asks.

"Sure," I say, trying to muster up some enthusiasm. It occurs to me that Neil's bed looks lonely without his cat, Sugar, on it. It will look even lonelier without me in it with him at night.

"You might want to change clothes." Megan giggles. "Unless you want to attract more demon hunters."

"I'll be fine," I insist. I'd have to search long and hard through my memory to find anything orange in my wardrobe, and I don't feel up to it right now. "I can't recall ever wearing orange, to be honest."

"It doesn't have to be something you wore, just

something you touched." Megan kicks up her legs. "I borrowed these socks from my sister's Halloween costume. She dressed up as a pumpkin."

Neil puts his hands behind his back and then grins widely, his dimples on full display. "Before we go, I want to give you something." He steps forward and extends his right hand, revealing a small box wrapped in silver paper, with silver bells dangling from a gold ribbon. It's an exact replica of the gift he gave me in the car before we crashed. And died.

My fingers fly to the hollow at the base of my throat. The skep charm. I never had the chance the wear it.

"Go ahead." Neil shakes it so that the bells swing back and forth. "I've been waiting for the right moment, but I think it's time we finally celebrate your birthday."

It's sweet how he's trying to make up for disappointing me concerning our living arrangements. I take the box from him and rip into the paper, unwrapping the white fabric-covered ring box. I pop it open eagerly. It's empty.

"The skep charm's not there." I slam the box back into his palm harder than I intended, and the hinge snaps closed.

Neil's face falls when he reopens the box. "I don't understand. Where is it?"

"Maybe you never touched what was actually inside," Megan suggests. "You have to have had physical contact with something in order to materialize it."

"I did touch it," Neil insists. "I put it into the box."

"Try again," Megan says.

Neil sucks in a breath and tips his head slightly forward. It's what he always does when he materializes something. But the charm still doesn't come.

"Wait," I say. "I touched it too. Let me try." I can see the charm's beehive shape clearly in my mind, but when I try to produce it, it doesn't work. I've never had that happen before.

"Maybe you can't make it appear because it was made out of traveler's silver," Megan says.

"But it was gold," I say.

"*Argentum viaticum* can be gold plated." Megan slips her hands into the side pockets of her dress. "Anyway, it's the only substance I know of that can't be replicated. But it's not found on Earth. It can only be mined in the higher levels."

Neil retrieves the crumbled wrapping paper from his beige carpet and deposits it on his desk with the empty box. "Well, obviously the charm was not made of that, then."

Megan shrugs and then jumps up from her chair. "Yeah, of course not. I've only seen traveler's silver in the obols that muses use to travel back and forth between here and Earth to do their jobs."

"Right! Muses travel back to Earth." That's what the brochure said too. It makes Level Three instantly more appealing. I could go back and visit my dad, and Grammy, if she's still alive. Even though it seemed like I was in Level Two for an eternity, Julian told me that time worked differently there and that only two Earth years had passed since I'd died.

Megan walks to the still-open door. "Shall we go?"

"Sorry." Neil draws me into a hug. I let him. He whispers into my ear, "Maybe I can find another way to cheer you up. Later." It's teasing and seductive at the same time, and it kinda makes me want to push Megan out the door and lock it behind her.

But we follow Megan out for the grand tour around the campus. She leads us down a side road between the dorm buildings. "First I want to show you one of my favorite places, Western Bridge Park."

When we emerge from the passageway, we're maybe twenty paces south of the bridge. It's massive stone, but the way it's constructed, it looks more like a footbridge you'd see over a babbling brook. It slopes gently upward from both ends with no support beams or girders. Its size makes it sturdy, and there are barriers and railings for added safety. Those who cross the bridge do so purposefully, but there's a group of healers wearing red dresses lounging on benches nearby.

The bridge spans a canyon approximately the width of a football field. Steep, rocky cliffs overlook a river that flows at least a thousand feet down below. It reminds me of the Royal Gorge above the Arkansas River in Colorado.

As we walk along the chasm heading north past the bridge, Megan answers our questions about Level Three. She explains that no one really knew why people stopped arriving from Level Two. The only new trainees that came in were people who had been murdered, so class sizes were small, and everyone got to know one another.

Then, after about eight years, the first refugees from Level Two trickled in and started sharing their stories about the battle with the Morati. It was also at this time that the records room was destroyed.

The bombing of the records room did not cause any structural impairment, and the population was told that there was nothing to worry about, and that the damage had been caused by an unfortunate accident. The only ones who knew otherwise were the heads of the careers, Libby, a few others, and now us. Those who'd been around during the era of limited arrivals questioned the need for the newly formed security force, but since those positions were filled mainly by seraphim guard trainees who were known to carry swords and knives anyway, the grumbles soon died out.

We cut through another break in the row of dorms that seems to go on forever into the distance. We wander along the edges of sports fields, watching the rivalries play out between the various careers. Cheers of "Don't lose your spirit!" erupt as a spirit trapper in a purple uniform tackles a green-clad caretaker.

"As you can see," Megan says, "no one is worried at all about the Morati. And personally, I don't think you need to worry either. Libby can be a bit of a drama queen."

Megan's assessment of Libby seems fair, but I can't let my guard down yet. The low hum of the Morati's signal buzzes through my veins, and if I can sense them, then they must be aware of me. With my luck they're probably waiting until I'll be alone and vulnerable in my room.

Once we reach Eastern Avenue, we turn right and enter a steady flow of students as they make their way to and from classes. Megan points out the classroom where a new muse orientation will take place tomorrow. She explains that most of the career tracks have new orientations every few days now that the population is rapidly expanding.

We've reached the lawn in front of the Muse Collection Library when Megan stops. "One of the demon hunters is flagging you down."

I turn in the direction that Megan's head is tilted. Coming toward us is a guy in tight yellow workout gear who seems incredibly familiar somehow. His dimpled grin is on full display, and he struts like he's a very big deal. When he gets closer, he holds out his arms for a hug. "Felicia! I thought that was you." I shrink away, and he drops his arms casually to his side. I have no idea who he is.

Megan gets giggly again and says, "Hey, Nate."

Neil whips his head around. "Nate?" His voice is all strangled and weird. That's when I place the guy. He's the one in the family portrait on Neil's mantel. Back on Earth whenever I'd ask Neil about the other boy in the photo, he'd change the subject or flat-out ignore me. The one time I pressed him, it led to a fight, so I finally gave up. I never saw him in any of Neil's memories either, because Neil was very careful to skip over anything from his freshman year of high school. Was Nate the reason? Nate has the same curly hair as Neil, though Nate's is darker, almost black, as well as longer and floppier.

Nate kisses Megan on the cheek, which makes her blush, and then slaps Neil on the back. "Good to see you again, Little Brother." If this is Neil's older brother, then Neil hid something seriously huge from me.

Neil pats Nate on the arm, as if trying to ascertain if he's real or not. Nate turns to me and squeezes my shoulders. Before I can ask how he knows me, Neil shoves him, and not in a playful way. "Leave her alone," Neil growls. I've never seen him behave so aggressively. If he hates his brother this much, it could be why he never told me he even had one.

Nate backs away from us. "Still haven't forgiven me?" He chuckles and then lets out an exaggerated sigh. "Guess you'll have to get over it, since I'm the head trainer for the demon hunters." He nods at me in approval. "Excellent choice of career, by the way."

"Oh, I'm not joining the demon hunters. I just like this dress."

Neil squares his shoulders and regains his composure. "I'm over it." He puts his arm around my neck like he's staking his claim.

Nate raises one eyebrow. "If you say so. Anyway, I'm glad to see you two back together. Always thought you made a cute couple."

"Um, thanks?" I scrunch my forehead. Someone who already came through must have told him that Neil and I were separated in Level Two. But that doesn't explain the "back together" part. That assumes he knew me on Earth, which he didn't.

Nobody says a word. The air feels charged between us.

"Well, it's nice to finally meet you, Nate," I say as sincerely as possible. "I wish I could say I've heard all about you, but I can't. Neil kept you a secret." I risk a quick glance at Neil and notice his clenched jaw and fists. Nate definitely gets under his skin. It's a side to Neil I've not seen much of, that's for sure. It hits me that as close as I am to him, I know only the version of Neil that he's shown me. He could be hiding countless versions of himself beneath his usually calm exterior. It would be a wholly different experience to see Neil through his brother's eyes.

Nate looks at me in confusion. "Were you hit over the head or something?"

Is he asking about my death? "Not exactly. I died in a car accident. I suppose a head injury could've been a part of it."

"Maybe, but head trauma and amnesia don't follow you to the afterlife." Nate rubs the back of his head. "If they did, my skull would still be caved in, thanks to that coward who did me in with a hammer."

"Somehow it doesn't surprise me that someone murdered you," Neil says with a very un-Neil-like smirk.

Megan gasps, looking wounded. Neil backpedals, realizing too late that Megan might have been murdered too. "I'm sorry, Megan. I—I didn't mean—"

"You get into a lot of car accidents?" Nate asks me, interrupting Neil's stuttering apology.

"No," I say. "Only the one that killed me. The day before my eighteenth birthday."

"What are you talking about?" Nate shakes his head. "You didn't die in that accident. I met you six weeks later in the hospital."

four

NATE'S WORDS do not compute. "You must be confusing me with someone else." I try to laugh, but it comes out choked.

"See for yourself." Nate darts forward and lines up his palm against mine.

I'm immediately sucked into his memory. He's walking down a hall that smells strongly of antiseptic and rotting flowers, and it takes me a second to adjust. Because exactly like all those times I rented memories off the net in Level Two, I'm inside this stranger's head. I'm seeing what he sees, thinking what he thinks, feeling what he feels.

Nate double-checks Neil's room number. He's been spaced out the past day—his jetlag is killer. Hence the "531" scrawled on his skin with a black Sharpie lifted from the nurse's station.

An orderly whizzes by, pushing an empty bed with rumpled sheets. Nate scans the room numbers until he's outside 531. He puffs out his chest and hopes for the best.

He makes his grand entrance back into Neil's life after nearly four years away. Neil is sitting up in his bed. He wears a normal T-shirt and a pair of shorts over a long cast on his left leg. The cast extends all the way from his midthigh to his foot, and it hangs on a pulley.

There's a girl next to him, holding his hand. Short, spiky brown hair. Long legs. Neil's so into this girl, it takes him a minute to notice that Nate is even in the room. Finally Neil squints up at Nate, and then his eyes widen, but he doesn't say anything.

Best to plunge right in. "Hey, Little Brother," Nate says. "Stoked you pulled through. Dad called and told me about the crash. Said some bastard stole a police car for a joyride."

"I wondered how long it would take for you to show your face around here again." Neil leans forward with a wince, and the girl tucks another pillow behind his back. "Have you been to see Dad yet?"

Nate ignores his question. Instead he swaggers over to the girl and extends his hand. "Name's Nate. Neil's brother. The pleasure is all yours."

She looks up at Nate with her huge brown eyes and shaky smile. She takes Nate's hand politely. "I'm Felicia.

Neil's girlfriend." There's an angry red scar on her temple. And fading bruises that clash with her porcelain skin. She's banged up. Picture-perfect damsel in distress. And she looks like Gracie, which could explain why Neil's in love with her.

"You never told me you had a brother," Felicia says.

"Half brother," Neil clarifies.

There are no free chairs in the small room. The windowsill is covered with get-well cards. Nate sits on the end of Neil's bed. Then he pulls the Sharpie out of his pocket and uncaps it.

"Better sign this before space runs out. How'd you get to be so popular? Dealing drugs?" Nate asks. Doodles and signatures compete for top billing on Neil's cast. The only splashes of white are in awkward places, like under his thigh and the back of his ankle.

Neil flinches. "Don't bother."

Nate shrugs and poises the pen above Neil's ankle. "I'm crashing at Vic's. Good to see the old gang again." He flashes his sincerest grin, the one he usually reserves for angry parents and highway patrolmen. "Ever hear anything from Gracie?"

Neil's eyes bug out, as expected. Felicia searches his face, and Nate can tell that there will be questions later. He regrets he won't be around to see how the Boy Scout lies himself out of this one.

But Neil tries for casual. "No. Why would I? How's Vic? I haven't seen him at church in years."

Nate is impressed with Neil's deflection. "Vic converted

to atheism. He spends his Sunday mornings worshipping his pillow."

Felicia laughs. She's giving Nate her full attention now, so she doesn't pick up on Neil's look of annoyance. "How long will you stay in town, then, Nate?" she asks.

"I want to be here for Neil. Dad says he has a lot of physical therapy ahead, and I'm happy to help any way I can." Nate is really laying it on thick now, but Felicia's buying it, even if Neil isn't.

"Oh, that's so sweet!" She leans forward in her chair. "Are you in medical school or something?"

"I'm a fitness trainer." Nate loves the way her eyes scan his body. The moment she sees the truth in his statement is worth all his hours in the gym.

"We could certainly use the help. I'm seriously out of shape."

She doesn't look it. Probably just sore from her injuries. "Give yourself a break. No one expects you to run a marathon so soon after a car wreck. How bad was it?" he asks gently.

"Three cracked ribs. Collapsed lung. Concussion. Bruises. They had to chop my hair off to pull me out of the wreckage." Felicia tugs at the ends of her hair and then reaches for Neil's hand and squeezes. "But they say I made a remarkably quick recovery and I got off easy compared to Neil. He had a torn spleen and whiplash as well as a fractured femur and tibia."

Neil pipes up. "If I'm lucky and all the bones set correctly, the doctors won't have to hammer me full of metal plates."

Nate makes sure his voice oozes sympathy. "It's great that you two have each other. And I'm sure Felicia will do all she can to help you get better." He waits until Neil catches Felicia's eye and then jots his initials on Neil's cast. *NIC*. Neil jerks his leg as far as the pulley allows.

A nurse comes in with a food tray. *Time to jet.* Nate takes out his wallet, extracts a dollar bill, and writes his number on it with the Sharpie. "If you need anything, here's my cell," Nate tells Neil. He places the bill on top of the tray. "Looking forward to getting to know you better, Felicia."

This time her smile is solid. Neil even cheers up, probably only because Nate's leaving.

When I come back to myself, I feel woozy. "I—I think I need to sit down." My legs give out, and I sink to the ground.

Neil jumps to my side, frantic. "Why? What did he show you?"

I can't do anything but stare at my sandals. Grammy said they were impractical, but I liked the way they showed off my pedicure. I always wondered if Grammy broke down when I died. I never saw her cry. I didn't even really think she was capable of it. I couldn't imagine it, in any case. And now there's Nate's memory. If it's real, and Neil and I survived that car accident, then it puts *everything* into question.

But we're dead now, or we wouldn't be here. Megan's hand is on my forehead, like she's checking my temperature. She's asking me if I'm okay. I want to scream, I'm not okay, Megan! I don't remember that hospital room. I don't remember anything after the crash.

I swipe at Megan's hand. Shoo her away like a fly. I need to concentrate on remembering. The girl Nate saw in this memory could be me, other than the short hair, except that she acted like some fragile waif waiting to be saved by a prince. That must be how Nate sees me. I've never been able to see myself through Neil's eyes. When I relive joint memories with Neil, my own point of view takes over. It's too strong because I remember the scene too. But I don't remember this, so that must be why I relived the memory from Nate's point of view even though I was present.

Nate kept going on about a mystery girl. Gracie. I have to ask Neil about her. I look up at him, and see him pushing Nate again. "What did you show her? Tell me now!" he demands.

Nate chuckles. He seems to be heartily enjoying himself. "See for yourself, Little Brother." He offers his palm to Neil, and in the few seconds it takes for the transfer, Neil spasms and shakes.

"What kind of trick is this?" Neil sits down next to me, and I lean my head on his shoulder. "We didn't die?" he asks. He sounds as stunned as I feel.

Finally I come out of my daze. "If we didn't die in the crash, when did we die?" I ask Nate.

Nate shrugs. "How should I know? We lost touch. I had my own problems."

"But you have more memories of us? After the crash?"

"The memory I shared is one of many," Nate confirms.

"But why don't I have them?" I ask in a small voice. What happened to mine? And more important, how can I get them back? If Nate's memory is real, then my death was a lie, and I don't know what to believe anymore.

"Show us the rest, then." Neil tries to grab Nate's arm, but Nate slaps him away.

"Level Three is all about detachment." Nate's tone is preachy, like he has finally decided to act like a mentor or something. "What happened on Earth doesn't concern you anymore. I was wrong to show you what I did."

Neil scrambles up, using my shoulder as ballast. "You're only saying that to rile me up." He glares at Nate as though he's three seconds away from punching him. We're attracting curious stares from our fellow students. I want to see the memories too, but it's pretty clear Nate won't show us any others.

I stand up and step between Neil and Nate, and kiss Neil on the cheek and take his hand. Then I whisper into his ear. "We need to talk. Alone." To Megan I say more loudly, "Thanks for the tour."

"Oh, it's not over yet." Megan takes hold of both Neil's and my free wrists so that we form a tight circle. "I have so much more to show you."

"Can we pick it up later?" I ask. "Neil and I are going to go back to our rooms now to rest."

She gives us her glinting, gap-toothed smile. "Sure thing!"

"Separate rooms? Really?" Nate breaks in, waggling his eyebrows.

Neil merely scowls at him, and Nate grins widely and winks. "Ah! I get it. Want to keep your options open, eh? Can't blame you. The afterlife has a lot to offer." A couple of girls walk by as if on cue, and Nate salutes them.

Neil trembles beside me. He takes a deep breath and exhales slowly. "You don't know anything about us."

"If Felicia gets lonely, she can room with me." A mischievous smile lights up Nate's face. Now that I've been inside his head, I know he probably can't help himself.

Neil tenses up again. His brother loves to push his buttons. I squeeze Neil's hand. Long, long, long. Short, short, long. It's the only Morse code I learned from Neil. It's the letters *O* and *U*, short for "open up." And, curiously, it was also the password for opening all the doors in Level Two. We used it as a signal after the fall of the Morati for when we wanted to make a swift exit from a conversation and for when we wanted to be alone. Not that there was any privacy after all the hives disappeared. Endless fields of wildflowers are pretty, but not practical for long-term habitation.

Neil understands my meaning immediately and squeezes back. The strength of our connection makes me giddy, and I throw my arms around his neck. "Neil's the only roommate I'll ever want."

Level Three may not be the safe haven we expected, but at least I'm here with Neil. We smile at each other, and he angles his face closer to mine.

The ground rumbles beneath us. A flash of light sears my eyes, and an impossibly loud boom explodes my eardrums.

The force of the explosion rips me away from Neil and throws me facedown into the grass, splaying my arms and legs. My head feels water-clogged, as though if only I could surface from this pool of confusion, I might be able to make out what the muffled voices around me are shouting.

Where am I? Where is Neil?

With effort I twist my neck to look for him. Looming large in my field of vision is a severed leg, the orange kneesock soaked in blood. Megan. As I dry heave, the leg fades away. Megan is gone.

This is not really happening. It can't be.

Through the blur of my tears, I can just barely make out Neil. His eyes are closed and his mouth is open. A giant beach-ball-size rock crushes his leg. Then I scream.

five

"NEIL." I CHOKE OUT HIS NAME. I can't understand why he doesn't open his eyes. I need to get closer.

Behind him lies the still-smoking ruin of the records building where we first entered Level Three. Everyone who can move crawls away from it. I reach out my arms, dig my fingers into the ground, and pull my body toward Neil an inch at a time. My muscles groan with the effort, but I won't stop. Neil's life is at stake.

When I reach him, I try to push the rock off his leg, but it won't budge. All I can do is cradle his head in my lap. He bleeds from a gash in his temple, and I search desperately for something to staunch the flow. My dress is torn and dirty, but I tear off a scrap from the full skirt, rip the hem, and press the clean side against his wound.

He's not breathing. But of course, in the afterlife, breathing is a habit, not a necessity. I run my fingertips over his eyelids and eyelashes, and then squeeze his shoulders with the little strength I have left. *Don't die. Don't die. Don't die*. If I lose Neil, I don't think I can go on.

Libby gets up right in my face. She shakes me, and all I can think is, *Where did she come from?* Her lips are moving, but no sound emerges. She seems to repeat the same word over and over. It finally dawns on me that she's mouthing the word "healer." She gestures at Nate and two guys dressed in black. The three of them lift the rock off Neil and carry him away from me.

"Take me, too," I croak out, but they ignore me and rush off. I try to lift myself to my feet, but my limbs don't respond.

"He'll be fine, and so will you." Libby must be yelling, but I can barely register her words.

That's when I notice the blood. The falling debris banged up my arms and torso. Libby is as pristine as she was before, and miraculously, she doesn't have a scratch on her. It doesn't seem possible that a blast that ripped Megan's leg off does not affect Libby at all and leaves Nate still strong enough to lift a boulder. Or maybe Libby wasn't in the records hall at the time of the blast. Was Autumn still there? Will I lose my best friend and my boyfriend on the same day?

People stream around us, and it is like I'm in the middle of an action movie with the mute button activated. Libby touches my forehead and enunciates, "You can hear fine." I'm blasted with sounds of anguished moans and frenzied shouting as more people in black and gray descend upon the injured.

Libby's up again in a flash, directing the crowd. I follow her gestures, hoping for some insight into where they've taken Neil so I can go to him when I'm able to get up. But so many panicked people run in all directions that I quickly lose sight of Libby.

My gaze flickers across a roman profile and shaggy blond bangs, and a sudden euphoria lifts me out of my worry and exhaustion. Julian! Julian will know what to do. I bite my lip, hard, when I realize it's not only Julian's competence but also his closeness that I crave. I can't afford to think that when Neil could be dying. I crane my neck back and forth trying to catch sight of that distinctively messy blond hair again, but it's gone. Maybe it was never there. Maybe it was merely a figment of my overstressed mind.

But it's not my imagination that Autumn heads straight for me, and she appears to be in perfect health. That's one blessing I can count.

"Felicia! I've been looking all over for you." Autumn sinks to her knees and inspects my cuts with deft hands. "Are you in pain?"

"They took Neil somewhere. Megan died in front of me." I touch my hand to my chest, over my heart, where it hurts more than I could ever put into words.

"Megan?" Autumn whispers. She sags into me and sighs

into my hair. "She was always so eager to include everyone. She wasn't here for more than a couple of months, but she made such an impression. I can't believe she's gone."

But gone where? I thought the one advantage of dying was that you'd finally know what happens to you after you die. But here I am, dead, and I'm still in the dark as to what comes next, if anything. A better place? A worse place? Or no place at all?

We don't say anything for a few moments. Autumn's grandmother, an early widow, always used to tell us that grief needs room to breathe. And here, in the midst of all this chaos, we form an island of calm, letting the sorrow sink in deep.

Finally Autumn pulls away, drawing in a ragged breath. "It takes most people a long time to adjust to their afterlife bodies. You still believe you can bleed. That you can die. It's something you have to unlearn." She tucks a strand of her blond hair behind her ear. "Watch this."

She pulls up a pant leg and slips a knife out of a sheath strapped to her shin. Arcing the knife downward, she jabs it into my middle finger, causing a pinprick of blood to well up at the tip.

"What was that for?" I scowl up at her as I suck on my finger, tasting the metallic tang of blood. I'm surprised she even carries around a knife, considering the way she died, stabbed to death in my bed. Maybe it's a coping exercise they've assigned in her training. I wonder if they know she goes around cutting people.

Then Autumn positions the knife so that it's pointing straight at her heart.

My eyes widen as I realize what she plans to do, and I reach my arms up to try to stop her. "No! Autumn!"

It's too late. She plunges the knife in, and I look at her, horrified, expecting a gurgle of red to stain her shirt and for the light to dim in her eyes as she falls over.

But she simply pulls the knife back out, flashes the clean blade in front of my face, and returns it to its hiding place.

It's horrifying that she is so casual about stabbing herself after all this carnage.

"Everything you feel, every physical reaction you have—it's all because you believe it can happen. You're still programmed to believe it can happen from your time in Level One. On Earth, you get cut; you bleed. You fall; you break a bone."

Very carefully she pulls me to my feet and drapes my arm around her neck to support my weight. We pick our way through the debris, heading away from the chaos and toward the dorms. "It's funny, though. You understand you don't need to eat or drink, of course, and that's why you're not starving or thirsty. But your body's hit with trauma, and *wham*—you react like you still have a functioning and tragically fragile system."

For most of my stay in Level Two, I was too drugged to feel anything at all. Then as the drugs wore off, I began to register pain. The drugs probably blocked my natural reactions to physical trauma. But there was also the man whom Julian punched in one of the hives so that I could use his memory chamber. The drugs didn't stop him from falling unconscious immediately. Obviously, what your mind makes you believe has a lot of effect on what happens to you in the afterlife. "But you're above all that now," I say. "You don't bleed."

"Exactly. I've evolved. I know I can't die, and so I can't."

"But Neil—"

"Don't be scared. I'm sure they got him to a healer in time."

"What can a healer do if all the physical stuff doesn't matter?"

"Healers enter a traumatized person's head and convince them they're not dying." Autumn taps her forehead. "It doesn't always work. Depends on the healer's talent. But for some, the power of suggestion is truly a skill."

"Libby fixed my hearing."

"Really? Hmmm." She stops and seems to ponder this for a moment. "Can you walk on your own now?"

Autumn's explanation has helped me to make sense of things. I tell myself I feel fine, and even start to believe it. "Yes, I think so."

She disentangles from me in one smooth motion, and I sway a bit on my feet before taking a deep breath to steady myself. I run my hand over the broken right strap of my dress to repair it, but I don't attempt a full overhaul yet. There are more important things to use my energy on right now than my appearance, such as helping Neil.

We reach the big double glass doors of my dorm. Autumn raises her arm, and the doors open for us. It's impressive.

We enter the foyer and turn right immediately into a large common room. Cots are set up in a triage situation, with about a dozen bodies lying down and three healers in long red dresses tending to them. I scan all the faces but recognize only the girls Nate was flirting with before. They're totally knocked out.

"Neil's not here," I say to Autumn, my voice tinged in panic. "What if they couldn't save him?"

It's now clear that Level Three may be even more dangerous than Level Two. I imagined a place of peace. A place I could finally rest. Not one shock after another. Arriving only to hear that the Morati did make it through after all. Discovering I didn't die when I thought I did. Surviving a bombing. Realizing Neil could disappear from my afterlife at any second.

Autumn hugs me fiercely. "I'll try to find out, okay? I'm sure he's fine."

"This can't be happening," I mumble into her shoulder.

"Cash," she calls to one of the security force guys, stepping back from me. "Did the team bring everyone here?"

Cash strides over to us and bows to Autumn, low and courteous like they do in Japan. Autumn bows too, but not as low. "The explosion damaged only the facade of the records hall. But there's a mandatory curfew starting now." Cash's voice is as slick as his dark hair. "Nate told us to take

Neil to Neil's room, but everyone else is here. Everyone who hasn't terminated, that is. Nine casualties so far." If Neil is in his room, that's all I need to know. I rush for the stairs and get caught up in the throng of people fleeing to their rooms. The atmosphere is tense. We are so jammed together, the waves of fear and unrest from the bombing cause my teeth to chatter.

By the time I make it to my floor, the crowd is thinning. But when I get to Neil's room, I come face-to-massive-chest with a burly guy from the security team. "Let me in," I demand.

I try for the door handle, but he blocks me. I have the urge to kick him in the shins, but a hand grabs me from behind. "Let me talk to him," Autumn says. "Go on into your room."

I don't want to, but Autumn stares me down until I do. Once inside my room, I pace over to the window and look out.

From this vantage point I can see the wide, treelined avenue that separates the dorms from the central buildings and courtyards. Beyond that is the lawn where we stood, where the explosion happened. Except there's no longer any outward trace of damage. Benches have been righted, rubble cleared away, and greenery revived. There's also a life-size stone statue of what looks like a samurai. The statue stands out next to the more Western-style buildings.

"I got you permission to visit Neil," Autumn says, making me jump at least an inch off the floor. I didn't even sense her coming in or up behind me. "They'll knock when they're ready for you. It shouldn't take long."

"Thank you." I stare out the window, trying to keep myself composed.

"That's weird. Furukama-Sensei is outside," Autumn says. "He's kind of like the president high commander of Level Three, but he never leaves his office in the administration building except for seraphim guard training."

"Where?" I don't see anyone.

"The statue. Turning to stone is Furukama's way of meditating," Autumn replies.

I look again at the stone figure. "Weird."

"I know, right? Furukama is by far the oldest human here. He claims to have left Level One sometime in the thirteenth century. Everyone else is from the twentieth century or later, since the older generations retire eventually and ascend to Level Four. No one knows for sure if Furukama made that story up to add to his mystique or if it's really true."

"Did Furukama call the mandatory curfew? Does he do it often?" Even though the room is relatively large and empty, the walls seem like they're closing in on me.

"This is the first time." She materializes an armchair. It's my dad's favorite chair, the patched-up one he always read in. "You look like you need to sit down, Your Highness." Her tone is solicitous but cheeky, like the court jester she used to play to my queen back when we'd pretend the chair was a throne.

I sink into the chair, running my hands over the worn leather and the smooth wood. Autumn knows instinctively what I need, like a best friend should. I took her friendship way too much for granted, and I have to make it up to her somehow.

There's a sharp knock on the door, and I dig my fingernails into my palms. A lanky guy enters dressed in black except for an enormous silver belt buckle. He heads straight to Autumn and whispers something into her ear. Alarm flits across her features, but she composes herself quickly. The guy glances at me before exiting and shutting the door firmly behind him.

"What did he say?" I brace myself for the worst.

Autumn doesn't answer me. She stares at the carpet, her eyes mere slits and her brow furrowed in concentration.

Is this the moment that will divide my existence forever? The moment when "before I lost Neil" slips cruelly into "after I lost Neil"? I try again, needing to know but not wanting to know at the same time. "Autumn? Tell me already!"

Autumn finally looks at me, her eyes shiny and sad. "William, the head librarian, was killed in the bombing."

I suck in a breath of relief. Not Neil. Not yet. Hopefully not ever. But if Autumn is this sad about the head librarian's death, they must have been close. "I'm so sorry."

"So am I." Autumn sniffles. "Because if William could die, any one of us could."

SIX

"WAIT. . . . I thought you said you couldn't die!" I cry.

Autumn leans against the bare, white wall. "Most things couldn't kill me, that's true. But William was one of the most powerful people in Level Three, second only to Furukama-Sensei." Her lips curl up, but in an ominous way that makes my whole being shudder. "If he could be murdered, we are all in trouble."

"Is there anything we can do? To protect ourselves?"

"Libby briefed you on the Morati, so you know they're here."

I gulp. "Yes."

"We think the Morati did this. They must have gotten

to William personally, and used their superior mind skills to convince him he was dying."

"They can do that?" If that's true, not even having Autumn around is going to keep me safe.

"It's speculation at this point, but it's the only explanation that makes sense." She sighs. "I don't know what they hope to gain by killing William, but I suspect it was a warning."

"A warning?"

"To the security team so that we'll stop looking for them. But it won't work. This makes us even more determined."

I'd rather lie low, avoid the Morati altogether. But if Autumn needs me, maybe I *should* help as much as I can. I owe her that as a best friend. "Libby told me I might be the one who can identify the Morati," I say tentatively.

"She said that?" Autumn's nostrils flare. "And you believe it."

She sounds upset, and it puts me on the defensive. "Back in Level Two the Morati thought I was important enough to put in their mainframe. They said they specifically needed my energy for their plan to eventually break into heaven."

"Really?" Autumn raises an eyebrow ever so slightly. "Why yours?"

"Remember that time I got mugged in Nairobi?"

She nods.

"Well, somehow as I was dying, our energies mingled, and they managed to break through to Earth for the first time. But then I didn't die. I just had nightmares."

"Okay, so the whole thing was random." She shrugs. "It

could have been anyone, so that doesn't make you inherently special."

Her dismissive tone annoys me. "I never said I was."

Autumn curls her toes into the carpet. "Sorry. I'm stressed. I didn't mean to take it out on you."

There's another sharp knock on the door, and I jump out of the chair, ready to run to Neil.

It's Cash, the security force guy from the lobby. He lets himself in, and as he strides toward me, he's all smiles. "I didn't introduce myself before. Things were kind of crazy. I'm Cash." He bows at the same time that I stick out my hand.

"What's with all the bowing?" I quickly retract my arm, embarrassed by my faux pas.

"Shaking hands means touching palms, and there's always the possibility of slipping up and going into a transfer," he says. For a memory transfer to work, the two people's palms and finger pads have to be aligned. It never occurred to me before, but I guess you wouldn't necessarily want to risk being dragged into the memories of every person you meet, even if the chance is pretty low.

"So, can we go to Neil now?" I ask, impatient. "Please?"

His smile falters. "Oh, I don't know anything about that. Sorry."

He's not here about Neil. He's another visitor for Autumn. I sit back down. I can't stand to wait another second.

When I don't answer, he continues. "You're lucky to have Autumn. She's amazing. Everyone in seraphim guard training thinks so, and seraphim reign supreme." Cash's mix of reverence and hype reminds me of the campus tour guide who showed me around Harvard my junior year of high school. Someone's been drinking the Kool-Aid.

Autumn waves away the compliment.

"So you're in that too? The seraphim guard?" I ask, more to be polite and pass the time than anything else.

Cash scrunches up his face as if horrified I'd imagine him in any other training. "It's only the most coveted job in the afterlife, even more than demon hunting or spirit trapping."

Autumn scoffs at this. "Of course it is. Demon hunters are losers."

Cash continues without losing a beat. "Word is, when you ascend to the next level as a seraphim guard, you get all the special assignments. Supposedly the squad is mostly actual angels, but elite humans also get on the rotation. Will you try out?"

Autumn's eyes narrow at his question. "Will you?" she asks me.

"No. I'm doing the muse program." Saying it out loud, in front of Autumn, makes it more real. "With Neil," I add, because he will recover. He has to.

There's a third knock on the door, but this time it's soft, barely there. When the door doesn't open, Autumn shouts, "Come in!"

A boy with a red baseball cap, the brim askew, takes a small step into the room. He wears jeans and a baggy T-shirt in a pink so pale, it's almost white. "Felicia? My sister says you can come in now." His cadence is gentle, like waves lapping at a boat.

I rise out of the chair, and my body tingles and then goes numb. I teeter forward, and for a second I think I'm going to fall flat on my face. But I manage to jerk my foot far enough in front of me to catch my balance. I lock my eyes on the boy, use him as a lifeline to pull myself across the room.

We walk together the few paces to Neil's. The burly guard steps aside, and the boy taps twice. A few seconds later a big brown eye fringed with long eyelashes peeks up at us. "Felicia?" asks a girl's voice.

"Yes. How's Neil?"

She squeezes into the hall through the door and shuts it behind her. She has a smattering of dark freckles across the bridge of her nose, and she looks as young as the boy. Like maybe fourteen, tops. "Before you come in, you should know that Neil is in a coma."

"Coma?" I can barely get the word out, my throat is so tight. I hope that doesn't mean he's like Beckah, who I found in Level Two, her brain waves only static.

"Not like you remember from Earth," she says quickly. "The body is a projection of the mind. Anything you feel is not a result of nerve endings but of your mind's memory of the feeling those nerve endings used to produce. If you're overwhelmed with pain, then your mind shuts down. In some cases that means complete disassociation from the body, or what you'd call death. In others it means a coma state."

"Don't worry," the boy says. "Kiara's got this. She's the best healer there is."

Kiara holds back a smile and straightens the boy's cap. She pulls us both into the room. "Keegan's not wrong about that." Autumn and Cash slip in behind us.

The room is the same as we left it hours ago, before our tour with Megan. I throw myself into the chair next to the bed and grab Neil's wrist, running my fingertips over his palm. It's warm and soft, and tears come rolling down my cheeks.

"I've stabilized him, so he's out of immediate danger," Kiara says. "And he's strong. I can feel that when I enter his head. His memories are compartmentalized, like he's worked at arranging them in a certain way. It's extraordinary."

The admiration in her voice makes me grin despite my worry, though I don't know quite what to make of her words. I've never really thought of Neil in such terms before. He always stood out to me for his kindness and his generosity and his passion for singing.

"It's good you're here for this." Kiara materializes another wooden chair and sits down on the other side of the bed, leaning over Neil to pat my arm reassuringly. "I'm going to go in and do a reboot, to try to shock him out of his coma."

"That sounds dangerous." I glance up at the door. Autumn and Cash stand at attention on either side of it. Keegan sits on the floor against a wall, hugging his knees to his chest.

"The procedure involves my dredging up a painful memory, something buried deep. Something he may have never accessed in Level Two. When I bring it to the surface, it should force him to wake up," Kiara explains.

"But wouldn't he have had to come to terms with all his worst memories in order to move on?"

"Actually, it's not uncommon for a person to still have some hidden painful memories in Level Three," Kiara says. "Especially with couples. If you're the one who called open the portal to come here, you might have pulled Neil through before he was ready. But don't worry. In this case it works to our advantage. We're not sure why, but these kinds of repressed memories work best. And I'm the best at digging them out."

"Okay. What can I do to help?"

"Keep thinking positive thoughts. And link up with me. I'll do the rest. He may look like he's having a seizure, but don't worry. That's normal."

A seizure doesn't sound normal at all, but she's so confident, it puts me at ease. I reach out my free arm, and Kiara clasps her hand firmly around my wrist. When she gets up and brushes Neil's curls back, I'm struck by the contrast of her dark hands against his pale forehead. She closes her eyes and begins to hum a low monotone.

Neil twitches and then spasms so powerfully, I lose my grip on his wrist and it slams into my chin. The blow propels me backward, and my chair tips dangerously, but Kiara's hold on me is like an anchor. She yanks me forward, and I fall across Neil's bucking chest. "Pin him down!" Kiara shouts.

I grit my teeth and position my knees against Neil's side. Pressing my elbows against my body, I put my forearms firmly onto his rib cage and throw my weight down as hard as I can. At the same time Autumn rushes over and holds down Neil's thrashing legs to keep him from kicking us.

Keegan jumps up to help too, but Kiara waves him away. "We're fine." He sits back against the wall again, but he's alert, ready to pitch in if Kiara needs him.

There's an insistent knocking on the door. I'm caught off guard, and Neil's next spasm pushes me forward into Kiara's abdomen. She absorbs this blow as if I were as insubstantial as a pillow, and continues to hover over Neil and press her energy into his pores with the tips of her fingers.

I scramble back to Neil's side, and as I do, I catch Nate demanding to be let in. Cash strides out into the hallway and firmly shuts the door behind him.

Kiara moans like an injured animal, and Neil goes deathly still. She removes her hand from Neil's forehead, loosens her grip on my wrist, and slumps back into her chair.

"What's happening?" I ask frantically. Autumn should assure me that this is normal, that Neil will wake up. But her face only registers confusion, followed by pity.

It may be only seconds before Neil's body fades away from me forever.

I gaze at his face, my fingers clutching at his dampened curls and my tears dripping freely onto his shirt.

Then Neil's eyes pop open and he sits up with a start, a look of horror on his face. "No! Gracie!" he shouts wildly. "Don't do it!"

seven

I SIT IN STUNNED RELIEF. Neil is alive.

But who is Gracie? Apparently Neil has been so intent on hiding her from me that he's repressed his memories of her. We shared so many memories after the collapse of the Morati architecture in Level Two, but I've never once seen Gracie.

Neil's expression vacillates between shock and confusion. And then he notices me. "Oh, Felicia—thank God! I've had the most terrible nightmare. There was an explosion, and you were hurt . . ." He reaches up to wipe the tears from my cheek.

"I'm fine," I say, trying not to cry all over again. "You were the one who was in a coma. Kiara"—I nod my head in the healer's direction—"was able to revive you by bringing one of your most repressed memories to the surface." I stress the word "repressed" and note that Neil's eyes shift downward for a split second.

Neil drops his hand back to his lap. "Coma? What happened?" He looks frantically around the room. "I saw Megan get hit. Where is she? Is she okay?"

The sadness of Megan's death wells up inside me like I'm experiencing it for the first time, burying my questions about Gracie. "She . . . she didn't make it."

"She *died*?"

I nod. "She disappeared from this level. Right in front of me."

Neil presses his balled fist against his mouth, as if to stifle a scream or keep from throwing up. His eyes are wild for a fiery moment, and I know he wishes that he could have done something to prevent what happened to Megan. But then he slumps into the headboard, and the fight fades from his face.

I want to comfort him, but there's nothing I can say or do that will make things better or bring Megan back. I don't even notice how badly my legs are shaking until Neil stills them with a firm grip on my knee. "We'll honor her memory," he says with a quiet desperation, "by not letting the Morati kill us."

Megan didn't think the Morati were a real threat, but Neil has seen their destruction firsthand. And he doesn't even know about William or that the librarian's death means the Morati can snuff out any one of us. Maybe I was the real target of the bombing, and they'll come after me to finish the job and to get their revenge. It's possible I'm putting everyone—in this room, in this dorm, in this level—in danger merely by being here. I should leave Neil's bedside right now. Get as far away from him as I can so they won't hurt him.

But I stay. Does that make me a bad person?

Cash comes back in and whispers something into Autumn's ear. She nods and clears her throat. "Cash and I have a security force meeting with Furukama." She strides over to Kiara and shakes her shoulder.

Kiara blinks and then rubs her forearm over her freckles. "That was intense. You've got a strong head, Neil. You should be feeling better soon, and it won't be long before you don't need us healers anymore." She tucks her wrists under the voluminous skirts of her red dress and stands up, a little wobbly.

Neil catches her arm to steady her. "Thank you, Kiara." His voice is warm.

Kiara curtsies and dips her chin. "It's nothing. Healing is my calling. You'll find your own soon enough." She pulls Keegan to his feet, and they leave with Autumn and Cash.

Neil and I are alone for the first time since we've arrived in Level Three.

"Come here." He scoots over against the headboard on his narrow bed to make space for me, wincing a bit as he does. He lifts his arm, and I tuck in next to him carefully. I melt into his side and lay my head on his shoulder. He might be safer without me, but he makes me feel safe.

Neil sighs into my hair. He runs his fingertips lightly over my wrist and then up my bare arm. It tickles, but in a good way. I bury my face into his shirt and breathe the scent of soap mixed with smoke.

"You almost died," I half sob into his chest. "If I had known Level Three would be so dangerous . . . Maybe we should have stayed in Level Two."

Neil shifts his position and draws me deeper into a hug. He tilts my face up and kisses my forehead. "We can get through this. We have each other."

"That's why we should share a room. I don't want there to be two doors and a hallway between us. I'll constantly worry about you. Won't you worry about me?"

Neil looks pained, and I can tell my words have caused a conflict within him. "I want you to stay. But . . ."

"But what?"

"I wouldn't have felt right about living with you on Earth." He doesn't quite meet my eyes. "How can I feel right about it here?"

I pull away from him. "In case you haven't noticed, the afterlife is not exactly what church taught it would be," I huff. "The morality police will hardly come knock your door down."

"Probably not. But even when there are no outside rules, you have to decide inside what's right. And I'm still trying to figure it all out. That's all."

"What if we materialize bunk beds?" Even as I say it, I know it's not going to fly.

He shakes his head, confirming my suspicions.

"I guess I can wait." I kiss his cheek tenderly, even though the rigidity of his belief system annoys me. I get up and smooth my dress, materializing clean fabric in place of the blood and filth as I do. "You've been through a lot, so I'll go to my room and let you rest."

"I didn't mean you have to leave right now!" He reaches for me, but I sidestep his grasp. He shoves out his bottom lip, and everything about him—the mussed curls sticking to his ears, his torn shirt and soot-blackened khakis—begs for me to lie down next to him and forget that he's pushing me away.

"Hey now, you're the one who insisted we get separate rooms." I try to keep my voice light.

"Oh yeah," he says with a lopsided grin. "That wasn't my smartest move ever, was it?"

I laugh and tap his arm with my fist. "Nope. Are you changing your mind?"

"I want to—" He catches my wrist, entwines his fingers with mine. He lies down and presses his cheek against the sheet.

"But you can't," I finish for him. He doesn't deny it, and my last bit of hope dies as he closes his eyes. His grip loosens, like he's fallen asleep.

I watch him resting for a few moments, caressing his arm lightly with my fingernails, dreading the return to my own practically empty quarters. But if Neil needs time to get used to the idea of rooming together, I should give it to him.

I trudge across the hall to my room. My dad's chair is still here, but I push it into a corner. Then I form a simple bed.

To cheer myself up I choose for the sheets and pillowcases a bright shade of Granny Smith–apple green that I admired in a department store once. I conjure up coordinating heavy drapes to cover the window. Back on Earth it always made me uncomfortable to sleep if I was exposed to the outside. Then I lie down and stare up. It should be too dark to see. I'm inside, the drapes are closed, and there are no artificial lights. There's no electricity anywhere. But I can still see. I guess seeing in the dark is a perk of the afterlife I never noticed in Level Two because everything was too bright.

The hum that warns me of the Morati's presence is a steady, low background noise to my whirring thoughts. Why is Gracie so important to Neil? Will he ever let me room with him? How can I get my memories back? Does Neil want to retrieve them as much as I do? And will we survive long enough to even have the chance to see more?

I sigh in frustration, turning my head to the blank expanse of white wall next to me. After being in the Level Two hives for so long, I can't stand the color white. I leap up off the bed. I will recreate the collage of photos I had up over my desk back in Germany.

There was a family shot in the center of my arrangement, and I can see clearly in my mind how my dad has his arm around me and is laughing so hard, his eyes are almost closed. My head tilts toward him, my eyes focused on the photographer. My mother's mouth is open, answering someone's question probably, her attention on anything but us, as usual. I materialize the print into my hand, and it seems pretty close to the original, with its glossy sheen and bright patriotic colors, even if it is merely a copy. Then I materialize a thumbtack and pin it to the wall.

Next I pin up photos of Autumn and me. My favorite is still the one where we dressed up as mermaids in the middle of August. We went door-to-door telling the neighbors we needed candy for our trip to visit the sea king, and my dad took a Polaroid of us when we returned from our scavenging with purple-stained lips and sticky hands. I also love the candid shot of us at the Blue Lagoon in Iceland, our heads close together like we're sharing a secret.

I don't have many photos of Neil. For someone who was so comfortable on the stage, Neil didn't like to pose. I did clip one from the newspaper, from the article about his performance in *Our Town* where he's kneeling at Emily's grave. There were a few on Neil's phone, but you can't materialize electronics here. Grammy snapped one before prom with her old camera, and I took arty photos of her rosebushes to finish off the roll so I could get them developed. The resulting print was a bit crinkled because I used it as a bookmark. I'd pore over it for hours, admiring the way Neil looked in a suit and tie. I pin it next to the one of my family and trace my finger over his crooked smile.

By the end of the night, one wall is completely covered with photos and mementos. If the Morati make me disappear from this dimension, at least part of me will be left behind.

eight

BELLS SOUND, signaling what I assume is the start of my second day in Level Three. I don't want to wear this sunny yellow dress when everything is falling apart around me. I materialize jeans and a plain black T-shirt, but black belongs to the seraphim guard. Instead I decide on a pale pink blouse with scalloped sleeves. Neutrality sounds good right now.

I go across the hall to Neil's room and knock. Hearing a muffled voice but not catching the words, I take for granted that Neil is inviting me in. I push open the door. Libby sits in the chair Kiara used last night, and Neil is on the edge of his bed. All his injuries seem to have healed, and he has also changed into a fresh orange polo shirt.

"Good morning, Felicia." Libby gets up. "I'm on my way out."

"Thanks, Libby." Neil rubs the back of his neck. "I'll think about what you said."

"You do that. Remember, the best thing we can do right now is stick to our routines so everything seems back to normal. Everyone should be in class today. No exceptions." Then she shuts the door firmly behind her.

"Did the bells wake you?" Neil bounds over and squishes me into a hug. I'm struck, all over again, by the easy way we fit together.

"No, I was up all night. I was thinking, with the Morati out there, and the bombings . . . maybe we should skip class and stay here. Maybe it would be safer."

"You heard what Libby said." Neil hugs me more tightly. "And besides, all we can do is stay vigilant. If the Morati want to find us, what's preventing them from coming to our rooms?"

He's right. I could ask Autumn to assign us a security detail. It wouldn't be effective against a bomb, though. Or we could materialize force fields and walk around with those. But that wouldn't work either. We'd tire out in less than five minutes.

"I have something for you." He practically skips over to his desk and opens the top drawer. He pulls out a long, flat box and hands it to me. "Birthday gift number two."

I pull the lid from the box and find a mini Maglite, like the one Neil was carrying on the night of our first kiss in the forest.

"It doesn't work here," he says, "but it reminds me of one of the happiest days of my life, so I thought you might like to have it anyway."

I place the package on Neil's bed and lean into his waiting lips, closing my eyes and picturing the looming trees and the way the light bounced through the darkness. I let the memory of that faraway kiss wash over me, intensifying the closeness of this moment.

Neil's door creaks open. "Ready to go?" Autumn calls from the doorway. Neil releases me from his embrace but laces his fingers through mine.

"Ready." Neil says it more convincingly than I could right now.

"Muse orientation meets in Hall One," Autumn says.

The trek to Hall One is short. We join a stream of other students on the way to their classes, over the avenue and through the grassy courtyard where Neil nearly died yesterday. Neil tenses as we walk past the spot where he fell, but he doesn't say anything. There's none of the chatting and joking we saw yesterday. Instead people hurry with their heads down and their shoulders hunched.

Autumn leads us into Hall One and into a corridor with a row of orange doors, each a richer hue than the last. She stops in front of the first one, painted an orange as pale as the first tinges of sunset. "This is where they hold orientation.

Miss Claypool will call everyone in soon. I'd wait with you, but I have to make sure everyone goes to class." She gives me a quick hug and leaves.

Neil and I wait with a group of about thirty other applicants. He retrieves the brochure from his back pocket and pores over it, like there's going to be a pop quiz or something.

"I wonder when they'll finally let us in," says a male voice beside us.

When I turn, the guy smiles ruefully at me. He looks like he's in one of those hipster rock bands, with longish dark hair that falls over one eye, a fitted long-sleeved T-shirt, and skinny jeans slung low on his hips. The awkward way he stands, though—sort of like a junior high kid who isn't comfortable with his height yet—makes me think he'd be the bassist rather than the lead singer.

Something about his manner sets me at ease. "Well, until they do, at least we can read over this amazing brochure." I elbow Neil in the side.

"I'm Moby. Nice to meet you." He tosses the hair out of his eye and sticks out his hand.

Both Neil and I look at his hand awkwardly and mumble our names. Then, hoping I don't piss him off, I say, "Uh, I think it's the custom to bow here. Shaking hands is too intimate because you might slip up and let the other person look at your memories."

Moby shoves his hands into the pockets of his jeans, pulling them down dangerously low. "Makes sense. Do you know anyone else in the muse program?"

"We used to," Neil says. A haunted look comes over his face. "Her name was Megan. She played the tuba, and made animal sculptures out of grass. But she died in the bombing."

With the side of his black boot, Moby kicks at the baseboard that runs along the hallway. "I also lost someone. He was this strung-out roadie who used to work our shows. I don't know anyone else here."

I guess I was right about Moby being in a band. "Now you know us." He seems nice, and obviously he could use some friends.

Moby nods. "God, I wish I had a cigarette. Maybe I could materialize one. But it's not the same." So far I haven't seen anyone smoking. I'm not sure it's even possible.

Neil looks at him curiously. "Did you consider other afterlife positions, other than muse?"

"Not really. I thought with my background . . ." He trails off.

"Yeah." Neil points out a section at the top of the second page of the brochure. "But I've been thinking that healer might also be interesting." He reads aloud from the brochure. "Healers tend to the perceived physical wounds of recruits who are still adjusting to afterlife physiology, as well as provide psychological counseling. Prerequisites include: one, honesty and integrity; two, demonstrated compassion; and three, agreement to a strict adherence to healer-patient confidentiality."

The scene in Neil's bedroom last night flashes before my eyes. I'm grateful for the healer's work, but I don't want him to be one, or to be one myself. "If we joined the healers, you'd likely end up with Nate on your couch. He's messed up enough to need counseling." This statement earns me a dimpled smile from Neil, so I snatch the brochure. "Let's see what else there is."

I scan the text for another alternative. "Listen to this. Seraphim guards are part of an elite force that performs highly secretive and sensitive missions. Prerequisites include: one, a strong mind; two, a highly developed sense of loyalty; and three, ability to follow orders." I materialize a highlighter and mark prerequisite one with fluorescent green. "Kiara said you have a strong mind, Neil," I say pointedly.

Moby whistles under his breath. "Seems like a sweet gig. Bet you have to be as tough as nails to get through that training."

The door opens, revealing a woman in a high-necked black dress with an orange lace overlay. She looks like she stepped out of Victorian England by way of a Halloween jack-o'-lantern. Her gray hair is streaked with orange too. "Come in, come in." She waves her arms. "Time's a-wasting."

The room is a typical lecture hall, with benches arranged to face a lectern and chalkboard. We all find a place to sit and murmur expectantly as our teacher writes her name—"Miss Claypool"—on the board with orange chalk.

She tilts her head upward, raising her fingers toward the

ceiling. "Repeat after me: We invoke thee, oh patron muse."

We repeat the muse slogan after her, like a chant: "We invoke thee, oh patron muse."

"Today I will introduce you to the art of being a muse. It's more than merely a job; it's a profession that will allow you to truly suck the marrow out of your afterlife," Miss Claypool says.

Neil scoots closer to me on the bench so that our shoulders touch. I shift my weight toward him. What would he consider would be getting the most out of his afterlife? Does he long to restore his lost memories as much as I do? We haven't gotten the chance to talk about it yet.

"To become a muse you will attend training sessions. At the end of the term, those who have earned enough credits, who excel at their audition in their chosen track, and who pass their detachment test will apprentice with career muses on their missions to Earth."

A girl raises her hand but asks her question before being called on. "What's the detachment test for?"

"Muses can be tempted to go rogue," Miss Claypool explains. "A muse's job is to inspire or help with memorization of text. But sometimes muses might feel the urge to give more story to their own lives or to right perceived wrongs. And to do this they might convince a writer to add them as a character to their movie or novel. The detachment test minimizes that risk."

It's not that I want to add more story to my life—it's that I want to know how my story continued after the car accident. It seems unfair that my natural curiosity might put me at risk for failing the detachment test.

Miss Claypool outlines what will be expected of us. She reveals that the course work consists of cultural immersion, for which we will have access to a curated collection of memory editions, which are readings of books or viewings of movies and art from the memories of people who experienced them on Earth.

This captures my full attention. "How do you get all the memories into the collection?" I ask. "Wouldn't the person who donates the memory edition have to be hooked up to the library for you to access it?" That's how it worked in Level Two. In order to rent a memory from someone else, that person's hive had to be part of the network. That's why I could never find Neil's memories, since his hive was isolated.

"Not at all," Miss Claypool says. "When a work is deemed worthy for inclusion, the memory holder allows it to be voluntarily harvested for the good of the program."

"But don't they lose it, then?" Neil asks.

"Not exactly. They can come back to the library and refresh their short-term memories with the material anytime they want. And when they retire, they can petition to have it returned to them in full. Once you get a library card, you can plug yourself in to access the memory editions."

That makes it sound like there is a way for human memories to be taken and packaged. Maybe that's what happened to my lost memories and to Neil's. If those memories are sitting around in someone's collection, though, I can't imagine why ours were chosen. Of course, it's also possible that the memories still exist in our heads somewhere, waiting to be unlocked.

The orientation goes on for hours and hours. At the end of our class, Miss Claypool hands out a workbook to everyone and tells us that we can skip class tomorrow if we'd like to check out the career fair. I want to ask her more about the memory extraction process, but my classmates mob her with questions, and Neil nudges me out the door.

Neil takes my hand and we start walking back to the dorms, Moby beside us. While crossing Eastern Avenue, my neck prickles, like someone's watching me. But when I turn, no one is looking my way. In fact, the few stragglers out at this time seem to be deliberately avoiding eye contact with anyone and curling into themselves to be as inconspicuous as possible. Still, I can't shake the feeling, and I shudder.

"What is it?" Neil asks, jumping behind me like a shield. He plants his feet wide, as if bracing for another attack. Moby goes on high alert too, scanning the rooftops of the row of buildings we just left. I guess we're all a bit jumpy right now.

"Nothing," I say. If I make a big deal out of it, I'll freak myself out. "How was it to go on tour, Moby?"

Moby relaxes and launches into a story about his tour bus breaking down. He might look like your typical mysterious loner dude, but it turns out he's quite the entertainer. He continues to regale us with self-deprecating anecdotes from his life on the road, and we find ourselves slowing our pace to snail speed to avoid parting ways.

Inevitably Moby excuses himself. "Thanks for cheering me up." He punches Neil and then me lightly on our arms. He holds up his tattered brochure and grins. "Time to go back to my room to decide what I want to do with my afterlife."

After Moby leaves, we run into Kiara and Keegan on Western Avenue. Kiara has a protective arm around her brother. His hat is pushed all the way down, so that the brim hides most of his face.

"Everything okay?" Neil asks. When even the healers look worried, it's not a great sign.

"All good." Kiara forces a smile. She elbows Keegan in his side, and he looks up at us and nods a somber greeting. "Want to come by tomorrow during the career fair?" she asks. "We don't get many visitors at the healers' booth. Might be nice to see friendly faces."

"Of course," Neil says. "We'd love to."

I touch her shoulder. "I wanted to thank you again for what you did for Neil. We're so grateful that you and Libby were there."

"What did Libby do?" Neil asks. I never told him about my own injuries.

"She fixed my hearing. The blast was so loud, I thought I went deaf."

"Libby used to train as a healer before she switched over to administration," Kiara says like it's an afterthought, and hitches up her long skirt. "See you tomorrow, then."

Kiara shuffles away with Keegan, and Neil and I exchange uneasy looks. The atmosphere of Level Three has changed so completely since yesterday. Now it's like a ghost town.

As we cross the street, I try to recapture some of our earlier lightheartedness. "Moby sure had some crazy stories of life on the road, didn't he?"

"Yeah, and he has such a vivid way of telling them. It was like watching a movie."

"That was hilarious how that girl threw a bouquet of flowers onstage and then the bees flew out and stung the lead singer." I mime a bee buzzing by his ear.

He swats my hand away. "You didn't think it was so funny when you got stung by a bee, did you?"

I tense. Is Neil scolding me? But then he smiles and I realize he's teasing. "It's not funny he got hurt," I say. "It's funny to picture all these bees lying in wait between the flowers, calculating the perfect time to strike. What was your favorite story?" We reach the double doors of our dorm, and he ushers me in.

"Not any one in particular. I enjoyed hearing what it's like to be a professional musician. That could have been me," he says wistfully as we make our way through the foyer toward the stairs.

"Maybe it was." It's the perfect opening to discuss getting our memories back. "I mean, we know now that we didn't die in that car accident. Think of all we might have achieved."

Neil takes the stairs two at a time, and I struggle to keep up with him. "Well, short of forcing memories out of Nate, or having the luck of finding someone else who knew us after, we'll never find out, will we?"

"We could always ask Nate again to share them with us."

At the mention of his brother's name, Neil's face puckers like he's eaten a rotten orange. "Keep your distance from Nate." We reach our hallway.

"Why? Because you think Nate might tell me all your deep dark secrets?" I'm half teasing, half probing. *Because he might tell me about you and Gracie?*

He whirls around to face me, his inside battle for control clearly showing in his eyes. "Nate's a jerk, and the only memories he'd likely be willing to show us are the bad ones."

"You must want to know what happened to us after the crash." He does. I heard it in his voice.

"Of course it bothers me," he confirms. "But in the end does what we did or didn't do on Earth really matter? We're here now. We're together. What more could we want?"

He's right in a way. Wanting to be reunited with Neil was the one thing that got me through Level Two. But that might not be enough for me anymore. I need to figure out who I really am. After all, we are nothing more than a collection of our memories. And if our memories are incomplete, we can never be complete people.

"But you were the one who told me that our experiences make us who we are—even the bad experiences. Don't you still believe that?" I ask.

Neil shrugs. "I did say that. But your memories are not all that you'll ever be. They're in the past. It's your choices now that make you what you'll be in the future. Libby told me this morning that the sooner we accept the loss of those memories, the better score we'll get on the muse detachment test. You *do* want to be a muse with me, right?"

We're standing in front of his door now. "Yes, of course," I say.

"Then let's try to forget we ever found out about our lost memories."

I suspect the muse detachment test is not Neil's only reason to want to put this behind us. He wants to close down this topic of conversation because it's too intertwined with his Gracie story. By putting all his memories in the past, he can avoid the ones he doesn't want to face. I hate that he doesn't feel like he can share his secrets with me. I'd love to tell him that I'll never be able to accept the loss of my post-crash memories. That I'd give anything right now to find out what happened to me on Earth and what happened between us. But obviously I can't, because he doesn't want to hear it. I can't afford to turn him against me, even a tiny bit. He's my rock. He's the one who showed me how to be good again—showed me that I *could* be good again. As much as it hurts, maybe this is something I have to figure out on my own.

"I'll try." What else can I say?

"I hope so. I think it's for the best." He holds up our

muse workbook. "I want to get a head start on this. See you later?"

"We can't study together?"

"I can't concentrate when you're around. We have to take this seriously."

"Umm . . . okay." I wait for him to laugh and say he's only joking. But he doesn't. He gives me a quick peck on the cheek and leaves me standing there in the middle of the hallway.

In a daze I enter my own room and flop onto bed, hurling my workbook at the wall. It lands with a thud on the carpet. A knock at the door a few seconds later perks me up. I rush to the door, thrilled that Neil has come around so quickly.

But it's not Neil. It's Julian.

nine

I CAN'T MOVE. I take in the sight of Julian, from his shaggy blond bangs, dark eyes, and sharp cheekbones all the way down to his black high-tops, halfway laced. He looks exactly like he did the last time I saw him, intense and maddeningly gorgeous.

All the nerve endings in my scalp tingle, but the buzzing that alerts me to the Morati's presence stays at the same background level instead of spiking in Julian's presence as I expected. It's crazy, but the one thing that stands out the most from this unbelievable reunion is that I'm not a human Morati detector after all. Libby will be so disappointed.

"Quick." He pushes past me. "Close the door. I don't want to be seen."

Julian struts in and makes a great show of searching the room, even bending down to check under the bed. "Where's Neil? Trouble in paradise already?"

I gape at him until I realize that my mouth hanging open is not that flattering. I swallow twice. "He's across the hall. We decided to take separate rooms for now." I hope the lump in my throat isn't noticeable in my voice. I cross my arms over my chest to prevent them from doing anything stupid. Like hugging Julian and making him think I'm the least bit excited to see him. Because I'm not. Am I?

Julian smirks at me knowingly. "Sure you did." Nope, definitely not excited to see him. He's as infuriating as ever.

"So you barge in here, acting like there's some kind of emergency, and really it's all because you want to tease me about Neil?" I shake my head in disgust.

"I'm in trouble." Julian sits down on my bed and then sprawls across it like he owns it. I'll have to remember to materialize new sheets when he goes.

"Why?" I materialize a beanbag chair and sink into it.

"The security team is going room to room, asking people questions. They're trying to find the angels they think blew up the records room and that are responsible for the latest bombing."

"But they don't know you're an angel—"

"Autumn does."

"Autumn knew you only on Earth." I shift in the beanbag chair. When Autumn finds out about Julian being here, it could complicate our friendship again. Or maybe she truly is over him.

His mouth drops open a bit as what I say seems to sink in. But then he says, "Well, Neil definitely knows."

"You think Neil has an interest in turning you in?"

"Neil is the type who always wants to do what's right. If he sees me here, he'll want to tell the authorities about me. He'll think I know something."

Julian does have a point. "Do you know something?"

"Not really. As soon as I got to Level Three—"

"How did you get here?" I interrupt.

"I can't tell you the exact mechanics, but I arrived at the portal like everyone does. There was no one on duty to greet me, and I could tell there had been an explosion. I was afraid I might be blamed, so I've been holed up in a dorm room these past four months, waiting for you. You're my biggest ally, and you'll help me." Julian radiates confidence. He's even cockier than I remembered.

"Umm . . . have you forgotten that you were sent to Earth to kill me so I would arrive in Level Two earlier?" Julian was driving the stolen police car that I thought killed me, and the Morati had put him up to it so that they could use my energy that much sooner.

"But I didn't kill you."

"Yeah. I know." I snort. "And you know how I know? Because Neil's brother, Nate, showed me his memory of meeting me at the hospital after the accident. The accident you caused."

Julian nods. "Exactly! You didn't die that day."

"You knew?" He knew all this time that I didn't die, and he never told me. I'll turn in the jerk myself. I go to leap out of the beanbag chair, but it's not really the best type of chair to leap out of. So instead of attacking Julian, I end up fighting with the chair, all awkward arms and legs and punching and falling.

Julian rewards my clumsy efforts with a throaty laugh. "God, Felicia, it really is great to see you again."

I flip my long hair behind my shoulders and zap the offending beanbag chair with a dose of dematerialization. I drag my father's armchair from the corner. And then I sit down with a huff, and glare at Julian. If he wants me to not turn him in, he'd better answer my questions to my satisfaction. Maybe Julian showing up is a blessing in disguise. After all, he's Morati. He must know something that I can use to my advantage. "Why didn't you ever tell me that I lived past my eighteenth birthday? You had plenty of chances."

Julian shrugs. "It wasn't relevant."

"Not relevant? This is my life, Julian. It's important to me!"

"Correction: this is your afterlife. And it was important that you stay focused in Level Two. To bring down the Morati. It worked, didn't it?"

I'm so upset, I don't know where to start. I open my mouth to protest, but all that comes out is a grunt of frustration.

"Well, that was eloquent," Julian remarks.

I push down my bitter feelings as much as I can, and I turn on the charm. "You must know what happened to me after the car accident. Can you give me the Cliffs Notes's version? How did I really die?"

"You won't believe me, but I have no idea." Julian throws his legs over the side of the bed and sits up straight, facing me head-on. "I mean, I made sure you survived the crash, but then I was banned from having access to you. That's why I was so happy to see you again when I found you in Level Two."

"You're right. I don't believe you. You have a habit of twisting the truth to your own advantage. And you've proven you aren't above using me."

Julian throws up his hands in surrender. "Sorry. The Morati's hives had to be dismantled in order for people to be able to move on. You were the only one who could set that in motion. We saved mankind. You should be happy."

"You took my place." All at once Julian's motive for sacrificing himself becomes clear. "But you didn't do it for me, did you? You did it because you thought it was the only way you could move on to Level Three."

"I did it for both of us," he says emphatically. "The mainframe was supposed to harness all the energy of Level Two, filtered through you, and allow the Morati to break through to the next level—something they could never do before. But if I hadn't taken over for you, it would have been too much for you to handle. The rebels were able to stop most of the Morati from ascending, but some made it. And when I took your place, I didn't save just you. I also broke through."

It makes sense now. Those few times in the mainframe when I lost connection with a Morati angel—they didn't die. They ascended. But I can't remember how many times that happened. Maybe twice, maybe more.

"Thank you, and you're welcome." I give him a huge fake smile. "You want my help. I want yours, too."

Julian's eyes narrow. "What is it that you want?"

I go straight to the heart of the matter. "I want my memories back. Obviously."

He shakes his head. "Didn't you get the memo? You're supposed to put earthly things behind you. Look to the future and prepare for your eternal afterlife. Your lost memories are extra baggage that would hold you back. Everyone here would tell you that you're lucky you have less to deal with. It makes you a better candidate for the really elite positions."

"How do you know all this if you were 'holed up' in a room?" I challenge.

"Chatter in the halls."

"Well, that's a load of crap," I spit out. "And I'll let you in on a little secret—until I get my memories back, I'm not going to be in the mood to cooperate with anyone. So will you help me or not?"

"If that's really what you want, I'll do what I can. But you must have been reprogrammed when you came to Level Two, so only the Morati will have access to your other memories."

"What do they want with them?" I ask.

"Insurance. Leverage. Control. A means of persuasion if all else fails. The Morati don't play fair."

"After the fall of the mainframe, Eli locked up all the Morati behind brimstone bars. What if my memories are with those Morati and not the ones who came here?"

"Brimstone makes angels go crazy."

"It does?"

Julian shudders. "We don't keel over immediately, and we have to be completely surrounded by it, but every minute of exposure to it drains us of a little power and sanity."

"So we have to hope that the Morati in Level Three have my memories. But they're all trying to blend in with humans. How will we find them?"

"I can recognize them." Julian smiles broadly, like he's won my allegiance to him or something. Which in a way he has. If I want a chance to get my memories back, I'm bound to him until he identifies the Morati for me. But once he does, all bets are off.

"We should start looking now. Go door-to-door if we have to."

"Don't you understand how dangerous that is?" Julian asks. "They want to be found as little as I do. If they hear we're on their trail . . . well, you saw what happened yesterday in the courtyard. They're not afraid to strike again."

"Okay, so what can we do? Can you track their signals?"

"They're actively masking their signals, like I am. I can't go out in public right now because Neil knows me and could identify me. But maybe you could talk to Neil. Convince him I'm not evil and that he shouldn't turn me in. Then maybe I can risk it."

I don't know that I can convince anyone that Julian's not evil, when I'm not convinced myself.

I stand up and stretch. "It's past curfew. I should rest up for tomorrow." I need to get him out of my room so I can think.

Julian grins and pats the bed beside him. "There's more than enough room for both of us."

Oh, wow. I totally walked into that one. "Why don't you get back to hiding in your hole? You're not staying here."

"Aww." Julian pouts. "Why not?"

"Look." I put on my sternest expression. "We can be allies or whatever. That's fine. But get one thing straight. Neil and I are together. And you're not going to mess that up for me. Got it?"

Julian vaults off the bed. He slides over to me until he's standing very near. He doesn't touch me but leans down and whispers into my ear so softly, it makes me shiver. "Got it."

Being this close to him again confuses both my body and mind. It's not like in Level Two, where I physically craved him like a drug, but he's so solid. So familiar. And I'm 100 percent sure he would never make me take a separate room. I don't know how it happens, if I close the gap between us or he does, but all at once my cheek grazes his shoulder and then his hands are pressed into my back. I have the unspeakable urge to pin him up against the wall, to pull up his shirt and run my hands over his bare skin. But instead I settle for allowing him to keep hugging me, far longer and more tightly than what's appropriate between friends. If "friends" is even the right word for what we are.

Finally I will myself to pull away. What am I doing, lingering here with Julian when Neil's the one I love? It's not because I want Julian. It's because I want the physical contact that Neil isn't willing to give me. That's all. I walk to the door and grip the doorknob, hoping Julian can't see how much he's shaken me. Before I can turn the knob, Julian strides over and puts his hand over mine. "I'll go. For now. But be careful, okay?" When I nod, he nudges me out of the way, opens the door a crack, and peers out into the hallway. He seems satisfied that it's all clear and ventures out. But as he does, Neil's door opens, and Nate steps out.

Nate raises his eyebrows and closes Neil's door. "Nice, Felicia. You sure work fast."

ten

"I'VE BEEN LOOKING for you," I say in response. Going on the offensive is a better strategy than reacting defensively with someone like Nate. The fact that Julian kisses my cheek good-bye before he swaggers down the hall, however, doesn't exactly strengthen my case.

"Really? Have you been thinking over my roommate offer?" he asks with a suggestive leer.

I fake the most carefree laugh I can muster. "Maybe I have."

Nate laughs too, and the way his eyes crinkle tells me that it is authentic. "It wouldn't be the first time one of Neil's girlfriends looked for an upgrade." My eyes dart to

Neil's closed door. I half expect him to come blazing out, ready to kick Nate where it counts.

"Who was that guy?" he asks in a bored tone, like he doesn't care. Now that Julian is completely out of hearing range, Nate's earlier flirtatiousness is gone. I guess it was all for show.

I match his tone. "Someone I knew when I lived in Germany."

We stare at each other a long moment. He leans against the frame of Neil's door like a drug dealer, overdone casualness with an undertone of menace. "Won't you invite me in?" he asks, the subject of Julian apparently tucked away to be exploited at a later date. "I believe we have something to discuss." Yeah, like the fact that he has hooked me on my stolen memories. What will it cost me to get another fix?

As much as I'd like to send him away, I play along. I usher him in and materialize a small table between two chairs and take a seat. The more this looks like a study environment, the less he's going to get the wrong idea. "So you were checking on Neil?" I ask.

"He's sleeping." Nate flexes his arms as he sits down, as if he can't help but show off his muscles.

Nate's comment confuses me. I haven't been able to sleep since I died, even though Neil seems to have managed it. I materialize a bottle of nail polish—clear but with flecks of gold—to have something to do with my hands. "Do you sleep too? Are these dorm rooms for sleeping?" I ask.

"That's not all they're good for." Nate's heavy-lidded stare makes me squirm.

"I'm sure no one knows that better than you do." I smile sweetly, but I'm barfing on the inside. I concentrate on the polish brush, making sure the stroke is even.

He grins. "There are so many notches in my bedpost, it's in danger of collapse."

"You must be positively swarming with STDs."

"Nah, none of that here." Nate waves his hand, dismissing what he presumes is my concern for his health. "It's like heaven even though it isn't. All the pleasures of sex with none of the complications."

I highly doubt there are no complications. I mean, maybe Nate's okay with bed hopping, but the girls he's with likely expect more, unless they have moved beyond emotional pain in addition to physical pain. That sounds wrong to me. If you're not in it emotionally, where's the passion? What's the point? I can't imagine my first time with Neil being only some physical exchange.

Physical. The word dredges out what Kiara said about our bodies here being projections of our minds. I grip the polish brush too tightly, and knock over the bottle, so that a gold stream pools out onto the table. If everything we feel is not a result of nerve endings but the memory of the feeling those nerve endings used to produce, then what if you've never felt something before? What if I can never know what having sex feels like because I never had it on Earth?

Nate notices my agitation. "What's wrong?"

"What about virgins?" I blurt.

"Not my type. Too clingy." Nate is not going to win any sensitivity awards, that's for sure.

"No, I mean, can virgins feel anything during afterlife sex?"

Nate scoffs. "How would I know?"

"Never mind." I'll obviously have to go to someone else with my concerns. Time to change the subject. "Tell me more about sleeping."

"We don't actually sleep." His voice is now robotic, as if he has switched over to a mentor mode and is reciting from a manual. "That's a biological function that's as obsolete in the afterlife as breathing and eating. Sleep is more like advanced meditation. It's a way for us to process our learning and development and grow stronger in our chosen path. Some people take to it naturally, like Neil. Others need more practice."

"Okay."

"You're boring me. I'm out of here." Nate gets up and turns to go.

"Wait." I take a steadying breath. "I have a favor to ask. I need to view another memory."

Nate's smile is tarnished with so much gloat, it makes me gag. This is exactly what he wanted me to say. "I can't do that."

I step closer to him. He can. He just doesn't want to. "Why not?"

He closes the gap between us, and I force myself not to

back away. Instead I smile up at him as nicely as I can manage.

Nate leans over and says clearly into my ear, "You do have something that I want." He places his hands lightly on my hips and pulls me toward him until our bodies touch. I'm revolted that he'd betray his brother.

"Is that so?" I brace myself inwardly, and suck in my breath as his lips near mine. I will shove him away if he tries anything.

"Yes, but clearly it's not what you think." He taps my nose twice and steps back, frowning.

I duck my head and let my hair fall over my face to hide the flame on my cheeks. This is super-awkward. "I didn't think *that*."

He doesn't challenge my fib. "I'll show you a memory, but then you also have to do me a favor."

Hope blooms in my chest, but then it's tempered with suspicion. "What kind of favor?"

"I haven't decided yet, but I trust you'll hold up your end of the bargain when the time comes?"

A blank check is a dangerous proposition. But he knows I'm desperate and that I won't refuse him, even though I'll most certainly regret it later. "Of course."

"What memory would you like to see?"

That's an excellent question. Since I can't rely on him to show me more memories later, this might be my one and only chance to find out what became of Neil and me. But on the other hand I also need as much context as possible, so skipping ahead to some random memory might not be the best idea either. "What was the next time you saw Neil and me together? After the hospital?"

Nate nods. "Give me your hand."

I raise my palm eagerly, and as soon as our skin connects, the memory transfer begins and I am inside Nate's head again.

These roses better be worth it. Nate can tell by the way the nurse at the front desk is eyeing him that she wishes they were for her. *Nope. Sorry, lady. You are so not my type.*

Nate saunters down the hall toward Neil's room. His father told him that Neil is being discharged today. Neil won't like that Nate's the one to come pick him up, but Neil will have to deal with it.

Nate stands outside the half-closed door, about to nudge it open, when he hears Felicia's strained voice and Neil's frustrated grunt in reply. Nate leans in closer, relishing the chance to to eavesdrop on an argument.

"But it'd be so much cheaper," Felicia says, with that annoying whiny edge women get that drives men to drink. "And we can get a two-bedroom if it makes you feel holier."

"Look," Neil says in an even, reasonable tone. "It's a tough break that your dad has to sell Grammy's house to pay her nursing home fees, but us living together is not the solution. Your dad suggested getting a roommate, right? Have you asked Savannah? Or Belen?"

Nate peeks into the room and sees Felicia with her arms around Neil's neck, all lovey-dovey. "They're both going to school here, so they can live at home. And besides, I want it to be you I see when I get home from work and get up in the morning. I mean, Savannah is nice and all, but she's got nothing on you in the kissing department." She giggles and pecks him all over his face.

Neil raises his eyebrows. He's out of his cast, but his leg is in a brace. "And how would you know that?" he asks, laughing.

"Maybe I better test you out again just to make sure." She kisses him, and they tumble into Neil's bed and fall quiet. Nate stands, impatient, for a good three minutes, but their lip-lock session doesn't look like it will end anytime soon.

Nate raps against the door. They break apart, startled. Felicia adjusts her tank top and tucks it into her shorts, and Neil stumbles off the bed.

"Hey, you two." Nate steps into the room, holding out the roses. "I brought you these, Felicia. I hope I'm not interrupting anything."

Felicia's eyes light up when she sees the flowers, and she skips over and takes them from Nate with a smile and thanks. But Neil's annoyed. No surprise there. "What are you doing here?" Neil asks. "I asked Dad to pick us up."

"And Dad asked me." Nate shrugs and points at an overstuffed duffel bag on the floor. "Is that ready to go?"

"Yeah." Neil pushes it toward Nate with his good foot.

"Well, pick it up and let's go," Nate says.

Felicia slings a backpack over her shoulder. "Let me get

that for you," Nate says, sliding it down her bare arm, making sure that his fingertips lightly brush her skin as he does.

She shivers. Exactly the reaction he was looking for. "Thanks, Nate." She exchanges a glance with Neil, who rolls his eyes.

"You've been discharged and everything?" Nate asks as Neil shuffles toward the door with a noticeable limp. He doesn't need crutches, but the bag slows him down.

"Yes," Neil says. Felicia offers him her arm, but he declines. She bites her lip.

Nate can't help thinking this is a perfect chance to stir up trouble. "So, where to?" he asks as they head down the hall toward the elevators.

"Home. Where else?" Neil answers.

"Thought maybe you two got yourselves an apartment. Or do you not plan on sticking around here after the summer?"

"We'll be here another year at least." Felicia scratches at a scab. "We're working to save up for college. Neil deferred a year. And I . . . well, I still need to apply." She hugs herself, squeezing so tightly, her knuckles go white. She glances at Neil. "I keep telling Neil we should get a place together—"

"It's none of Nate's business." Neil grits his teeth.

"Oh, are you worried what the church will think if you live in sin?" Nate asks innocently, hitting the down button to call the elevator. "You could always get married. I mean, seriously, you two belong together. Everyone can see that."

"We've known each other only a little more than seven

months." Felicia fiddles with a charm that's hanging from a chain around her neck. It looks like a beehive.

The elevator dings, and everyone steps in. "So what?" Nate says. "Time doesn't matter. When it's right, it's right." Not that he actually believes this, of course. Marriage is for suckers. Living with his mom and all her various husbands over the years taught him that.

Neil punches the button for the lobby, and the doors close. "Just drop it, Nate. In fact, why don't you go? We'll call a cab."

"But that's so expensive," Felicia moans.

"Or we'll take a bus, like you did to get here."

The elevator descends. It's old and it lurches, pitching Neil, who is unsteady on his feet, against the mirrored wall and making him drop his bag on his injured foot.

"Why don't you let me carry that for you?" Felicia picks up his bag at the same time he does, and they both pull on the straps in a comical tug-of-war. The elevator doors open, and Neil reluctantly lets Felicia take his bag. She groans. "What do you have in here, bricks?"

Nate pulls the bag from her hand as they exit the elevator. He doesn't find it heavy at all. "I'll be your packhorse. And your chauffeur. No arguments." He heads to the right, through the automatic doors that lead to the parking garage.

"Fine," Neil mutters. "But let's talk about something else."

Nate smirks. *Showtime*. "I got the 411 on Gracie. Vic's mom is still in touch with her mom."

Neil sputters like someone's hit him on the back, and then throws Nate a look of pure venom. Nate wasn't aware that Neil was even capable of such a look.

"Gracie?" Felicia asks Nate, intrigued. "You mentioned her before. Is she an old friend of yours?"

Nate winks. "You could say that."

Once at the car Nate pops the trunk and dumps the bags into it. He unlocks the doors and opens the front passenger door for Felicia.

"Neil should sit in front, with his brace and all." She helps Neil get settled and then smiles when Nate opens the back door for her. "Thanks."

"My pleasure."

Nate gets in and starts the engine. Neil stares straight ahead, his lips pressed into a thin line.

"So what did Vic tell you about Gracie?" Felicia tries for casual by sniffing the roses, but it's obvious she's deadly curious.

As Nate maneuvers the car out of the narrow parking spot, he glances over at Neil, whose jaw is set so tight that his face is twitching. "She is thinking of coming back for a visit," Nate says. "She hasn't set foot in Ohio in years. I don't blame her, after what happened."

"Oh, well, that will be nice for her family." Felicia looks like she wants to ask more but is too polite. But that doesn't matter. She'll definitely be pumping Neil for details later, so mission accomplished. Nate can't help grinning.

○ ○ ○

Nate scrutinizes me as I process what I've seen. It's funny that Neil and I seem to have had the same differences of opinion on Earth regarding our living arrangements as we do here. If I only knew how it resolved then, it might help me form a strategy now, and allow Neil and me to get closer. Nate's thoughts about Gracie hint at something deeper, but I still haven't gotten any answers to what would cause Neil to shout out her name in Kiara's healing session.

"I need to view more." I lift up my palm so I can connect again.

"Nope, not part of the deal." Nate shakes his head slowly. His patronizing tone makes me want to punch him.

"I could do you two favors."

"Let's not get ahead of ourselves."

"Fine." And then I ask him what I swore I wouldn't. "What about Gracie? Why was she such a big deal to you two?"

"You need to ask Neil."

"He didn't seem like he wanted to talk about her."

"Give him time. It's a traumatic time in his past." Nate pats my arm. "I can tell you that Gracie's the reason Neil doesn't like me much."

So Gracie caused a rift between the brothers. At least that's a small nugget of truth I can work with.

"Well, did Neil ever tell me about Gracie when I was alive?" If I can view Neil's confession in one of Nate's memories later, then maybe I don't have to press Neil for answers now.

"Not when I was around."

I sigh in frustration. "Can't you tell me anything? Did Neil and I move in together? Did we go to college? Did we get married?" This is torture.

"You don't want to know what I know, trust me."

"What do you mean by that?" All my nonexistent blood rushes to my head. Maybe I'm about to cross a line that I shouldn't, but right now I don't care. I need to know. "Stop teasing me and tell me!"

Nate grabs my shoulders. "Remember, you're the one who forced this out of me. You have no one to blame but yourself."

I nod, gulping.

Nate lets go of me and steps back, opening the door to leave. "As far as I know, you and Neil broke up."

eleven

"WHAT DO YOU MEAN, 'as far as I know'?" I run after him and block his way out.

"It means that things got bad between you two. And then I left town. But I didn't need to be psychic to see you were headed to Splitsville."

"But you must have heard something later, from your dad maybe?"

"Hey, it might not have worked out then, but that doesn't mean you have to break it off with him here. Don't overthink it." He taps me twice on the nose again. "Neil's the type who absorbs himself in other's problems so he doesn't have to deal with his own. He's a fixer. But who will fix him?" Nate swishes past. "I've got to jet. But I'll be back at the morning bells to pick you two up for the career fair."

As Nate walks down the hallway, I stare daggers into his back. All he really gave me in exchange for some future unspecified favor was a look at twenty-five lost minutes of my life. Like the roses he gave me at the hospital that day, the memory is fraught with thorns. They poke at my mind, demanding answers. Nate says Neil and I couldn't go the distance. If we broke up on Earth, it could be only a matter of time before we implode here as well. I can't allow that to happen. Not after pining for him for what seemed like centuries in Level Two and finally reuniting with him. Neil and I are good together. I feel it through my entire being. But still, the thorns draw blood and create even more doubts in my mind.

Neil's closed door taunts me. He's right behind it, and yet right now he feels miles away.

Retreating back into my room, I push aside the table and chair and walk to the bed.

I slip under the covers and close my eyes, trying to concentrate on one thing and one thing only: the look Neil gets on his face right before he kisses me. But it's no use. All my questions and insecurities burn within me, and there's no way I'll be able to meditate my way to a state approaching sleep. If I even knew how.

I pick up my muse workbook and thumb through the pages, and settle on the chapter that details the history of the muses, starting all the way back in ancient Greece. It's like reading mythology, except that this part at least seems to be actually true. I spend the rest of the night caught up in the intrigue and inspiration of muses throughout the centuries. It distracts me from thinking any more about the implications of all the conversations I had today.

Eventually the morning bells ring out, signaling the dawn of my third day in Level Three. I rub my eyes and trudge over to Neil's room. How is he going to act this morning? Hot or cold?

As soon as I enter his room, I get my answer. He rushes over and kisses me, running his hands up and down my back and leading me backward until we fall into his bed.

But I can't lose myself in the sensation like I always did before, and I don't know what's wrong with me. His lips are as warm and inviting as ever, and his fingertips are whisper soft against my skin. I'm doing exactly what Nate warned me not to—I'm overthinking things.

I break away from Neil, and he gives me a questioning look.

"Why don't you get along with Nate?" I ask, because I'm so great lately at ruining moments and blurting out things that should stay locked away. Maybe Neil can give me some tips on how to compartmentalize thoughts and repress memories.

Neil frowns. "Because Nate's only objective is to stir up trouble. He loves messing with people. Our family counselor diagnosed him with abandonment issues."

"You never mentioned him. Your family had only one photo of him up."

Neil gets up off the bed and sits in the chair facing me. "We didn't even know Nate existed until I was fourteen. His mom contacted my dad and told him he was Nate's father and that now was the time to step up. Nate was already seventeen, and she didn't want to deal with him anymore. Nate stayed with us a year, and that was the worst year of my life."

He looks so wrecked, I almost feel guilty that I forced the issue, but I'm also relieved that he's talking. That he's finally sharing some of his own pain instead of only absorbing mine. "But maybe he's changed for the better," I offer. As much I wish that were true, based on last night I can't imagine it is.

Neil grabs my hands. "Trust me, Nate poisons everything he touches. Don't let him play mind games with you."

"You can tell me anything. You can tell me about Gracie." I hold my metaphorical breath.

Neil leans back in his chair, letting go of me in the process. He obviously doesn't relish talking to me about her, so he's probably throwing me a tiny bone to get me off his back. "Gracie went to our church. She was a year older than me. Beautiful." The longing tone of his voice when he says "beautiful" makes my heart flutter. "I think all of us were in love with her. She was always nice enough, but she had this way of avoiding our clumsy attempts to get closer to her. She didn't want to date anyone. Until Nate." His face darkens.

"So she went out with Nate, then?"

He nods. "Long story short: Nate used her, like he uses

everyone. She was so upset that she stopped coming to church, and even started skipping school. And Nate didn't care. He left town the day he turned eighteen and never looked back."

"But you cared." The parallels between Gracie and me are obvious. We were both broken. It's a big leap to take, but maybe Neil's initial interest in me had to do with the fact that he couldn't have the girl he really wanted to fix.

Neil smiles sadly. "Yeah. At the time, too much. I told you once, at my house, if it hadn't been for Eagle Scouts and my guitar, I don't know what I would've done. Hunted Nate down, maybe tried to punch an apology out of him."

His statement comes with such a sweet mix of vulnerability and bravado, I sweep him up into a tight hug. I ignore the stab of jealousy.

There's an insistent knock, and the door opens. I break away from Neil reluctantly, turning to find Nate. "Hey, Little Brother. Am I interrupting something?"

"Good morning." Neil's greeting is more cheerful than I expected. I'm irritated by Nate's timing, but Neil seems almost relieved. If hanging out with Nate is preferable to talking about Gracie, then it's even worse than I thought.

"Career fair today, and I told Libby I'd take you." Nate crosses his arms. "I'm due at the demon hunter booth, so let's go."

"We've already decided to be muses," I say. "So we'll stay here and you can go on without us." And then Neil and I can continue our talk.

"We should go," Neil says. "Kiara is expecting us at the healers' booth."

Unfortunately, I can't argue with that reasoning unless I want to look like a total ingrate. But when Neil reaches for my hand as we follow Nate out the door, I pull it away and pretend to examine my nail polish.

As we walk toward Assembly Hill, Nate acts the part of a perfect older brother, pointing out various landmarks and telling us more about the various afterlife positions. "Have you read your copy of the 'Guide to Afterlife Occupations'?" he asks.

Neil was pretty absorbed in it yesterday before class, but I haven't done more than skim it. "No," I say at the same time Neil says, "Yes."

Neil squints and then pulls out the rumpled copy from his back pocket and hands it to me.

"I've been meaning to ask, why is 'guardian angel' on here?" Neil asks Nate. "Don't actual angels do that?"

"Surprisingly, no. Guardian angel is the most boring job you can get, and actual angels couldn't be bothered. Sure, once in a while you get to save someone's life, but what does that get you? A pat on the back from your supervisor? A plaque on the wall? No, thanks. But it's the job with the most openings because of all those desperate people on Earth. The recruiters are out at the career fair in full force. Steer clear, is my advice."

Nate is right about the guardian angel recruiters. When we reach the fair, which is a jumble of plywood booths that resemble street-side lemonade stands, recruiters in white suits and dresses descend upon us like vendors in a third world country, shouting their slogan "Protect and Serve!" and waving white sheets of paper in our faces. Taking Nate's advice, we don't respond to any of them and keep our faces resolute, as if we know exactly where we're headed.

Once we've lost the recruiters in the crowd, we relax again. At a booth flying a yellow flag, Nate ducks under a support beam. "This is me." He positions himself next to a girl built like a professional weight lifter. Her black hair is tied up in knots and pushed off her tan forehead with a yellow headband. She rifles though a stack of folders, so intent on her task that Nate has to poke her arm to get her attention. "Shan, meet Neil and his girlfriend, Felicia," he says.

Shan salutes us. "Interested in demon hunting?" When I shake my head, she licks her thumb and returns to her paperwork, pushing half the stack over to Nate.

Nate groans. "Okay, then. See you later, Little Brother."

Neil and I spend the morning and early afternoon visiting the various booths and listening patiently to the different groups' sales pitches and stories of life on the job. Finally we come to a red booth at the edge of the fair. The sign says HEALERS with the slogan first in Latin and then in English: *Primum non nocere.* First, do no harm. Odd that the slogan isn't in other languages too. No one is here to greet us and try to sell us on their profession.

"I wonder where they are," Neil says. "Kiara said she would be here."

He cranes his neck to look behind the booth. "Oh my God!" he breathes, his eyes widening in horror.

"What?" I ask, alarm racing through me. I press myself against the booth to get a better view. What I see would make me throw up if I actually had anything in my stomach—Kiara lying on a red blanket, her body slashed and seeping blood.

twelve

NEIL SKIRTS AROUND THE BARRIER and dives over to Kiara. I'm right behind him. There's blood trickling from her mouth, and she stares up at us in a daze of pain and confusion. If a powerful healer like Kiara is bleeding, this has to be the work of the Morati, who can apparently make anyone believe anything. The skin on my neck prickles, and I turn my head to scan the immediate area, but there is no one.

"What happened?" Neil kneels beside her, his hands hovering like he doesn't know if he should touch her. "Is there anything we can do? Where are the other healers? You need a healer!"

She coughs, grabs Neil's forearm. "Keegan. Where is he?"

"I don't know." Neil materializes a pillow and props her

head on it, trying to offer her a small comfort. I take a corner of the blanket she's lying on and press it to her abdomen, where the most blood is.

"Protect. Him. Promise me." Her eyelids flutter.

"I will," Neil promises. "What happened?"

"All the healers. Have been murdered."

"Who did this to you?" I ask her.

Her head lolls to the side, her strength at an end. "Angel . . ." The word is so soft, I almost don't even catch it. The light leaves her eyes, and I watch helplessly until her body disappears, gone now. Maybe gone forever.

"Did she say 'angel'?" asks Neil, his voice wet. He stares in disbelief at Kiara's bloody handprint on his skin, and falls back against the wall of the booth.

I materialize a cloth and wipe the blood from his arm. "I'm so sorry." I can't believe Kiara is gone. She was strong. I could never thank her enough for saving Neil's life. Was there something I could have done to save hers?

I shiver. Standing up, I survey this section of the fair. The healers' booth is not only at the very edge, but there are several empty booths between it and the next closest, a poorly constructed hovel occupied only by the caretaker representative that we talked to a few moments ago. Now he lies in a green hammock, his attention elsewhere.

Kiara said they didn't get many visitors down this way, and she wasn't kidding. When did the attack happen? Most people would fade out rather quickly if they had injuries as serious as Kiara's, but Kiara was a powerful healer. She might have been able to hold out for hours.

"The Morati killed them. We have to tell Libby about this." Neil gestures wildly at the red blanket, now stained dark. "They specifically targeted the healers. You know what that means."

I do. It means Level Three is even more dangerous for everyone now. Without the healers, we're more vulnerable than before. Maybe it means the Morati are planning large-scale attacks. The Morati's ultimate goal is to ascend all the way to heaven, but how does weakening the people here help them do that? Julian might know.

I should have told Libby about Julian's visit. It's not that I think he did this, but he is still Morati. I've protected him because of our bargain, and because I care about him more than I dare to admit. But now that all our lives hang in the balance, I can't rationalize keeping his presence here a secret.

If he's truly innocent, if he works with Libby and Furukama and helps them as much as he can, they'll have to treat him fairly. They wouldn't expose him to brimstone and make him sick. Maybe once they capture the Morati, they'll also let me question them about my stolen memories.

But considering Libby's insistence on detachment, I'm deluding myself if I think for a second that they would allow me any access at all. It comes down to a choice: a chance to view my memories or a chance for everyone's safety. Obviously, the latter is much more important.

"Um . . . Neil . . . I need to tell you something." I've been dreading this conversation about Julian. Neil is not going to understand why I didn't alert the authorities immediately.

"What is it?" he asks warily. "We need to find Libby. Now."

"Well . . . ," I begin, but I'm cut off by a girl's screams. I whip around. The girl stands in shock just outside the booth, staring down at the red blanket. She sees me, gulps, and runs back toward the fair. She stumbles and flies to the ground, and begins to sob and point toward the healers' booth. Toward me. My shirt is covered in Kiara's blood, which has sunk into the weave of the cotton fabric and caked into an ugly brown.

Soon enough the girl's hysterics attract the attention of the security force, led by Autumn and the guy with the silver belt buckle who came to my room while Neil was in a coma.

"What happened here?" Autumn guides us out of the booth onto a patch of trampled grass behind it. I give her a report of how we found Kiara and what she said about all the healers being killed by an angel.

"It's terrible." The shock of it all is clearly etched on Neil's face. "I owe Kiara my life, and now she's gone." He sinks down onto the stump of a tree.

Silver Belt Buckle escorts the shocked girl away while the others roll out yellow-and-black crime-scene tape to cordon off the area from the rubberneckers who've already started to gather, wide-eyed and curious.

Autumn lets out a piercing whistle. "The career fair is

over. Curfew is in effect until tomorrow, as of immediately. Please return to your rooms." The Careers shutter their booths with worried glances. A trickle and then a flood of fair attendees bump into one another in their haste to get back to the dorms. I reach for Neil to return to our rooms, but Autumn calls out, "Stay for a minute, will you?"

She returns to my side. "Did Kiara say who did this? Give a description?"

"No. She was really weak by the time we found her, and then . . ." I trail off. It's surreal to be talking about Kiara's death to someone who was murdered similarly and in my own bed.

Autumn shakes her head. "It's okay. I've come to terms with the way I died. It has only made me tougher."

While Autumn gathers evidence, I sit next to Neil on the stump and put my arm around him. Kiara's death has hit him harder than I would've expected, especially considering they barely knew each other. But then, I'm starting to see several new sides to Neil. It must be all the upheaval and change he's gone through lately. As someone who moved a lot, I've come to expect change, sometimes even crave it. But Neil spent his whole life in the same town, his days set to a familiar rhythm. No wonder he's so moody.

Libby arrives and consults with Autumn. As Autumn hurries away, Libby approaches us. "I understand you found Kiara." She offers her wrist to Neil to help him stand. He takes it and scrambles up, flustered.

"What will we do? Now that the healers are gone?"

Neil is visibly calmer, almost as if Libby's touch took away his sadness. She fixed my hearing, so it's possible that she can affect emotions as well.

"I'll have to train new healers," Libby says. "I'll brush up on my skills and take over the program. It's a priority now."

Kiara mentioned that Libby had once been a healer. It's a good thing she switched careers, or she'd be dead now. "But won't that make you a target? And anyone you train?" I ask.

"You should know as well as anyone else that sometimes the good of the many comes before the good of the few," Libby says.

Guilt hits me hard. It's time to tell her about Julian.

As I glance over at the healers' booth, the security force starts to run toward Eastern Avenue. There's a commotion at one of the distant booths. "What's going on over there?"

Libby follows my gaze. "We've found one of the Morati."

"You have? That's great!" Neil says.

I paste on a bright smile. The capture of a Morati means we're all safer, which is the best news of the day. It also means I don't have to turn in Julian, and Neil won't be disappointed in me. But how did they capture one? Libby told me that they hoped I would be the one to find the Morati, and then they managed it themselves after all. It's doubtful I'll get the chance to grill their prisoner about my stolen memories, which is a shame.

The group of security officers strides toward us. They form a tight circle around a prisoner and are at high alert, all ramrod-straight postures and shifty eyes. Autumn argues with Silver Belt Buckle, and she's vibrating, as if she's trying her best to maintain control over her reactions.

"He's not responsible for this, Brady!" Autumn shouts. "Let him go."

The prisoner's head finally becomes visible.

Julian.

thirteen

"SOMEBODY GAVE US an anonymous tip," Brady says in a southern twang as big as his belt buckle. "This one might be an angel. We're fixin' to take him somewhere to make real sure."

Julian blanches. Brady must mean some sort of brimstone enclosure, like a jail. If they hold him too long, he'll go insane. As much as Julian frustrates me, I don't want that for him.

I wonder if it was Neil who gave the anonymous tip. Did he somehow find out that Julian was here and turn him in already? I have to try to stop this.

I march over to Julian, elbowing the security goons when they try to stop me. "Julian is innocent. I'll vouch for him."

"Tell it to Furukama-Sensei at his trial." Brady's towering stance is formidable, but his chin quivers. He is waffling.

Libby breaks in. She materializes a cashmere wrap and bundles up in it, which makes her look softer, an impression that is counterbalanced by the stiff way she holds her head. "If he truly is an angel, he is our main suspect. We'll find out soon enough."

At this point I risk another glance at Autumn. Despite all her years of training, the fact that the three of us—her, me, and Julian—are all back together again has to have made the events of that last Halloween, when she caught us kissing in the taxi, rush to the surface. At least the boiling red color of her face makes me think that.

"Take him away, Brady," Libby says. Brady looks over at Autumn for confirmation, and she nods, jaw tight. Apparently Libby outranks her.

The security detail regroups and blocks my access to Julian. I start to approach Libby to protest, but Neil pulls me back. "Let him go."

The steel in Neil's voice stops me in my tracks, and all I can do is look at the back of Julian's head. Autumn, Libby, and Brady fall into step behind Julian's captors, and the procession moves back in the direction of the hill.

I close my eyes and press my fingertips hard against my temples. The Morati are still on the loose. We're all in danger. Right now Julian is the only one who can help me find my lost memories, something he can't do in custody—and something he can't do if he's exposed to brimstone and goes crazy. I don't want Julian to get hurt, even if he has hurt me countless times. I'm concerned for his well-being. I *care* about him.

"Come on, Felicia." Neil prods me in the side with his folded-over brochure until I open my eyes. "If he's the criminal, then things will go back to normal."

"Do you think Julian's the one behind all this?" I ask, trying to keep my voice measured, but apparently failing, if Neil's sudden defensive posture is any indication. "He rescued you. He brought us back together."

Neil scoffs. "He did that to serve his own agenda. You know that even better than I do."

Julian is a master of twisting the truth. He screwed up my life, and he's messed with my death. And yet I am drawn to him. I yearn to give him the benefit of the doubt. There is obviously something wrong with me.

"Were you the one who gave the anonymous tip that Julian is an angel?" I ask, half-scared of the answer.

Neil narrows his eyes. "Me? I didn't even know he was in Level Three. Did you?"

I get the distinct vibe I should keep my conversation with Julian to myself. "Why would I know?" I ask so I can avoid an outright lie. "There must be something we can do to help him. You seem pretty chummy with Libby. Maybe you could ask her to release Julian."

Neil tenses. "Let's let the security team handle this. If Julian's innocent, he'll be fine."

If they expose him to brimstone long enough, he won't

be fine. But I can't tell Neil that because he'll wonder how I know about brimstone's effects on angels.

As we walk, Neil taps the brochure against his thigh. I'm used to him redirecting his nervous energy into a driving beat to a song only he can hear in his head, and for several minutes I try to guess what it might be. I peek over at him, expecting his features to reflect the calming effect of music. But instead of gaiety I get grim, as if we're on some sort of death march. I think back to the easy way Neil and I were able to interact in those months after the fall of the mainframe in Level Two. How we created top ten memory lists in different categories, even silly ones like top ten car rides and top ten root beer floats. How we recited poetry to each other and he sang me songs. And how he kept me close, even when intently counseling others on the best way to face unpleasant memories so they could move on. Now in Level Three, with Nate in the picture, and Gracie, and Julian, there are so many tiny land mines to avoid in the space between Neil and me lately.

For Julian's sake, though, I have to try one last time to persuade Neil of Julian's importance to us. "But what if Julian knows a way to get all our memories back? Think about it. The Morati could have stolen our memories when we got to Level Two. They might still have them. What if Julian could help us?"

"If Julian is some kind of evil mastermind, I wouldn't want him to do me any more favors." Neil squints at me. He shakes his head and opens the door of the dorm.

"Deals with the devil never turn out well."

"Maybe Julian isn't as evil as you seem to think."

We climb the stairs in silence, and when we reach his room, he takes my hands in his. "Promise me you won't get caught up in this Julian mess. Let him lie his own way out."

"But—"

"We're still in this together, right?" His blue eyes search my face. I'm never going to be able to adequately explain to him why Julian is important to me, not only as someone who is willing to help me but as a friend. I'll have to drop it for now.

"Of course. And we always will be," I say forcefully, as if mere determination could make it true.

"Good." He brushes back the hair from my face and kisses my forehead, then my temple, my cheek, and finally my lips. "I love you, you know."

My heart soars within my chest, because this is big. Because despite all we've been through, this is the first time he's ever said it out loud. I don't hesitate to say it back. "I love you." His grin is contagious, infecting me with desire and delight. My lips long to spread kisses all over his body, and my limbs itch to spontaneously break into dance.

He opens the door and then steps back into his room. I move to follow him, but he blocks me with his body. "I . . ." He swallows hard. "Can you give me a little time? After what happened to Kiara, I need to be alone to process all this . . ." He trails off, leaving all the other things he needs to come to terms with hanging in the air.

He finally tells me he loves me, and then he sends me away. He might as well have smacked me across the face.

"Yeah, okay." My smile is wobbly but far more generous than is genuine. He closes the door on me for the second time in two days.

I return to my room and spend the next couple of hours flipping through my muse workbook and wrestling with myself. If I'm a good girl, I won't break curfew. I'll stay here and meditate on my future until Neil comes to get me for our class tomorrow. But the sting of Neil's rejection and the lure of getting my memories back are too strong. I didn't actually promise Neil I wouldn't go to Julian. He's over there mourning a girl he barely knew. He doesn't care about our lost memories or about finding out what happened in our relationship back on Earth. I need to know, so in case the same obstacles come up again, I will be able to conquer them, for the benefit of both of us. After the way Neil so thoroughly shut me out, he won't miss me tonight.

Still, as I skulk down the hallway and descend the stairs, I have to shake off the mantle of guilt that weighs down my shoulders for both sneaking out and looking for Julian without telling Neil about it.

When I slip out the double doors downstairs, it is the semidark of twilight. I can't imagine there are actual rotations of this afterlife realm around a sun, but who knows? Dividing time into day and night is probably something the powers that be do to help us acclimatize, like the campus construct. But it seems almost counterintuitive, like it would make it even harder for us to detach from our lives on Earth with so many reminders of it.

I run over to the nearest tree and press myself against the rough bark. The realness of the texture against my bare arms makes me homesick for Nidda Park and the stubby pines in Grammy's backyard in Ohio. I breathe in the earthy scent and peer up at the utterly gorgeous pattern the green leaves form against a sky filled with stars, so much more inviting than the bright, blurry whiteness of Level Two. I might have a million more moments like these missing from my memory banks because of the Morati.

That thought only reinforces my determination to find a way to restore my memories. I have to find Julian. In Level Two, Eli taught me to think of the person I was seeking and then scan for their brain waves. It had to be someone I recently touched or knew well. I successfully used this technique to find my friend Beckah, and if it worked for me in Level Two, maybe it will work for me here. I picture Julian, his strong arms reaching out to me, drawing me toward him. A signal tingles at the base of my skull. It's weak, but it's coming from Assembly Hill.

I hurry from the tree to the shadows of the Muse Collection Library to a gigantic tree in the center of the lawn. It is covered from trunk to branches with scraps of paper of all colors and sizes. One of them says "My sister's locket." Another says "My letterman jacket." This must be the Forgetting Tree that Megan mentioned. I take a moment to remember Megan. It's heartbreaking that she will never have the chance to write "My braces."

I continue on to the north side of the administration building. With proximity Julian's signal from the hill has grown stronger, but it has a strange shape to it, and it makes me worry that the brimstone could already be harming him. I seek cover behind some bushes and survey the scene in front of me, looking out for the security force.

All the booths from the fair are gone now, and no one at all is outside. Maybe Julian's brimstone cage inside the hill is so secure, they don't feel the need to patrol. But I don't want to be too reckless and show myself prematurely.

During the next few minutes there is no movement whatsoever. Not even a false breeze rustles the leaves on the trees.

As I'm about to step from my hiding place and run for the hill, I spot Cash and his team. I duck down lower in the bushes, praying they don't see me. As silent as ninjas, Cash's team continues on by.

Once enough minutes have passed, I work up the courage to make a break for it. I flex my feet and propel myself forward. But I don't advance a single step, because a hand clamps down on my shoulder. And a deep voice commands me to stop.

fourteen

I TURN MY NECK SLOWLY to get a look at the face connected to the fingers currently immobilizing me. It belongs to a young man with tanned skin, almond-shaped brown eyes, and dark hair shaved in the front and pulled into a topknot in the back. The man wears a heavy, dark gray kimono, straw sandals, and the sort of socks the Japanese wear to separate their big toe from the rest. Despite the sword sheathed on his left hip and the scar over his right eyebrow, he doesn't seem threatening, merely curious.

"You are Felicia Ward," he states. "I am Furukama-Sensei." The most important person in Level Three knows who I am.

He lets go of my shoulder and bows. I return the bow

and then stand awkwardly while he stares at me.

"You wish to visit Julian."

Am I that obvious in my intentions? "Julian is innocent. I know it."

Furukama grips the hilt of his sword, and for a terrifying moment I think he's going to punish me for breaking curfew. "You are sure of this." He nods, as if pleased.

"Yes."

"Julian will be released tomorrow."

"But—"

He cuts off my argument. "This is my final decision. You may visit him now. My guards know to let you enter."

The emotional part of me begs to appeal to Furukama to release Julian immediately. But the calculating part decides it is a better tactic to appear agreeable and to try to gain him as an ally, not an adversary. He's obviously a step ahead of me if he predicted I'd come for Julian. "Thank you." I bow low.

He bows and then glides away.

Not wanting to lose any more time, in case Neil decides to check on me and finds I'm not there, I rush toward the oddly shaped hill and walk around to the other side. Carved into the hill itself is a stone door, flanked by two of Furukama's security force. Both carry swords on their left hips. One of them is Brady, the member of the security force who took Julian away. The other one copies Furukama's traditional samurai hairstyle, though his hair is so pale blond, it's nearly white. His buckteeth cut into his bottom lip, and he wears his acne like a geek badge of honor. When I approach, they both wave their arms straight out in front of the door. It slowly creaks away from the stone boulders surrounding it to reveal what appears to be a dank hole. The guys look straight ahead, taking their jobs as seriously as guards at Buckingham Palace.

Carved hieroglyphs partially covered with moss and ivy decorate the entrance. I step over the threshold. The walls are a sickly yellow, which must be brimstone. The strong smell of sulfur sends me into a coughing fit, and I have to stand still and remind myself that it can't affect me. I'm not an angel, and I'm already dead.

I test the first step of a narrow spiral staircase that curves down counterclockwise, like in a medieval European castle. It is solid gray slab under my feet. As I descend, high-pitched squawks reverberate against the walls, and my skin crawls as I imagine bats. Moisture drips from the drab ceiling, making plunking sounds as it hits stone. At least the entire place is not made of the suffocating brimstone.

I tread carefully, both because the stairs are uneven and because I don't want to touch anything. When I reach the bottom, a quick scan reveals a vast underground chamber lined with cells on either side. Only one of them is lit up with the soft glow of candlelight. It is fitted with bars forged from brimstone instead of iron, giving it the appearance of the pillars that form when stalagmites and stalactites meet.

But it's the sight of Julian hunched over in the corner on

a threadbare rug that really sets me shaking. The glow of his cell, which appeared to be candlelight, is actually emanating from his weakened body. I drop to my knees, and the thud I make prompts Julian to wearily lift his head and gaze in my general direction with unfocused eyes. There's yellow foam at the edges of his mouth, and his hair is plastered to his forehead.

"Julian!" I gasp. Fortunately, the space between the bars is relatively wide, allowing me to stick my arms through them so I can reach out to Julian. It's unconscionable that Libby and the security force threw him in here without even a trial. I can't believe I ever thought about turning him in to those monsters.

"Who . . . who's there?" His voice cracks. He begins to crawl toward me, but he collapses after only a couple of feet.

"It's Felicia." If the brimstone has reduced him to such a fragile state in only a few hours, I don't know how much longer he can take this.

He turns his head, his cheek pressed against the rug, and mumbles. "Felicia. I know that name."

He must be joking. So like Julian to play me like a fool. "C'mon, knock it off." There's no way someone as obsessive as Julian has forgotten me. I refuse to believe it, in any case.

"I didn't do it. I didn't. Felicia can tell you. Ask Felicia." His eyelids flutter and his pupils dart back and forth. It makes me dizzy.

I can't even talk normally to Julian. Julian said himself that brimstone makes angels crazy, but he didn't mention that it makes them forget everything. I can't afford to have Julian forget anything. I need him to help me get my memories back. But it's not only that. I care too much about him to let him rot away.

"*I* am Felicia, and you're getting out of here soon," I say in the most soothing cadence I have at my disposal. "Try to rest." What else can I say? Don't turn crazy while I'm gone?

I rise and march back toward the stairs, but before I climb a single step, an unearthly screech rings out, followed by several sets of heavy footfalls from above. Coming toward me.

My pulse racing, I run down the hallway of cells until I reach a wide hole with a safety railing all around it. I peer down into the hole, but it goes down so far, I can't make out the bottom. The screeching comes closer.

I slip inside the open door of the last cell on the row and make myself as small as possible in the corner, hoping that whatever is coming will overlook me.

The racket gets louder. "Shut up, demon," a rough female voice shouts.

Demon? What's going on?

"Hold it tighter, Shan," a man growls.

The group stops in front of my cell. The demon glows like blue flame through its paper-thin, clear skin, illuminating the whole corridor. If it turns its head, it will see me. I shrink back even more. The demon's face is contorted into a hideous grimace sure to emotionally scar me for the rest of my afterlife.

The man wrestling with the growling demon is Nate. And he's dripping wet, so he must have just returned with the demon from Earth, via the Styx River. After a short scuffle Shan and Nate pitch the demon down the hole, and its curses reverberate through the jail, getting farther away until they finally cease. Nate slaps his hands together like he's dusting off demon germs, but fortunately, he doesn't look in my direction. I don't want him to know I observed him down here.

"Good work, partner." Shan gives Nate a fist bump. Afterward they laugh and jostle each other roughly as they make their way toward the stairs.

I take a deep breath and press one hand to my abdomen and the other to my forehead. My stomach is in knots and my head is pounding. Still, I wait at least five minutes before daring to move. I stumble to my feet. When I reach the spot where Nate pushed the demon, my shoe connects with something metal and kicks it across the floor. I bend over and pick it up. It's a gold charm in the shape of a beehive that hangs on a thin gold chain with a broken clasp. It looks just like the skep charm Neil gave me the day we allegedly died. But if it is, how did Nate get it?

Pocketing the charm, I drag myself toward the stairs and climb them quickly.

The great stone door is still open, the two sentries looking as stoic as before. After witnessing a demon disposal and Julian's breakdown, seeing them so detached pushes my patience over the edge. Summoning a burst of energy, with my mind I unsheathe their swords and try to fling them away. They fly only about two feet before falling to the ground. The skinny, geeky one with the samurai topknot gapes at me as I grab Brady by his biceps and collapse into him, my knees buckling. "How could you do this to Julian?" I shout in his face.

Brady lifts me carefully and doesn't let go until I've regained my footing. "Calm down," he admonishes as he flicks his wrist to send his sword flying back to him. He catches it by the hilt and sheathes it.

"Sorry." I sway a bit. "I'm really upset right now."

Brady straightens his posture, his lanky frame a head taller than me at its full height. He rubs the back of his right hand over the stubble on his jaw. "Yeah, you sure are." He materializes two canvas camping chairs, and I sit down gratefully. I feel woozy all of a sudden. Probably from the shock of seeing Julian caged like a sick animal.

When Brady sits down across from me, his partner clicks his tongue and curls his upper lip into a disgusted snarl. He stalks over to retrieve his sword and then refuses to look at me once he's back in position.

Brady rolls his eyes and mutters "Samurai poser" under his breath. It's clear he's not as serious as he appeared to be before. I could maybe get along with this guy.

"Furukama-Sensei claims it takes an awfully strong dosage of brimstone over many weeks to cause an angel any lasting damage," Brady explains. "Julian'll be set loose before long."

"Tomorrow. But he shouldn't be in there at all. He's innocent!"

"It's not my place to decide, is it?" He shakes his head, hangs his thumbs in his belt, and drums his fingers on his tarnished silver belt buckle, drawing my attention to its depiction of a bucking bronco superimposed on an outline of the state of Texas. "You know, I've been around four months, and tonight was my first demon sighting. They sometimes follow a demon hunter back from assignment on Earth, hoping to kick up a ruckus."

"Couldn't a demon have been responsible for the bombings and the murder of the healers?" I am genuinely curious, so I don't even mind that he's changing the subject.

"No. Demon hunters have got a protocol on how they open their portal to and from Earth. If a demon does get through, they always catch it immediately and bring it here."

"So that pit down there, where Nate threw the demon, where does it go?"

"I'm not supposed to tell anybody, but since you saw it, I'll tell you. This hill and the chamber below have been here since Level Three's creation. That hole is a one-way passage to the negative levels."

I shudder. "Negative levels? Like hell?"

Brady nods. "I don't know much about it, but there're rumors. You ever hear of Dante's *Inferno*?"

"Of course."

"I reckon it's like that, nine circles of suffering. But like I said, I don't know. The demon hunters always try to get the demons who have made it up to Earth to talk about what the negative levels are like, but it turns out demons aren't that cooperative." Brady guffaws. "Who would have thought, huh?"

"Well, thanks for talking to me."

"Anytime." Brady gets up and dematerializes his chair. "Oh, and with your ability to sneak up on people and disarm them like that, you have to try for the seraphim guard."

"So I've been told. Numerous times," I say wryly.

"If you do feel like trying out, the last open call of the term is tomorrow. Gym Three." Brady smiles as he helps me up. He bows, eliciting a scowl from the samurai poser.

I grit my teeth and reluctantly head back to my dorm room. I can't believe I have to leave Julian in such dire circumstances. He could barely crawl! What condition will he be in after spending the night locked up in there? And how can I hang out safe and sound in my room while he suffers? The look on his face will haunt me every time I close my eyes.

Once I'm inside the dorm, I push the day's events out of my head. I would check on Neil, but he made it clear he wanted time alone. I sigh and open my door.

Neil jumps up from where he was sitting on the end of my bed. He shoots me a look that's half-accusatory, half-hurt. "Where have you been?"

fifteen

I SWEAR I'M ABOUT to break out in hives, and then I immediately realize that there's no reason for me to have such a physical reaction. I need to learn control. "Uh, I went for a walk. To clear my head." Which is not false, but is exactly the kind of half-truth that Julian would tell. "I didn't think you'd be ready to see me again so soon."

"You shouldn't have broken curfew." He cocks his head and narrows his eyes, like he doesn't quite believe me but he doesn't want to call me on it either. Then he sighs and slumps back down onto my bed. "I was pacing back and forth and berating myself for being so stubborn with you. If someone like Kiara could be killed, well, it made me think about priorities and how I need to make the most of my afterlife while I have the chance."

"Yeah?" I hope he's here to help me get our memories back, or to reveal to me what he has repressed. "So what does that mean exactly?"

"I shouldn't have shut you out. When I'm upset, I guess I prefer to be alone."

"But you don't have to be. You can share stuff with me. That's what I'm here for." I sit down on the edge of my bed, facing him.

He nods. "I like what you did to your wall." He points at my crazy photo collage. "And I have something to add to it."

"Really?" I don't like that he's changing the topic, but I do like presents. I touch the skep charm in my pocket. If I tell him about the charm—which would have been his first present to me if he'd been able to materialize it—I'll have to tell him where I got it, and I'm not ready to do that yet.

He slides a package out from under my pillow. It's about the size of a book, wrapped in a brown paper bag. "Remember when you told me you used to be in Girl Scouts? And then later you gave me a photo of you in your green uniform as proof?"

I laugh. I didn't learn anything useful from my short stint in the Scouts, not even how to tie a proper knot, so Neil teased me and said he doubted my story. I told him my troop was mainly occupied with sleepovers and selling cookies. "Yeah, and then you claimed I Photoshopped it."

"Anyway, this is your third birthday gift."

I pull away the paper to reveal a framed five-by-seven of

Neil in his Boy Scout uniform. He's not exactly smiling, but he looks friendly all the same. The photo makes me want to reach back in time and meet the boy he was then.

"That's me at fifteen. Right after I got serious about it," he says.

"You look cute."

"I look like a dork."

"If that were true, would I give you a place of honor?" I spring up and hang his photo smack dab in the center of my wall, moving a few snapshots of Autumn and me to the corner.

"Thanks."

I sit down again, this time closer to Neil but still not close enough to touch him. "So what was it you wanted to tell me?"

"Libby came by to drop off the information for our muse apprenticeship auditions, so we could start practicing."

He's still keeping me at arm's length. I should have known. He'll never tell me the truth about Gracie. And forget about getting back our lost memories.

"Libby has taken quite an interest in you," I remark.

"She's generous with her time," Neil enthuses. "She said she could tell that the two of us were special, and she wanted to tell us about the accelerated muse program."

"What's that exactly?" I cross my legs.

"Muse 101 is a prep course. It's designed for students with little or no performing arts experience. But when I told her that I'm a singer and you're a semiprofessional pianist, she told me we didn't even have to go to the first weeks of class if we didn't want to. We should spend our time preparing our audition instead."

That means we don't even have to leave our rooms. "What do the auditions entail?"

"There's a solo portion and then a group portion. So for solos you can play piano and I can play guitar and sing, and then we can do a scene together from a play." Neil leans back against my headboard. He's perfectly in his element now.

"I've never been in a play. I'm probably not a very good actress." With my fingers I pull at the bedspread, forming little molehills of fabric all around me.

Neil shakes his head. "But listen. I still think we should be muses. Eventually."

"Eventually?"

"I mean, we should practice, for when things go back to normal. But right now we're at war." His voice gets dead serious. "I can't act like everything's normal when people I care about are dying around me. I have to do something to help."

He's right, of course. And this is exactly why Neil will always be too good for me. His first inclination is to think of others, and mine is to think of myself. The Morati have already caused too much pain while I stood selfishly by, not wanting to get involved. Libby told me I should join the seraphim guard to develop my skills so I'll be able to face down the Morati killers and bring them to justice. It's time for me to step up, and Brady said the last open call is tomorrow. "I do too. I'm going to train with the seraphim guard."

Neil takes my pledge in stride, not batting an eyelash. "You should. And I'll train to be a healer."

A lump wedges in my throat, and I throw my arms out toward him. "But, Neil, that's like painting a bull's-eye on your chest!"

He leans forward and puts his hands over mine. "I couldn't save Kiara. She died right in front of me. I can't let something like that happen again."

I know what it's like to feel helpless, so it must be a thousand times worse for Neil. "But you'll be careful."

"And even though we'll be in separate classes during the day, we'll still be together every evening," he says.

But not every night. I don't say it out loud, though, because it will make me sound petty. There's so much more at stake than our relationship at the moment.

"Right."

"Now that we've settled that, shall we practice for our muse audition?" He lies down on his side, propping himself up on his elbow.

"So what scene do you want to do?" I ask.

"I thought we could do something from *Our Town*. I know that play well. And I could teach you via my memories of it."

"Sounds like a plan." It's something to pass the time until tomorrow.

Neil holds out his palm to me, and I press mine against his without hesitation. He's chosen to show me a memory of a dress rehearsal instead of a performance, so it's easier for me to concentrate on Emily's lines.

After we surface from the memory, we discuss which scene to perform and decide on the middle of act two, where George walks Emily home from school, starting from where George asks if Emily is mad at him.

The choice is kind of ironic, because Emily insists that George should be perfect, and George counters that men aren't naturally good, whereas women are. Obviously Emily needs to meet Neil.

I materialize a spiral notebook and a pen to write down all the lines I can remember. Neil has all of George's lines memorized, and most of Emily's, too, so he helps me. We enter the same memory several times before I'm satisfied that I have everything written correctly.

We do a read-through, and Neil performs the part of the stage manager as well. The stage manager has only a few lines, but they're important ones.

Neil puts so much emotion into his reading, especially in the part where George decides to stay in town for Emily instead of going off to college. But my favorite line is when George says, "I'm going to change so quick—you bet I'm going to change." That's something I could never imagine Neil saying for real, though I wish he would.

We spend half the night practicing the play and some duets on piano and guitar. Finally I say, "You realize you're essentially staying the night, right?" I lie on my side and poke him in the ribs.

"It's called pulling an all-nighter." Neil settles in beside me and stretches out. "A perfectly acceptable practice for college kids." The need to rehearse isn't exactly urgent, since the audition won't be for weeks or months, if ever, but I don't argue with him. I want him to stay.

"Can you teach me how you get to sleep?" I still haven't figured out how he or anyone else is able to do it, and I yearn to zone out for a while. To forget that Julian is in jail right now, foaming at the mouth. That Neil and I will be going down dangerous paths tomorrow, apart. And that the Morati are out there, somewhere, waiting to strike.

He shifts positions until we are lying with our knees interlocked and our foreheads touching. "Back when I was on Earth, I used to count sheep. Now I count goats." The corners of his mouth twitch upward.

I splay my fingers on his chest and push him gently. "Shut up! You do not."

He hides his face behind his elbow. "I do! And the goats have these bells that play a melody when they prance. . . ." I can't see his smile, but I hear it.

"And that puts you to sleep?" Neil likes to revisit that memory with me, of the time I went with my father to the Turkish hills to find a special goatherd and his musical goats, but I can't fathom how he could use it to meditate his way to sleep.

He moves his arm so that he's touching my hip and scoots back slightly. Our eyes meet. "I focus on one detail and let it run through my mind over and over. Eventually it all runs together and I blank out. If you can call that sleeping, that's how I do it."

"Is that what you did after Kiara healed you?"

"No. There I think I passed out from exhaustion." He shrugs. "When I was in Level Two, I liked to relive my memories of sleeping. Times when we were like this, in bed together."

"Me too." I sigh. "I even had a top ten of best stretches of sleep. You were in most of them."

"Most of them?" He gives me a look of mock chagrin. "Why not all of them?"

"There should have been so many more memories of us sleeping." And I'm reminded yet again how unfair it all is. If stopping the Morati is my main goal, getting my memories back is not far behind. It must be possible to do both. "All those memories are lost to us now. Doesn't that make you sad? Doesn't that make you angry?"

Neil crashes down on his back and blows air up at the ceiling. "You really want to start with that again? I thought we were letting it go."

"But what if I can't?" I ask in a small voice. "I have a pathological need to know what comes next."

"Getting your memories back would only show you what the future held for that version of you. The living version. It doesn't matter now that we're dead."

"It does matter." I materialize a throw blanket and tuck my legs under it. "And I'm going to prove it."

He rubs his eyes as if I am exasperating him. "Whatever."

Ugh. He can be so unsupportive sometimes. It's because he's hiding something about Gracie. "Didn't you come over to tell me why you shouted Gracie's name?" I blurt.

He goes completely still. "When did I do that?"

"When Kiara pulled you out of your coma."

"I don't want to talk about Gracie anymore." He hops off the bed. "She's in my past, and that's where she'll stay."

"Just tell me!" I say stubbornly.

Neil shakes his head on the way to the door. "Good night, Felicia. I hope you can get some sleep." Then he leaves.

sixteen

I SLIP BACK UNDER my blanket and pull it up to my chin. Neil has no problem talking about other people's problems, but when it comes to talking about himself, he can't seem to do it, which frustrates me. My brain is too full and I'd like nothing more than to shut it down until morning. I might as well try Neil's prancing goat method for meditating your way to sleep.

In Level Two, using the net architecture, I could call up any memory I wanted to as long as I plugged in. But it doesn't work that way without the net. Without someone else's palm to touch, I can't access even my own memories in full, only the snippets that remain archived in my mind, faded like old photographs. By now I've visited the goat memory enough, so I call it up and picture the black goat with the white spot on its chest. I watch it jump, over and over and over.

Soon enough the morning bells ring, and I stretch my arms out, satisfied. I actually did it! I meditated my way to sleep, even if it was for only a few hours. I remove the skep charm from my pocket and fix the clasp on the chain so that I can wear it around my neck for luck today.

I get up quickly and materialize a pair of pale pink yoga pants and a pink T-shirt, because I assume that seraphim guard training will involve some sort of physical activity. But I'm not ready to commit to black. Not yet. I tuck the skep charm under my shirt.

Smoothing my hair, I open the door and run smack into Neil's knuckles, raised in the process of knocking.

"Hey," he says sheepishly. "You look good."

"Thanks." But I can't return the compliment. Because he looks terrible: dark circles under his eyes, rumpled shirt with spots of blood, grass stains on his khakis. He looks like he was on the losing end of a fight with a lawn mower.

He rubs at a grass stain, materializing it away. "Nate visited me after I left your room. He wrestled me down outside. Made me break curfew and eat grass."

"What? That's horrible."

Neil bursts into laughter. "Can't say I didn't deserve it. I was kind of hysterical, and I punched him in the face. Surprised him so much that his nose actually bled."

"Yeah, I can tell." I touch each spot of blood on his shirt

with my finger, making them disappear as I do. "Why did you fight?"

"I plead the fifth." His breezy tone of avoidance hints that Gracie was the topic. But I've had enough arguing for a while, so I don't press him. In fact, maybe if I am supernice, it will make him comfortable and he'll confide in me.

Several other doors open, and fellow students join us in the hall, making their way toward the stairs.

"No big deal." I cram as much sunshine into the statement as I can. "Maybe I can pick up some useful tips from Furukama in my training today. Like how to turn into a statue."

It wins me a half smile. "Ooh, then you can teach me." I bet turning into a statue would be something Neil would be good at. He's got the art of stonewalling down already.

We head out of the dorms and walk until we hit the avenue. "I'm supposed to find Gym Three. Do you have any idea where that is?" I ask.

"I have a map." He pulls out a crinkled map from his back pocket and stretches the paper out by the edges until it is readable. "Gym Three is up here, near Assembly Hill, but across Eastern Avenue."

Because I'm heading farther north than usual, we take a different route. I'm anxious about Neil and me going our separate ways today, because something terrible could happen while we're apart. I try to cover it up with small talk.

"Have you ever tried to materialize food and then eat it?" I ask.

"No, have you?"

"We should. After class. It could be a fun experiment to see what happens. Maybe start with gazpacho. Then move on to escargot."

"Snails? Gross!" Neil makes an exaggerated gagging sound.

"Have you ever had them?"

"No way."

"They're really good. I always ate them in Paris with my dad when we went."

"Maybe I should be in charge of our menu. I could really go for a Fourth of July barbeque. Hamburgers. Hot dogs. Potato salad. Apple pie."

I giggle. "That's so American of you!"

Neil bristles. "You're American."

"Sure, but I went out and tasted the world." I can't help but let a note of pride slip in.

"Because you had the chance to," he says matter-of-factly. "Not all of us did."

I fall silent. I want to point out that we might have taken trips together and that we probably did. Our lost memories could reveal so much. But we'd only be rehashing the same argument. So instead I swear to myself that I'll get the memories first, and then show him. He won't be able to refuse them when they are right there in front of him.

"Have you seen this yet?" I point out the Forgetting Tree as we draw near.

Neil ducks his head. "Uh, yeah. I came here with Libby. Early this morning before the bells."

"Breaking curfew twice in one night. Nice." So he was hanging out with Libby this morning and didn't even tell me. At least he has the decency to be embarrassed about it.

He stops in front of the tree and looks upward at its heavy branches. Thousands of paper scraps ripple in the breeze. "She brought me here, and I pinned up my paper. It's the first big step in the detachment process. You should also do it."

It's a step I'm certainly not ready to take, and I'm annoyed that Neil's so eager to prove that he is. "Where's yours? I want to see it."

Neil pulls me away from the tree. "Oh, it's way up there. We'd have to materialize a ladder, and then you'd be late to class." The only thing that stops me from asking what he wrote is the horrible thought that he wrote my name. That I'm the one he wants to get over.

As soon as his grip is loose enough, I slip out of his grasp and pick up my pace. "No, we certainly don't want to be late," I say under my breath. So much for my attempt at being supernice.

Neil matches me stride for stride, and we walk in silence.

When we reach Eastern Avenue, we face each other awkwardly. "Okay. See you later." I step closer to Neil and hold out my arms. He gives me a quick hug, doing that annoying flutter pat thing that people do when they don't really want to touch you, or when they hug a stranger. It totally freaks me out for a second, because I don't ever want Neil to be a stranger.

Once he's out of sight, I turn to head off to Furukama's class and crash right into someone.

"Oh, sorry." I back away, looking up. I've run into Libby. Maybe I'm not so sorry after all.

"It's fine." Libby tucks the red silk scarf at her throat into the open collar of her white button-down blouse. Her skirt and heels are red too, which must mean she's firmly committed to rebuilding the healers now.

We size each other up for a moment. Finally she gives me a prim smile. "I assume Neil is doing well."

"You should know." I try not to let my irritation show. "You saw him this morning."

"I'm surprised he told you about that," Libby says innocently.

I don't want her to think that Neil doesn't confide in me, so I suck in a deep breath. "Of course he did." Unfortunately, my voice cracks a bit, undermining my show of false confidence. "We tell each other everything." A huge lie, but Libby doesn't need to know that.

"I used to think Jeremy told me everything," Libby says, and I groan inwardly. I don't want to hear about her doomed relationship again, especially because it is clear Libby thinks she's imparting some kind of lesson to me. "I wanted to forgive him for our murder and for us to stay together. We roomed together. We joined the healers together. We spent every moment together. I thought it would be enough. It wasn't." She pauses again and regards me expectantly, as though it's my turn to deliver my line of a script.

I want to run in the other direction. Instead I settle for what I think she wants to hear. "What happened to him?"

"He became a spirit trapper. He lives in Area Three, and from what I hear, he's always on assignment on Earth, rounding up the malevolent spirits that haunt humans." There's a deep well of regret in her words. She runs her hands over her skirt as if to smooth it, even though there's not a wrinkle to be seen, and I notice her fingernails, jagged and chewed down to the quick. "But I can't change the past. I chose to live forward, not backward."

That's easy for her to say. She still has all her memories. "Um, that's great."

"You should be in class," Libby says abruptly. Girl talk is over. She has closed back up, returned to her unruffled, chipper default.

"On my way now."

She nods at me absentmindedly and waves me across the avenue.

When I get to the building marked Gym Three, the door is ajar, kept open by a yellow rubber duck with an orange beak. The area out front is deserted, but voices buzz from within. I slip in and stifle a curse. There have to be more than five hundred applicants and trainees, and each and every one of them except me is wearing black.

seventeen

I DIDN'T EXPECT *THIS* MUCH competition. Perhaps I am overestimating my talents by even trying out. If I thought I could simply show up and they'd give me a place automatically, this full gym of gung ho applicants proves otherwise.

"Felicia! You made it." Brady calls me over. He's perched on a balance beam that's shoved up against the wall. The samurai poser sits next to him, and when I approach, he scowls.

"Angel sympathizer," he whispers roughly. "If it weren't for you, that traitor would still be rotting away."

"Stop picking on her, Wolf." Brady bends and puts a hand on Wolf's shoulder. Wolf shakes free indignantly, his eyes like twin puncture wounds. He stalks off.

This exchange makes me think a whole bunch of things at once. First, Julian isn't in jail anymore, which is a great relief. Second, if he isn't in jail, where is he? Third, Brady has got my back. Fourth, Wolf is about the most unlikely name I can think of for the samurai poser.

Before I can form any of these thoughts into words, Autumn enters the gym. She kicks the rubber duck outside, and the door slams shut.

At the front of the gym, she bows. "Seraphim reign supreme," she says.

"Seraphim reign supreme," the entire gym repeats. They know the drill.

"Who is here for the first time?" Autumn asks. I raise my hand, as does almost everyone else in the crowd. They seem to belong here more than I do. It's not only their black outfits; it's their fearless stances and fierce expressions. Any one of them could fit in with the military, whereas I'm sure I'd wash out in a second. "Okay. Listen up, newbies, because I'll be blunt. Most of you won't pass Furukama-Sensei's test today, and you can go elsewhere tomorrow." She snaps her fingers to materialize a bowl with slips of paper in it, and places it on a table. "Come up and take a number."

My fellow newbies rush to grab a number, as if being first will better their chances. I'm the last to draw, and when I do, Autumn squints at me as if she wonders why I'm here. I end up drawing number 425, meaning I'll be one of the last to take the test. At least this is the perfect opportunity to do some stealth investigation. Once I return to the back of the gym, I close my eyes and focus on Julian's brain waves so I can find out if what Wolf said was true, if Julian really is out of jail. After a few seconds I find him in the dorms, but his shape is still off, like last night. I hope that he's not still in such an awful condition that he doesn't know who I am. As much as I want to rush over and check on him, I have to take my test.

I roam over to Brady on the balance beam. "Hey, thanks for defending me."

"Don't sweat it." He pats the beam. "Come on up."

I accept his invitation, and as I settle in next to him, I scan the room. Most of the crowd watches Autumn, waiting for testing to start, while some stand or sit along the edges of the gym, joking with one another. The latter must be trainees who've already gone through testing. I lean back and dangle my legs.

"Are you here to help out with the testing?" I ask.

Brady plants his hands on the beam and stretches out his arms, lifting his body in the air. "Nah, I'm scoping out the competition." He smacks back down on the wood surface and then blows into his cupped palms. "There're only twelve spots open this rotation, and one of 'em's mine."

"You mean on Ascension Day?" a voice approaching us asks. It's Moby. And he's with Cash. I'm surprised to see Moby here after meeting him at the muse training. He seems surprised to see me too.

"That's right," Brady says. "At the end of each term Furukama-Sensei chooses the twelve best candidates to ascend to the seraphim guard when the portal opens for all the retirees." Cash gives Brady a fist bump, which is a good alternative to bowing. Moby follows suit. "The name Brady Sandoval is going to be on the list. Count on it."

Cash flashes a smarmy grin. "Right after mine," he boasts. The more I'm around him, the more he reminds me of a used-car salesman. "Have you met Moby yet? I ran into him at the career fair yesterday, and convinced him to take the test."

Moby leans on the beam casually, and I admire the snake tattoo that wraps around his forearm. Brady appraises it too. "Nice ink. And what's cool is that if you ever don't want it anymore, you don't have to laser it off. Dematerialization is all it takes."

"What's even cooler is this." Moby twists his arm, and the tattoo morphs into an actual coiled snake, which promptly opens its fangs as if to strike, startling me and making me bang my elbow against the wall.

"Whoa, dude, put your snake away," Brady jokes. "There are ladies present."

Moby's arm shimmers, and the snake recedes back into the tattoo. His theatrics have gained us a few curious onlookers among the newbies, including a petite Asian girl with dreadlocks who can't take her eyes off Moby's tattoo.

"So you love snakes, like, a lot, I guess," she remarks. "I love them too."

Moby crosses his arms and runs his hands from mid-biceps, where the sleeves of his black T-shirt end, to wrists, elongating his shirt so it covers up his tattoo. "I used to love them, but now I can't stand the little buggers. A snake is the reason I'm here."

"Death by snake bite, huh?" Brady says sympathetically. "And yet you keep the tattoo. Respect."

Everyone starts trading stories about how they died. Brady died of a brain tumor at a children's hospital in Dallas. Snake lover, who introduces herself as Zhu Mao, cracked her head on the side of a heated pool in Aspen while diving, and drowned. A girl built like a weight lifter who says her name is Maria Lucia tells how she choked on a bagel in a deli in Boston. Then they all look expectantly at me.

"Um . . . I didn't die." I hug my arms tight around myself. "I mean, I guess I did at some point or otherwise I wouldn't be here, but I don't remember anything about it."

A shadow crosses over Cash's face and he frowns, like he's trying to solve a difficult equation.

"Oh, so, like, you hit your head so hard you got postmortem amnesia," Zhu Mao says, as if it is some kind of afterlife medical condition, easily cured with a trip to the healers. I wish it were that easy.

"No." I jump down from the beam, irritated. "I'm saying someone wanted me to think I died in a car accident and then stole a bunch of my memories. Sometimes I think I'd do anything to get them back."

"But who could do something like that?" Brady asks. "That sounds impossible."

I'm about to answer, but the way they're all looking at me like I'm crazy makes me pause. So far there is no evidence that this type of memory loss is widespread. I know of it happening only to Neil and me, and in our case it seems to be related to my role in the Morati's plans. And even though Brady and Cash are aware of the Morati because they are part of the security team, I'm sure they don't know everything the Morati are capable of. Despite the bombings and the murders, Libby and Furukama, along with the rest of the career heads, have tried to keep everything as normal as possible. With the exception of the mandatory curfew and going door-to-door in the dorms questioning people, they've taken no public security measures that I'm aware of. It'd be wise to keep this to myself for now. I might have already said too much.

"I don't know," I say. "Maybe I do have some sort of amnesia."

Us newbies compare our testing order and find out that we're all very close together, with Zhu Mao being first.

The conversation moves on to other topics, but I'm only half listening. Instead I focus on the action at the front of the gym. Furukama has arrived and begun testing.

The screening appears simple enough. Autumn whispers instructions into each candidate's ear. The candidate steps up and touches his or her palm to Furukama's. Evaluations take anywhere from ten seconds to two minutes. Afterward Furukama points to either the left or the right. Considering there are so few to his right, I'm guessing those are the ones who have passed. Those to the left don't leave but simply take a seat on the hardwood floor.

Finally, after an agonizing wait, Autumn calls Zhu Mao's number. She takes her test and is sent to the right. Then Maria Lucia has a turn. After her test she shuffles to the left, her shoulders drooping. When Moby finishes his test, he is sent to the right.

When Autumn calls my number, my throat constricts. If I pass, I can build up my skills and have a chance to expose the Morati. I'll have a choice about whether to serve or not. But if I don't pass, the choice is taken from me, just like my memories were. I make my way past the seated candidates who now take up most of the left side of the gym. Autumn approaches my ear and cups her hand over her mouth. "Find the horse."

Furukama gives me a slight smile as he holds out his palm. The second I connect, a bright white light pierces my consciousness and hard surfaces press up against me from all sides. I panic. It's like I'm back in the Morati's mainframe and everything I've experienced since being captured by the Morati has been an elaborate fantasy.

I reach out with my mind to try to latch on to Julian's brain waves. Nothing. I try again with Neil, but I can't find him, either.

The walls start to crush me, and I push down the scream rising in my throat. A horse. Look for a horse. I reach deep into myself and pour all that I am into one thought: horse. Slowly the pressure on me lessens, and I'm rocked in a gentle side-to-side motion before being jolted upward and then smacking down hard. I'm riding a horse bareback, speeding through a bamboo forest, with arrows whizzing past my head. I squeeze my legs together so I can sit better. Just as my horse is about to leap over a narrow stream, I'm pulled out of Furukama's memory and back into the gym. He points to the right, and my head spins. I passed.

While Autumn breaks the bad news to those on the left, I concentrate on staying upright. Being inside Furukama's head was even more disorienting than being inside Autumn's, almost like he knew my fear and tried to use it against me. I'm not sure I really want to train with him if it will continue to be like this. But I repeat my pledge to track down the Morati for the good of Level Three. Seraphim guard training will not be easy, but I have to try.

Amidst groaning and complaining, the failed candidates exit the gym. That leaves thirty candidates who passed previously—including Autumn, Cash, Wolf, and Brady—and ten new recruits, including Zhu Mao, Moby, and me. Forty candidates vying for twelve spots. Well, thirty-nine, since I don't ultimately want to ascend. Not without Neil.

After the long day Furukama dismisses us with the guard's motto "Seraphim reign supreme." He reminds us of the curfew and tells us to come back tomorrow. He bows, and we all bow back. Before we leave, those of us who passed today pick up a huge binder with our syllabus and required reading.

While everyone chats animatedly about what their tests entailed, I make a beeline for the door and slip out.

Autumn catches up to me. "You did great in there!"

"You're not mad?" I ask. I know she wasn't superkeen on me trying out for the seraphim guard.

"No way," she protests. "It will be fun to spend more time together. I didn't get to see much of you yesterday."

I saw her only briefly at the healers' booth crime scene and defending Julian when he was arrested. "Thanks for putting in a good word for Julian. Do you know where he is now?"

"He's under house arrest while he recovers. It's unfortunate that Libby insisted on jailing him. Now we can't get anything coherent out of him."

"But you don't think he's guilty?"

"Not of the stuff he's accused of, at least," she says flippantly. Something in her tone makes me wonder if she's really over Julian. Perhaps it's best not to discuss him. No need to pick at old scabs.

"I'll have to build up my strength to make it through training. Are there some techniques you can teach me?" The more I can learn from her, the better equipped I'll be to survive whatever the afterlife throws at me next.

"Concentration and practice are the main tactics." Autumn holds out her palm to me. "Try to read my memories again. But focus."

"Okay." I suck in a breath and let my palm connect to hers. Like the first time right after my arrival in Level Three, I'm plunged into an inky blackness and I find myself spinning out of control. I grab on to an image fragment as it speeds by, and I hold tight, but I can't quite get inside the memory to experience it. Instead I merely get a glimpse. Autumn and Julian are at the movies. She's laughing as Julian throws kernels of popcorn at her. He starts to say something, and then the scene shatters into a million shards, and I'm thrown out of Autumn's mind.

She stumbles slightly when we break apart, surprise showing in her face for an instant before it's gone. "You're getting better at this. We can practice more later."

"Thanks. I'm lucky to have you as a friend."

Autumn laughs. "Damn straight you are!" Then her eyes narrow. "Hey, where'd you get that?" She reaches out and touches the skep charm. It must have come loose from under my shirt when I was trying to get inside Autumn's mind.

"Neil gave it to me for my birthday. Right before our car crash, actually. It's one of the last memories I have."

"Oh. Sure looks like what we call an obol. In ancient Greece, obols were coins that were buried with the dead so that their souls could pay passage on the river Styx into the underworld. But our obols are shaped like your beehive instead of coins." She taps her foot, her classic tic for when she's pondering something.

I shrug and hide the charm beneath my shirt. Megan mentioned obols and said they were what Careers used to travel back and forth to Earth. So if this *is* an obol, I guess that explains why Nate had one. It's a strange coincidence that it looks so much like the skep charm that Neil gave me.

"So I've been meaning to ask how you met Neil." She has this breathless vulnerability in her voice that makes me want to confide all my secrets. We stayed up late so many times in the glow of the television, whispering in our sleeping bags about boys. Until Julian.

"If you can believe it, I met him at church." I give her a few highlights—the day when I first admitted to myself that I was crushing on him, the walk in the woods that led to our first kiss, and the numerous times that he pulled out his guitar to sing me a song to cheer me up.

She listens with rapt attention, nodding, laughing, and oohing in all the right places. "He sounds too good to be true." She's right. The Neil I'm presenting to her is the idealized version, the one I want him to be all the time. The other version of Neil, the side I'm seeing a lot more of lately, is closed off emotionally, stubborn, and can be a little too self-righteous. I don't want to talk about that Neil.

"How about you?" I ask instead. "Anyone here you like?"

"Me? Not really." She shrugs and looks away. She must have boy trouble that she doesn't want to talk about either.

"I'm dropping off my binder. Want to come with?"

"I wish. But I have a security team meeting with Furukama-Sensei in a few. Stay safe."

"You too."

I race back to the dorm. When I get there, I materialize a desk and dump my binder onto it. First I'll check on Neil, and if he's not back, I'll look for Julian.

As I turn to leave, my whole body goes on alert. There's a small table next to the door, and sitting on top of it is an orb glowing with a white light, set into a base that makes it look like a snow globe. I draw closer, wary. In front of it is a note that reads, "Felicia Ward: Memory #35025."

eighteen

THE SOFT LIGHT of the orb draws me in, and I'm compelled to reach out for it, much like Aurora couldn't resist the call of the spindle that doomed her to one hundred years of sleep. Does a similar fate await me? Or is this more like Eve's apple, a gift that will forever wake me up to certain truths?

I force myself to pause. I need to report this, because if this is really one of my stolen memories, it could have only come from one of the Morati. The security team will want to examine it for clues. Then it will probably be entered into evidence, and my one chance to view it will be gone.

Or at the very least I should tell Neil about this. After all, it's probably one of our joint memories, so it concerns him as well. But Neil would take it to Libby.

Why does the Morati want me to have this memory? It

must come with strings attached, and I already owe Nate a favor.

But all my concerns fade into the background as the orb grows brighter and more tempting. This is mine. I deserve it.

I poise my fingers over the surface, shiny and as smooth as glass. As my skin comes into contact with the orb, the surprisingly thin membrane pops like a soap bubble. The room fades and crackles around me, and in a rush of icy water I'm pulled into my memory.

"Ramen noodles for the sixth night in a row. Yum." I grab the only two bowls I own off the drying rack and pour in the dry wormy noodles, the orangey powder from the spice packets, and boiling water. I pop a spoon into each bowl and carry them over to the tiny white table in the corner of the cramped kitchen.

"Lucky for us it's pizza night tomorrow." Neil pokes at his ramen listlessly.

"You don't have to eat with me. Maybe your parents don't want me over for dinner, but you're still welcome at your own house."

"I told you. They ban you from dinner, they ban me." He dunks the noodles with vigor now. Neil's parents made it clear that they held me responsible for Neil giving up the worship leader position at church, for him deferring college for a year, and for the car accident, too. It's no wonder they don't want to make small talk with me over pot roast and carrots.

"At least my dad likes you." I sit down. On the phone Dad was going on and on about how helpful Neil was with

Grammy's move and the estate sale. "Today he said, 'Hold on to that one, Felicia.'"

"Your dad gives excellent advice." Neil smiles broadly. Seeing his dimples makes me realize how little he smiles anymore. Working so much overtime to save up for college on top of all the physical therapy for his leg has caused shadows to creep into his face.

"Sometimes," I tease.

We both stir our unappetizing noodles a few minutes longer until they are finally soggy enough to eat.

I choke down the ramen. The faster I eat it, the less I'll have to taste it. The rapidity with which Neil shovels his ramen into his mouth tells me he has the same idea. "Oh, you should apply for a passport," I say casually.

"Why?"

"My dad is being sponsored by some French arts organization to put on his *Prancing Goat* Symphony in Paris in a couple of months. And they're going to pay to fly me over to play the piano."

"That's awesome." The chair squeaks across the floor under him as Neil gets up to pull me into a congratulatory hug. "I'm sure your neighbors will be thrilled to hear all your practice has paid off. Maybe they'll even stop beating on the ceiling with broomsticks."

"Very funny." I tap him on the chin with the end of my spoon. "The broomsticks are for the kids, not me." To pay for my apartment and living expenses, I give twenty hours of piano lessons a week.

He retrieves his bowl from the table, slurps up the broth, and rinses it out with water. "You done?"

"Yeah." I hand him my bowl, and his eyes narrow in that silently reproachful way he conveys so well. He pours the liquid remains of my ramen down the drain. "What? I ate the noodles."

I lean against the counter as he washes our bowls. "Imagine it. We're sitting at a sidewalk café on the Champs-Élysées eating *soupe à l'oignon* and drinking a Beaujolais wine . . ."

"Ooh la la!" Neil does an exaggerated French accent and bats his eyelashes at me.

"I can show you my favorite paintings at the Louvre, and we can go with my dad to our favorite restaurant. It serves the best escargot."

"You mean snails? Gross!" Neil makes a face.

"Trust me, they taste light-years better than ramen noodles from a package."

"I can't." Neil puts the bowls on the counter and throws a dish towel at me.

"You can at least try them." I dry the bowls in two smooth motions and slide them onto the shelf with the other dishes. I wish Neil would be more open-minded when it comes to food. He sticks his nose up at anything spicy or the least bit exotic. "I'm not suggesting you eat cockroaches or anything."

"No, I can't go to Paris." Neil walks from the kitchen into my tiny living room, and I follow him. He sits on the sofa and flips on the television to the news.

I stand between him and the screen, blocking his

view. “What do you mean you can’t go?”

Neil sighs and pushes the off button on the remote. “I have too much going on. I have work. Physical therapy. The play. Boy Scouts. Not to mention I can’t afford it.”

His money problems are my fault. Because if it weren’t for me, Neil’s parents would be paying for his college and he wouldn’t have to wait, wouldn’t have to work so many hours to save up for it. It makes me hyperaware of all that Neil has given up for me. “But I want you to come. There has to be some way.”

“I don’t want to live on ramen for the rest of my life just so we can splurge on *snails* one time.”

“If it weren’t for me, you could go.” I blurt it out before I can stop myself.

“If it weren’t for you, I wouldn’t even have a reason to go.”

I curl up on the sofa next to him and let my fingers inch up his arm, across his shoulder, over his neck, and into his hair. He shivers. I dip my hand into the back of his shirt so I can trace circles into his back. He doesn’t say anything, but he must like it, because he closes his eyes and the muscles in his face relax.

I get onto my knees and lean over to kiss his eyelids, my lips whisper light on his skin. Then I kiss his temple, his cheekbone, his smooth jaw. Once I get to his mouth, the dizziness of being close to him takes over. I kiss him deeply, throwing my leg over him so that I’m straddling him and letting my hands explore his chest under his shirt.

But as is typical, when I unbutton his shirt and try to push it off, Neil groans and breaks away. "You're killing me, you know that?" He looks me in the eye, and his expression is so anguished, it makes me a little bit crazy.

"Just this once we can break the 'all clothes stay on' rule." I lift up my tank, daring him to stop me. He doesn't reply, so I take that as an invitation and whip my top off and resume kissing him before he can change his mind.

He's careful at first and keeps his hands firmly on my lower back, but slowly he gets less cautious. When he touches the clasp of my bra, I want to scream at him to open it. But when he doesn't, I reach my arms behind me to undo it myself.

"No, we can't." He catches me by the wrist. "It's too much temptation."

He tries to stand up, but I scoot even farther onto his lap until my knees are pressed into the sofa cushions behind him, pinning him in. "God, Neil, why can't we live a little? Do you want to die a virgin saint or what?"

His eyes grow wide, a curious mix of fear and anger, like a feral animal that's been shut in a cage. "Felicia," he says with frightening calmness. "Please let me get up. And put your shirt back on."

I slide off him and wrestle into my tank top while he buttons his shirt. "What's wrong?"

He stands. "Maybe I shouldn't keep coming here. You living alone . . . it's making me weak. I don't want us to do anything we'll regret."

"But I won't regret anything I do with you." I mean it. I

rearrange the throw pillow behind me on the sofa and cross my legs.

"That's what you say now. But you don't know."

"Oh, I get it. This is about the pledge again," I say, more bitterly than I intended to.

He sighs. "Look, I don't want to fight about it. You know how I feel about this. We laid down the ground rules for a reason." He walks to the door and picks up his keys from the shelf. "Anyway, I have to go. I have PT early and I should get some sleep."

"Yeah, okay." I don't get up to kiss him good-bye.

As he opens the door, he turns like he wants to say something, but then shakes his head like it's not worth it and slips out. And yet another evening ends in frustration.

I come to again on the hard carpet of my dorm. Judging by the dull ache in the back of my head, I must have fallen when I went into my memory. I moan and open my eyes. Neil looms over me, his eyes wide.

"Thank goodness you're okay!" he exclaims. "I came in, and you were passed out on the floor." He half turns. "She's fine, Keegan. I'll meet up with you again later," he calls out the door.

My eyes shift up to the table that held the memory orb, but from this angle I can't tell if anything's been disturbed or if Neil has seen the note.

Paper crinkles, and my heart sinks. He's holding the Morati's note in his hand. "Oh, are you looking for this?"

nineteen

NEIL SHOVES THE PAPER into my face so I can clearly read my name and the memory number. "What does this mean?" he asks.

I'm not going to let Neil make me feel guilty for viewing something that belongs to me. "It's a note that came with one of my stolen memories." I hold out my arm so he can help me up.

He pulls me to my feet. "You mean a memory from after our car crash? Did you watch it?"

"I did."

"But how?"

"There was an orb," I say. "I came in, and it was sitting on that table. The package disintegrated as soon as I touched it. But the memory is part of me now."

He ponders this for a moment, sizing me up carefully. "If you have it, let me view it."

"I thought you didn't care about our lost memories."

He rubs his collarbone and then the back of his neck. "What do you want me to say? That I do care?"

"It's a start." I cross my arms. I won't make him grovel, but I am growing tired of his sanctimonious attitude and his cold shoulder.

"I care about them," he admits, to my great satisfaction. "But we don't know where this came from, or what it might cost."

"I'll pretend I heard only that first part." I lift my palm in offering to let him have access.

He hesitates, but in the end the pull of curiosity is too strong even for him, and he relents, lining his hand up with mine. As I relive the memory again, sharing it with him, I'm almost embarrassed by the intimacy of the scene on the sofa and the way it ended with Neil pushing me away.

Neil must be too, because when we emerge from the memory, he's blushing and fidgety. "That was . . . intense." He seems about to ask me a question, but then something clicks. "That wasn't Nate's memory. It was really yours. But that means the only ones who would have access to your memories are the ones who stole them in the first place. The Morati."

"I guess so, yeah."

"This is so dangerous, Felicia." He grabs my wrist. "If

the Morati are giving you these, they're up to no good. I can't believe you didn't immediately go to Libby with this. What if they coated the orb with poison or something?"

"I'm fine," I insist. He wants to go to Libby with everything. I'd be more inclined to take it to Autumn, if anyone.

"But still." He lets go of me and rubs the back of his hand across his forehead. "If you get any more of these packages, you have to tell Libby. You can't view these memories. It's like . . . withholding evidence. Don't you want to catch whoever killed Megan and Kiara? Whoever nearly killed me?"

"Of course I do!" But my joining the seraphim guard training is enough, isn't it? Libby isn't going to get anything from one of my memory globes.

"Good. Then you'll give it to Libby if you get one again."

More like, if I'm lucky enough to get another stolen memory, I'll view it and tell him it was an accident. He'll be as curious to share it next time. "I'm sorry," I say instead. "I was so surprised to see it sitting there. I wasn't thinking straight."

He hugs me, which I guess means he bought my story. "I couldn't take it if I lost you again."

"Again? Did Nate show you a memory of us breaking up or something?"

"No. I meant being apart from you in Level Two." He narrows his eyes. "Why? Did Nate show *you* another memory?"

Crap. How am I supposed to answer that? I materialize

my piano and sit down in front of it, letting my fingers run over the familiar keys. I play the first few measures of the *Prancing Goat* Symphony. I wonder if I ever did go to Paris to play it for an audience. Maybe I'll use it for my muse audition.

When I don't respond, Neil gets agitated and slides his arm under my hands so I can't keep playing. "He did, didn't he? Why are you keeping things from me?"

With a sigh I close the lid of the piano over the keys and I turn to face him. "You're the one who won't tell me about Gracie."

"Don't twist this around. What did Nate show you?"

I shrug. "It was a memory of the day you were discharged from the hospital. He told us that Gracie was planning to visit Ohio after being away for years."

"Show me."

With the desk, my father's chair, the bed, the small ornate table from the Morati, and now the piano, the room is pretty full. But there's still enough space along the wall for a two-seater sofa, so I materialize the one I saw in my apartment in the memory. Being able to materialize it proves without a shadow of a doubt that these memories are real, because I wouldn't be able to if I had never touched it. I like how wide the cushions are. "I would if I could." I sit down, crossing my legs under me.

He nods, slapping the top of my piano in frustration. He knows we don't archive memories of our afterlife, just our lives on Earth; I couldn't even show him a memory of my viewing Nate's memory. "What did he tell you about Gracie? I'm sure you asked him." The way he says it is very accusatory, like wanting to know the truth is a cardinal sin.

"He said it was up to you to tell me. When you felt the time was right."

"That's all?"

"He also said he thinks you and I broke up back on Earth. But he didn't know for sure."

"Don't believe a word he says." Neil balls his hands into fists.

"Well, you can't say we looked amazingly happy together in this last memory." It definitely has some disturbing parallels to our current situation, with us fighting and Neil retreating.

Neil finally sits down next to me, and I adjust my position so that I'm facing him. "Every couple argues sometimes. That doesn't mean we broke up. There might be one hundred happy memories to balance that out."

"You're right about that. We need context. That's why I've been saying that we need to get the rest of our memories." I can't believe that we didn't somehow solve our problems and stay together, and I want to know how we did it.

"No, that's why we need to forget about whatever happened on Earth and focus on now." He's slipping into some serious self-righteousness again.

"If you're so over everything, then why don't you

practice what you preach? Why can't you forgive Nate?"

"That's different."

"How?"

"Nate's a jerk."

I can't help but laugh. "True. But he is your brother."

"Stop trying to make this about me. We're talking about you willfully putting all of Level Three in jeopardy so you can view some memories that don't mean anything anymore anyway."

"If the Morati took our memories, they must have had a reason. Maybe there's a clue hidden in there. Something we can use to defeat them. What if *not* viewing them is what would put Level Three in jeopardy?"

"You'll say anything to justify your actions, won't you?" Neil asks, his eyes flashing. "But think about it. If the Morati give you memories, they won't give you ones they don't want you to view. Why would they?"

"Every memory is valuable," I retort. "Every memory is a piece of the larger puzzle of my life. Of our lives. Why should I have to let them go?" This is starting to sound a lot like our last conversation.

"If you don't, you won't be accepted in the muse program one day."

Of course he brings up the detachment test again. I just want the chance to experience the moments that I already did live, so that I can know my whole self. But I don't need to rehash this with Neil, or have him trying to interfere with my plans anymore.

"How was the healer meeting with Libby?" I ask. Neil's always so good at ending discussions by changing the subject, so I'll steal a move out of his playbook.

He brightens. "Libby sent me to muse class after all, because she's still preparing for students. Miss Claypool told us more about the Muse Collection Library."

"Cool. Did she talk more about the memory extraction process for getting the memory editions that the students use to study? Maybe I can go to her for more insight on that."

"I really don't know what the point of that would be. Shouldn't you be putting your energy toward something useful, like strengthening your skills in guard training?"

I hate the way we keep talking in circles. He won't convince me I should give up my quest, and he's never going to understand why it's so important to me.

"Maybe we should agree to disagree on this one," I suggest.

Neil takes my hands in his and looks at me seriously. "You need to really think about this. You have choices here. You can choose to let this make you crazy or you can choose to let it go and move on."

I withdraw my hands. "I don't think it's that black and white. We are victims of a crime. I certainly didn't choose to have my past stolen."

Neil tries again. "But I told you before—it's not your past that defines what kind of person you are now. It's each and every choice you make. A good choice elevates you, and a bad one brings you down. You can't let this fruitless pursuit of your stolen memories get in the way of going forward."

"I think you're afraid of what I'll find out about you."

Neil glares at me. "You are unbelievable." He gets up from the sofa, stalks across to the table, and throws the note on top of it in disgust. "Go ahead and do what you want. I don't care anymore."

Maybe this is what it was like for us back on Earth, and our breakup there began with these same kinds of words.

I slip my hand under the neckline of my shirt to rub the spot on my chest that burns in fury, and my fingers brush up against the skep charm. "Fine! I will."

As soon as the words are out of my mouth, a pulse like an electric shock sears through my body. The floor shakes under us, rattling Neil's framed portrait on my wall. There's a painful screeching sound followed by a series of gigantic thuds. We both race to the window and pull aside the drapes to look out. Neil slams his palms against the windowpane and then keels over, clutching his stomach.

The Muse Collection Library lies in ruins, and the lawn around it is pure chaos. The Morati have struck again.

twenty

I PAT NEIL'S ARMS and back. "Are you okay? Did you feel the electric shock too?"

"Some of my classmates were heading to the library for a tour after class, but I rushed back here to hang out with you and then I met Keegan." He rights himself, hands drawn into fists at his side. "I have to go check on them."

"I hope no one was hurt." And I hope all those memories weren't destroyed. Or that they made backups.

He looks over at me, dazed. "What?"

I touch his arm gently. "Should I come with you?"

"Not yet. But keep watching out the window for when the site is secured. I don't want anything to happen to you."

"Be careful." Our anger from before is momentarily

forgotten, and Neil draws me into a tight hug before leaving.

I survey the damage from the safety of my window. This bombing was different from the last one. It seems to have been something akin to an electromagnetic pulse rather than a gunpowder type of explosion. There's no trace of smoke, or ash, or blackened stone. Instead it looks like someone pressed a giant die-cutter into the Muse Collection Library and environs, cutting grooves in the shape of a perfect circle into the earth. What kind of bomb does that?

After a few minutes of watching people in agony, I can't take any more.

To keep my mind off the horror, I concentrate on searching for Julian's brain waves. I lock onto them. He's on the top floor of the dorm, and as I make my way toward his room, I pass my fellow students, and the heightened unease radiates off them onto me. They talk in low voices about the bombings and how they can't trust Furukama or his security team to keep them safe.

When I get to the room that must be Julian's, I don't bother knocking. Julian's space contains only the eggplant-colored sofa Mira was so fond of in Level Two, and he's lying facedown on it, wearing a pair of board shorts. That combined with the way his hair is tousled makes it look like he's been at the beach, not in jail. When I approach him, my insides are in a topsy-turvy whirl of worry. I nudge his thigh with my knee, and he lifts his head.

"Felicia," he mumbles. So he knows who I am again. That's a huge relief.

I sit down on the carpeted floor in front of him so that our faces are inches apart and run my fingers along the skin of his forearm. He's no longer glowing, clammy, or foaming at the mouth.

"How are you?"

He squeezes his watery eyes shut, and a couple of tears escape. "I have a headache. I've never had one before."

"You've never had a headache?"

"Thanks to our excellent control over our minds and our unique physiology, angels don't usually have to feel unless we want to. But since I was exposed to the brimstone . . ." Julian trails off, his meaning clear.

"Can you sit up?"

"I'd rather not. When I do, I get dizzy."

"What are your other symptoms?" I rise to my knees and start massaging his temples. "How does that feel?"

"It hurts more in the back of my head. My thoughts are fuzzy, my muscles are sore, and my throat hurts."

The position I'm in, leaning over Julian, is awkward and doesn't give me enough leverage to apply adequate pressure. I stand up and look him over, trying to figure out how to help him. I kneel on the sofa near his hip and throw my leg over him so that I'm straddling his narrow waist. As I look at the broad expanse of Julian's back, I'm struck by how Neil would never so casually lie around half-naked. Not around me, in any case. Lead us not unto temptation but deliver us from the evils of bare skin.

I flex my fingers and slide them into Julian's thick

hair and press circles into his scalp. "That okay?"

"Yes," he says, barely above a whisper.

"You're really tense. Long overdue for a massage." I work on the left side of his head for a few minutes and then ask him to face the other direction. After I concentrate for several minutes on his right side, his body relaxes under me. I relax too, and I don't understand why, but I feel compelled to run my fingernails lightly over his skin. First under his shoulder blades, then right above his hipbone.

He flinches. "Are you tickling me?" His voice is ragged, like he's having a hard time talking. And not just because of the effects of the brimstone.

I mentally kick myself. What am I doing? "Um . . . sorry. That was very unprofessional of me." I continue with his massage, kneading his neck, his shoulders, down his backbone and ending right above his tailbone. "I hope you don't ask for your money back," I joke. "Because I tickled you."

He shifts under me, turning completely around so that my hands fall onto his chest. It catches me off guard. The look in his eyes is so intense, it brings me right back to my living room in Germany, the day we shared our first kiss. Never breaking his gaze, he lifts himself into a sitting position until our chests are nearly touching. He's propped up with one arm, and the other is on the nape of my neck, so hot it might be burning a brand into my skin.

He parts his lips, leans even closer. I'm under his spell, and all I want is to lose myself in his kiss again. I remember the taste of him, intoxicating like a summer wine, and my thirst becomes unbearable. Every nerve ending in my body is on fire, begging me to close the gap between us.

But then he winces in pain, and our strange connection is broken. I scramble up off him and stumble over to the window, not daring to face him until I can cool off. I have no idea what possessed me to give Julian a massage, let alone to straddle him and practically seduce him. Seeing the dust clouds still billowing from the ruins of the library sharpens my mind again. What almost happened between Julian and me is not allowed. I love Neil, and I won't betray anyone else I love because of Julian.

"Did you know there's been another bombing?" I ask, needing to put emotional distance from the moment in Julian's arms.

"I heard it. But I didn't get up to see what was hit."

"The library." When Julian doesn't reply, I risk a glance at him. He's collapsed back onto the sofa and stares at the ceiling. I materialize a wooden chair and set it so the back of it forms a barrier between us when I sit down.

"The Morati delivered one of my memories to my room today," I tell him. "It's the third memory I've viewed of my stolen life, after the two Nate showed me."

He tilts his head in my direction and squints. "And you absorbed it." Julian knows me all too well.

"Of course I did," I say forcefully. "It belongs to me."

"Hey, I'm not judging you. But you do have to admit it is odd timing."

"What do you mean?"

"You view a memory, and then . . . boom!" He says the last word so strongly that I jump.

He's suggesting that the Morati strike every time I view a memory. The first, that Nate showed both Neil and me, was followed by the bombing that hurt Neil. The second, that Nate showed me in my room, was followed by the murder of all the healers. And now the third, delivered to my room, was quickly followed by the destruction of the library. But it has to be a coincidence, because the alternative is too troubling to contemplate—the possibility that each time I view a memory, it comes at a high price to all of Level Three, and it's my fault. But I don't know how that would be possible or probable, so I dismiss it immediately. I'm being paranoid.

In fact, it's more likely that the Morati are targeting me. The blast that injured Neil went off right next to me. The healers might have been killed to make me more vulnerable. And I went to a muse class, so the Morati might have assumed I'd be on the library tour. But then the Morati wouldn't have given me a memory if they just wanted to get rid of me. It doesn't add up.

"In any case, you have to realize that absorbing the stolen memory will cost you something," Julian says. "Whoever gave it to you has plans for you."

"So what are you saying? You think I should tell Furukama if I get another one?" If I do alert the authorities, it'll be "So long, memory." But if even Julian won't support me, maybe it's time to give up.

"What? No." He reaches out and rests his hand on the middle slat of the chair, like he wants to reassure me with his touch but it's too much effort for him. "We'll come up with a plan. We have to figure out who left the memory in your room." He lets his hand drop.

"That's where you come in."

"As soon as I recover. That may take a while."

"But you know how the Morati operate. What do you think their plan is?" I ask.

"Their goal is to ascend to the highest level they can to regain their former high positions. After the Morati were cast out of heaven and trapped in Level Two as servants to humans, we called out for eons to the higher levels, petitioning for an audience and hoping for a second chance. We never got a response. A radical faction formed, and the members aren't afraid of employing extreme measures to be heard. There are presumably only two ways for them to get to Level Four. The first is to serve many long years in an afterlife career and then be awarded a retirement spot. The second is to get selected to the seraphim guard."

They might have the patience to go for option one, but I think it's more likely that they'd pretend to be humans in order to win a coveted spot on the seraphim squad. They have to be good, of course, but not so good that they draw suspicion. "Lucky for me, I passed the initial testing for the guard today."

"You did? Congrats."

"But Furukama might find them first. I mean, couldn't

he expose all the candidates to brimstone and see which ones weaken?"

"Someone would have to tell him the Morati might be attending his classes with ascension in mind. And then he'd have to take every single candidate in training down to the jail," Julian says. "But he won't do that because he doesn't want word to get out that the jail contains a one-way passage to the negative levels."

"Why not?"

"Think about it. For example, a seraphim guard position is the most sought-after job there is. Training is highly competitive. If a candidate knew about the jail, what would stop him from pushing a rival down the hellhole? It'd be a concern, I'm sure." Julian has a point about Furukama's possible motivation to restrict knowledge of the jail's features to only a few guards. Trainees might be working on detachment from their human lives, but that doesn't mean they've lost their humanity and all the good and bad that goes with it. Furukama must really trust Brady and Wolf.

"Can't I suggest to Furukama that you attend a class? Then you could look at all of them and see if you recognize them."

"They're disguised as humans. I'd know them only in their angel forms."

I sigh. "And you're too weak to look into their memories right now."

This time he makes more of an effort when he reaches his hand toward me, and his fingers brush against mine.

"Keep your eye out for suspicious behavior. Angels can show you what they want, even fabricate whole pasts for themselves."

I get up from the chair and carry it over to the corner of his room. "I will."

He props himself up on his elbow, and a full-blown smirk forms on his lips. "Thanks for the massage."

Now that Julian's brought it up again, the shame settles in the pit of my stomach. I have the urge to find Neil and silently beg for his forgiveness for my near brush with infidelity.

I go downstairs and check both our rooms, but don't find Neil. And he's not down in the common room either. I go outside, and walk toward the ruins of the Muse Collection Library.

The bombing has left its traces in the hollow eyes of those who stumble by me, in the displaced clumps of soil and shrubbery, in the rubble that litters my path. Miraculously one of the towers of the library is still standing, and the stone gargoyle atop it looks down on me with what I imagine is disapproval.

The cleanup crew is out in full force, and the gusto with which they are already dematerializing debris makes me think it won't be long before the physical proof of the bombing will be erased forever. It will take longer to heal emotionally. If Neil hadn't hurried back to meet me, he might have been in the library. He might have been killed. The thought chills me. Instead of plotting with Julian, I should have come here with Neil to offer my help.

Victims that survived the blast have been brought to a makeshift tent near the explosion site. But with the healers gone, I expect their prognosis is grim. I duck into the tent. Maybe it's not too late for me to offer my assistance. The tent is packed with people, some lying in cots, most standing. Straining to see over those in front of me, I step on my tiptoes, and I spy a familiar head of curls at the front of the tent.

The first strains of music hit me with déjà vu. It's the song "Blessed Be the Tie That Binds," the song that Neil played the first Sunday I met him.

twenty-one

LIBBY SITS BESIDE NEIL with her hand on his shoulder while he plays. How dare she touch him so possessively? Why are all these people clapping along to the music as though nothing is wrong? Shouldn't they be in their rooms?

I lurch back, accidentally stepping on someone's foot. "Excuse me," I mumble as I turn.

"Didn't feel a thing," Autumn whispers, smiling. Her arms are folded across her chest, and she looks alert, as if she's on duty.

"Right, of course not. Mind over matter." Annoyed, I glance around the tent and see Cash off to one side, also standing at attention.

Neil finishes his song to wild applause. He laughs and

elbows Libby. "Sing this next one with me."

Even though few know the words to the next song Neil launches into, I recognize it from my church days. It's one of those repetitive ones that's easy to learn, and soon enough the sides of the tent ripple with the voices contained within.

Peace washes over me, an assurance that everything will be okay, that there is no reason to panic. Autumn sways behind me. She reaches out for my hand and then spins me in place until we're dancing.

Neil plays several more songs, and my cheek muscles hurt from smiling. The faces of my fellow students glow with something powerful that's been all too scarce lately: hope.

Libby stills Neil's guitar playing by patting his arm. She thanks the audience and asks them to return to the dorms. They comply, even those in the cots, and with Autumn and Cash directing traffic, the crowd eventually thins. Up front Neil slaps Keegan on the back and turns the bill of his baseball cap from side to front. Keegan gives him a high five and follows the others out. Neil and Libby confer in hushed tones and animated hand gestures. I trace figure eights in the air while I wait.

"You could've gone up there and joined him," Autumn says, startling me. Now that she's finished leading everyone out of the tent, her arms hang loosely at her sides.

I giggle. "Me? No. The last time I sang in front of anyone was our performance of Crocodile on Your Rock."

"Croc, croc, croc, stay up on your rock," she warbles.

"That's it!" I pull up a snippet of the memory of the silly musical we wrote and then performed at our neighborhood picnic back when we were about ten or eleven. I bust out with the second line. "Croc, croc, croc, don't bite and don't shock."

Autumn mock grimaces. "Wow, we were terrible, weren't we?"

"Oh, everyone loved it, though. They even let us go first in line for the hot dogs, remember? And your mom told me I had tons of talent."

"I remember." A shadow passes over her face.

Libby approaches, done with her private chat with Neil. "Great concert." She runs her hands down the tight skirt of her suit. "Neil has a real knack for bringing calm to a tense situation."

"After the bomb went off," Autumn explains, "people panicked and raced for the bridges to cross over into Areas One and Three."

My heart bangs in my chest, bursting through my happy haze. I frown. It makes sense that people would want to flee. All the incidents have been isolated to Area Two so far. "Why not let them go?" I ask. "If they'd be safer?"

"Right?" Autumn shakes her head. "But Furukama-Sensei says if we don't retain as much normalcy as possible, we're letting the Morati win. The rest of the career council agrees. The security team blocked off the bridges and sent people here."

"And I used Neil's music as a conduit to distribute mood

stabilizer," Libby says. So that's the reason she was touching him the whole time. She had to in order to amplify her healer skills to the crowd. It's pretty genius, actually. "Instead of being on the edge of rebellion, they're now happily returning to their rooms."

Libby smiles at us, waves at Neil, and then she's off in a cascade of red curls and a puff of pressed linen. Autumn follows her out. "I'll come by later," she calls to me.

Now that the tent is empty except for me, Neil, and two lone metal folding chairs, the flaps flutter noticeably in the wind. Neil sets his guitar case on his knees and lovingly tucks his instrument into it. He closes the case and pats the chair next to him, inviting me to sit.

"You know why I always went to church?" Neil asks.

"Because your parents went. Because your friends went," I say, even though this more accurately describes the reason I went. Neil's a true believer.

"Well, yes, that's part of it." Neil smiles ruefully. "But the reason I loved going was the music. Everyone singing and worshipping together, it made me believe I was a part of something bigger, that I was communicating with a higher being. I was given a talent that I could use to minister to others. And when I was sad or angry, the first thing I did was pick up my guitar. If I learned anything on Earth, it's that music has the power to heal. Did you see how those people looked tonight? When I first got here, after the bombing, they were inconsolable."

"I bet." Neil was always in his element singing in front

of a large group, so it's no surprise, really, to find him so engaged in it in Level Three. But I hadn't expected him to become some sort of revival tent leader.

"I think this is my calling. This is what I'm supposed to do. Like maybe even permanently."

I don't like Neil using the word "permanent," especially when I'm not in the sentence. "But what about our plan to join the muses together?" I ask. What about me? Did he really mean what he said in our fight right before this bombing? That he doesn't care anymore?

"This might fit me even better. In any case, the muse program is on hold indefinitely until they can replenish the library. Miss Claypool already announced a muse collection drive, where anyone can go in and donate a memory."

I notice he uses the word "me," not "us." And he's glowing, excited about this. I can't deny that his music was effective. My mood was certainly lifted, at least until he hinted at abandoning me. "You are exceptionally good. I've always said so. Wouldn't it be great to use your talent as a muse to inspire those still living? It could be your legacy."

"I'm needed more here, in Level Three." He snaps the closures of the guitar case and stands up. "You could accompany me on piano."

He's throwing me a bone. "And be a healer, too?" There's no way I could switch to healing right now. I'm on a mission to uncover the Morati posing as seraphim guard trainees.

"Sure. Why not? We'd probably start small. Maybe in the common room in the dorm. If the demand grows, we can move to a larger venue, like Assembly Hill."

"Seems like you have a pretty big following already."

"Nah." Neil blushes and ducks his head slightly, his usual way of receiving compliments. "It's not me they stayed for. It was the music."

I give him a playful shove. "Only because you were the one playing it."

He smiles, but as we walk back to the dorms together, he doesn't say a word. Once we get to our rooms, Neil gives me a quick good-night peck on the side of my mouth, says good-bye, and closes his door firmly behind him. I stand in the hallway, drained after all this drama. I have no idea where I stand with him.

I press my ear against the wood of the door, straining to hear the muffled strumming of his guitar. He starts off with an upbeat song, but stops after a few measures and segues into a ballad. And not just any ballad but the one he played for me that first day I went to his house. The one that dredged up all my pain and brought it so close to the surface, I thought I might burst with it. He played it for me to show me that he understood what I was going through. That he had moments in his life he longed to forget too. And that he would be there for me, anytime I wanted to talk.

His closed door is a broken promise. If I can't go to him to talk, who can I go to? Not Julian. I almost crossed a line with him today, and what if I can't help myself next time? My relationship with Neil is fragile enough as it is. I could talk to Autumn. I never would have believed it five days ago, but I've gotten my best friend back. She's my one comfort right now.

I wrench myself away from the sound of loneliness and shuffle over to my room. Autumn walks down the hallway toward me. "You look like you could use a friend," she says.

My eyes well up with tears. It's like she instinctively knew I needed her. I invite her in.

She heads straight for my collage wall. "I like what you've done with the place. No pictures of Julian?" she teases.

Her delivery is light, but I can't help thinking that if she's bringing him up, she must still hold at least a shadow of a grudge. Maybe it *is* time we hashed out my betrayal and completely cleared the air. "About that . . ."

Autumn holds her hand up. "I know what you're going to say. I'm not angry with either of you for what you did. All of that is so far removed from me, it's almost like it never happened."

She could be a role model for detachment. "So you forgive us?"

"There's nothing to forgive." She gives me a wistful smile that makes me nostalgic for the early days of our friendship, when she was the first person I thought of when I got up and the only one I wanted to whisper my secrets to. Impulsively I hug her, tracing a crude outline of a dolphin between her shoulder blades. It used to be what we'd do every time we met, to make sure the other was still herself, and not a clone or possessed by an alien. She hugs me back, laughing. "It's so amazing, isn't it? How buildings can crash down around you but you feel like nothing can touch you because you're in the company of a friend?" she asks.

With Julian incapacitated and Neil mad at me, my reserves of hope are running dangerously low. But Autumn gives me a vital boost. I regret the way our relationship soured in those last months before Autumn's murder. I'd once thought her moodiness charming. I'd told myself it gave her depth, made her interesting. But the unrelenting nightmares of my mugging in Nairobi had left me sleep deprived and brittle, increasingly unable to keep myself together. I took it out on her, and became hostile when she pouted. I gave up on trying to appease her. That's the way it is sometimes with the people you love the most. You pile abuse on them because they're the only ones who will take it from you. Until they don't anymore, and you find yourself alone.

"I want to return something of yours." Autumn extends her palm, revealing a dolphin charm. Autumn gave me two dolphin charms as a symbol for our friendship, but after she caught Julian and me kissing in the back of the taxi, she ripped one away from my bracelet, telling me I didn't deserve it. I never imagined I could ever earn it back.

"Are you sure?"

She smiles. "Just a little something for passing the entrance exam today. I'm proud of you."

"And I am in awe of you." I take the charm and hug her tightly.

"Pedicures?" she asks. Whenever we had bad days, Autumn would always bring over her nail polish, and we'd cheer ourselves up with the bright, glittery colors. No amount of polish can fix all my current troubles, but maybe being with Autumn can take my mind off them for a while.

"Definitely," I say. We spend the next several hours chatting. She comments on many of the photos, and we reminisce about our travels and afternoons after school together. By the time she gets up to leave, my heart is full of joy.

I walk her to the stairwell, where we bump into Nate. They glower at each other.

"See you in training tomorrow," Autumn says to me before rushing down the stairs.

Nate is the last person I want to deal with right now. He reaches out to tap me on the nose in that annoying way of his, but I dodge his finger. He plucks at the air and produces a single yellow rose, which he holds out to me with a flourish. "I brought you this."

I make no move to take it from him. "Why are you here?"

He snaps the stem of the rose between his thumb and forefinger and lets it drop to the floor, all pretense of friendliness gone.

"I heard that you impressed Furukama at your seraphim guard screening today."

"How would you hear that as a demon hunter? I didn't think you all got along with us." The "us" is stretching it, since I've been to only one session so far, but Nate's left eye twitches ever so slightly. I've rattled him. I walk back to my room, and he follows.

"You have a good chance of getting one of the open ascension spots this rotation."

"I doubt that." I'm suddenly feeling very worn out, and I don't want to invite him in. I crouch down and sit on the floor, slumping against the wall outside my door. "Nearly all the trainees have more experience than I do. Like Autumn. She's been here forever."

Nate sits on the floor too, across the hall, next to Neil's door. He stretches his left leg out completely but rests his right arm on his bended right knee. "Don't you think it's odd that Autumn has stayed in Level Three? She's content to serve as Furukama's assistant while term after term others ascend to serve in the guard."

"Maybe it's because she enjoys her position." Or maybe it's because no one knows what the seraphim guard actually do in Level Four, and she worries that she would like it.

"Maybe." Nate regards me with a calculating expression. "I think it's suspicious. She has what it takes to move on, and yet she stays. It's almost like . . . she's been waiting for someone." Is he implying that the someone she's been waiting for is me? Did Autumn sacrifice her place in the guard in order to have the chance to repair our friendship?

"Who? Me?"

Nate barks out a laugh and then mumbles under his breath, "And people tell me I'm self-centered."

I let his insult roll right on by. "Whatever."

"Think about what's been going on lately . . . the bombings . . ." Nate looks pleased when my eyebrows jump about two inches.

"Wait. . . . You think Autumn's involved in all this?" Autumn's no criminal mastermind, and since she skipped right over Level Two because she was murdered, there's no way she could have met or had any contact with any of the Morati, unless they recruited her in the past four months. "That's impossible."

Nate shrugs. "There's more to Autumn than your experience with her. I wouldn't underestimate her if I were you."

It seems to me that Nate's trying his best to cast suspicion elsewhere. That makes me even warier of him than I already was. "She's helped me practice so I can view the memories others are trying to hide. Maybe you're worried that I'll soon be able to get whatever I want out of you without having to make shady deals." Okay, so maybe we've practiced only once, but Nate doesn't need to know that.

"Speaking of which . . . your debt has come due," Nate says. "I'm calling in my favor."

I tense up. This can't be good. "Oh?"

"That's right. You will threaten to quit seraphim guard training. Unless Furukama kicks Autumn out immediately."

twenty-two

"WHAT?" I SHAKE MY HEAD and press my fingertips into the carpet. He can't seriously be suggesting that I betray Autumn again. It's ludicrous. "Why?"

"Explaining my reasons wasn't part of the deal." Nate gets up and brushes off his pants. "I expect to enjoy the fallout."

"There are two problems with your request. One, Autumn is my best friend. Two, Furukama isn't going to choose me over her. He barely knows me!"

"I guess that's the chance you take." He shrugs and starts off down the hallway.

I jump up and run after him. Of all the favors Nate could have asked for, this one punches me right in the gut.

I can't bear to lose Autumn again. Plus, Furukama will throw me out on my ear for making such a demand. I won't be able to improve my skills or suss out the Morati among the seraphim guard candidates myself. I'll be totally reliant on Julian, once he recovers, to get my memories back. "I won't do it."

Nate stops and spins so quickly, it throws me off balance. He grabs me by the shirt and twists the fabric in his fist. "Don't test my patience." Then he lets me go and gives me one of his patented jerk smiles. "You'll do it. Tomorrow. Or I'll throw you into the same hole I threw that demon into." So he did see me down there. Furukama is right to keep the jail and the hellhole top secret. I fervently wish Nate didn't know about them.

"I don't believe you."

"No?" He waves his arm menacingly in the direction of Neil's room. "How can I prove it to you?" His voice is flat and hard. He's threatening Neil's life now too.

"Stay away from Neil." Oh God, Neil was right. Nate is a psychopath.

"I better not hear that you warned Autumn about this beforehand. In fact, she's never to know. I want there to be public fireworks." He punches his fists together. "BOOM."

As he struts away, I smooth the wrinkles from my shirt. I run through my options. If Julian were full strength, I could go to him. Maybe we'd be able to form some sort of emergency plan B. But in the state he's in, talking to him would be futile. I could go to security, to someone other than

Autumn—Cash maybe, and tell them how Nate threatened me. But it would be my word against Nate's, and Nate has a high position here, while I'm no one. Who will believe me? I'm too ashamed to go to Neil. He'd ask me how I even knew that a demon hole existed. If I tell him about this, he might never open the door for me again.

The stupid thing is, Neil actually made me believe that I had become a better person, and that I had somehow redeemed myself. But it's clear that deep down I am still bad. It's easy enough to rage against Nate, and obviously I hate him for taking advantage of my weakness, but in the end I have no one to blame but myself. I got myself into this mess out of selfish greed, and out of the need to view another memory at any cost. I'm powerless to stop what's coming. I don't deserve Autumn's friendship, or anyone else's for that matter. I deserve to be alone.

I reenter my room and flop facedown onto the bed. I squeeze my eyes shut and try to block out all the images of Autumn's smiling face staring out at me from my collage. Instead I think of goats rearing up, one by one. Eventually, the monotony of my thoughts puts me into a trancelike state.

Light streams between the curtains I forgot to shut last night. I roll over and sit up against the headboard, the horror of what I have to do today making me want to retch. I don't want to do this to Autumn, but Nate threatened Neil's life, and I can't take the chance that he'd follow through and murder his own brother. I hold my stomach and do some slow breathing exercises.

Finally I get up. I materialize into a black tracksuit so that I'll match everyone else at training. If I have any chance at all of Furukama choosing me over Autumn, I need to be dressed for the part of seraphim guard. It could be the tipping point. Still I allow myself the small rebellion of keeping the light pink glitter polish on my toenails inside my black shoes.

I pull my hair into a ponytail as I walk over to Neil's door. I knock, but there's no answer. I check, and he's not in the room. It takes me a few moments to process that he left without me. It robs me of my last bits of confidence. I walk over to his desk, where he's displayed Megan's grass animals. Next to them is the box he gave me, with the useless flashlight. Gift number two of the week of gifts he promised me in the car before our accident, though he stopped with three. It's not practical to carry the Maglite around with me, so I leave it where it is. I pat my chest to make sure the skep charm is still there. At least I have this reminder that at one point Neil truly thought I was good enough to love.

When I arrive at Gym Three, the rubber duck is once again being used as a doorstop. I give it a tiny good-bye wave, since this is almost definitely the last time I'll be welcome at seraphim guard training, thanks to Nate. The duck's yellow cheerfulness seems to mock me, especially when I'm confronted with the somber atmosphere inside. All the other candidates have arrived already, and from their semicircle on the floor, Wolf stares at me with a sneer. I ignore him, my eyes locking with Autumn's. She's sitting with Furukama at the opening of the semicircle. I look away quickly. Moby and Brady are on one end, and when Brady pats the floor next to him in invitation, I don't hesitate to join them.

Once I'm seated, Furukama goes down the line, examining each of us, with the exception of Autumn, from head to toe. He doesn't touch us physically, but the way his eyes drill into me is invasive enough. Can he see the blackness of my soul?

"Seraphim reign supreme," Furukama says, and we repeat it after him. "Your minds are strong. We train. Your minds get stronger. At the end of term, on Ascension Day, I will choose twelve to join the seraphim guard and ascend to Level Four. The rest will continue to train until they are one day chosen, or leave to seek another career." Furukama materializes a binder, the same one we were all given yesterday. The one I left in my dorm room. This day is not at all going in my favor.

Wolf has his binder with him, of course, as do about half of the other students. Because I never touched my seraphim guard binder on Earth, I can't materialize it now. I could materialize a similar-looking binder, but it wouldn't have the same content, so it's no use.

Autumn takes over. "If you looked at the syllabus yesterday after class, you know that our first unit is on meditation. And you would have read the required chapters provided as well as practiced deep breathing techniques." She pauses to look knowingly at those of us who didn't bring our binders and probably also didn't read or practice. "But considering the bombing of the library yesterday, we will not penalize anyone today. We will have an open session to talk about your concerns. Who would like to go first?"

Wolf's hand shoots up, and Brady groans beside me. "It's obvious who's setting off the bombs. It's that angel," Wolf says. Some of the others around Wolf mumble in agreement. Even though most of the populace of Level Three doesn't know about the Morati being here, it's an open secret among the seraphim guard trainees, many of whom also serve on the security force.

Furukama nods. "You refer to Julian."

"Julian continues to be in our custody," Autumn explains. "Therefore, we can be sure that he is not responsible for the latest bombing."

Wolf sticks out his lower lip like a bratty child. "Maybe he didn't blow up the library, but that doesn't mean he wasn't responsible for the other crimes. It means he has an accomplice." When he says the word "accomplice," he looks straight at me. *Real subtle, Wolf.*

"I assure you, we are pursuing every lead." Furukama's tone is polite but firm. Wolf nods, satisfied for now.

"Anyone else?" Autumn asks.

Zhu Mao clears her throat and straightens her posture. She has pulled her dreadlocks back into a bun, which gives her a more serious edge. "So these people in my hall were complaining that the security force sucks." The trainees that are also part of the security force chime in with unhappy groans and denials. Some cast uneasy glances toward Furukama, waiting for his reaction. After all, if you criticize the security force, you are in essence complaining about its top commander.

"And everyone's, like, totally freaked," Zhu Mao continues. "The bomb chopped a girl in half yesterday. So is this, like, Armageddon or something?"

"There is no reason to believe that." Autumn's voice is tight. "If we stay calm, and lead with our calm examples, everything will go back to normal soon. To assist on this account we've enlisted Libby's help. Some of you might have heard about, or attended, Libby's first mood-enhancing concert last night. The results were extraordinarily positive."

"But, like, isn't that a Band-Aid for the problem? Drugging everyone up? I mean, not that I mind drugs," Zhu Mao says, eliciting chuckles from the group, "but they don't protect anyone from bombs. Won't we be like lambs on a chopping block? Can't we stop preventing people from leaving here to go to Areas One and Three?"

"You think we'd all be safe from the Morati if we moved? Why wouldn't they follow us?" Autumn challenges.

"I don't know."

"If you have a better suggestion, you're welcome to share it with us," Autumn says.

Zhu Mao shakes her head.

Furukama stares at me. "Are there other concerns?" It's like he can read my mind.

I gulp. Here goes nothing. I'd rather do this in private, but I can't risk that Furukama will go back into his statue mode before I have the chance to do Nate's dirty work. "Yes. I do have something I want to say." I stand up. "I've thought it over, and I have to quit."

Brady and Moby look up at me in surprise, and Wolf lets out a very inelegant cackle. Brady pulls at my arm. "What're you doing?" he whispers. "Is this because of what Zhu Mao said?" I sway on my feet, fighting the urge to run.

Furukama's face reveals nothing. "Class dismissed," he says. "Only Felicia stays."

My fellow trainees file out, eyeing me with a mix of curiosity and disdain as they go. They can't fathom why anyone would voluntarily leave guard training and all the cachet that comes with it.

When the gym is empty but for me and Autumn, Furukama wastes no time in getting to the point. "Do you disagree with my tactics? Is that why you wish to quit?"

"No. The Morati drugged us in Level Two for selfish reasons. What you and Libby are doing is trying to help people."

"Explain your problem," Furukama says. "You are a valued trainee. You could find the Morati. I have high hopes for you."

"I do as well," Autumn interjects, the concern clearly showing in her eyes. Autumn's acceptance makes this even harder for me.

I bow my head. I can't bear to look at Autumn while I say what I have to say in order to keep Neil safe. Even though my afterlife will be bleak without Autumn's friendship, it would be even more so if Nate were to dispose of Neil. "Thank you, but . . ." I pause, my voice cracking. "I can't train with Autumn. It's either me or her."

Autumn yelps, like a dog that's been kicked in the side. "What?"

Furukama reaches out both arms, placing one hand on Autumn's shoulder, which silences her, and one hand on mine. His concentrated stillness fills my mind, pushing out all my thoughts.

He lets go of us abruptly and grunts. "Autumn, you are dismissed. Permanently." Then he morphs into his stone statue mode as if to ward off any protestations.

My jaw drops, and Autumn careens into me in a free fall. I catch her and lower her to the floor. She slaps at my legs, and I let her. I want it to hurt. "Why, Felicia? Why? You have to explain this to me, because I don't understand."

"I'm so sorry. So sorry." I could say it a million times and it would still never be enough for what I've done. I never could have anticipated that Furukama would choose me. I was fully resigned to be the one who had to leave. Autumn would still have her position. Nate would have his sadistic fun. And I would be reliant on Julian for helping me find the Morati. Maybe Autumn would have forgiven me again at some point down the road. But she's not going to now, especially because I can't tell her that Nate forced me to do this.

Her forehead creased in confusion, she lowers her cheek to the floor and stares at the balance beam against the wall. For a moment she's the old vulnerable Autumn. "Do you have any idea how hard I've worked to get this? To become Furukama's confidant? To have a position where people look up to me? And then you waltz in here, smile your pretty smile, and he dumps me for you."

"I wish I could take it back. I am so, so, so sorry," I repeat helplessly.

"Oh no, you're not." Autumn's pupils dilate, making her look a bit crazy. A bit dangerous. "Not now you aren't. But you will be."

Is that a threat? "More sorry than now?" I squeak out. In all my fear of Nate throwing me into the hellhole if I didn't do his bidding, I didn't even consider what Autumn might do.

She sits up. "There is so much more going on here than you'll ever understand. I shouldn't give you this advice, because you certainly don't deserve it, but don't trust anyone." Autumn glances at Furukama's statue, and when she does, her lip twitches. "Especially not him." Then she goes to the door, kicks the rubber duck viciously, and lets the metal door slam behind her.

The slam echoes through the gym, driving it into my skull how very cut off from everyone I am. Autumn said I shouldn't trust anyone, but I know the truth. No one should trust me. Not even I can anymore.

I walk back to my room, kicking idly at stones and

pebbles. Now that Furukama has put his faith in me, I should check out the syllabus and do my meditation homework so I can be prepared for tomorrow, but I get no joy from the thought of doing so. When I reach the lobby of the dorms, I'm greeted by the sound of Neil's singing voice. He leads a large group of our peers in some songs. I don't stop. I can't deal with his cheery public persona right now. I need to get to my room and be alone.

Safely inside, my eyes automatically go to the table by the door to check if the Morati have delivered. They have. And this time there's not one memory globe but two.

twenty-three

THE TWO UNLABELED milky-white memory globes are nestled in a cream-colored silk scarf. They look so innocent for objects that hold so much mystery and temptation. I should alert Libby or Furukama, but I won't. Not when the globes pulsate with truths that have been kept from me all this time. Truths that could be my salvation—the keys to improving my relationship with Neil, maybe even salvaging my friendship with Autumn. And until I have these truths, nobody has to be aware of this but me.

I inch closer until I'm poised directly over the twin globes. Their soft glow illuminates my greedy hand as I make contact with the one on the right. The globe pops and the memory dissolves into my skin, rushing my mind with images and sucking me back in time. Back to my earthly life.

It's nearing midnight and I'm sitting cross-legged on my narrow bed in the tiny Paris hotel room I'm sharing with my dad. The score to the *Prancing Goat* Symphony is laid out all around him on his own narrow bed, and he scrawls notes in the margins.

"Isn't it a bit late to be making changes?" I ask. "The concert is tomorrow." I've been practicing for months, but my nerves are so frayed that my hands are tucked under my legs to keep them from shaking. It's not only worry about my performance. It's also that I texted Neil earlier and asked him to call, but he hasn't. And I don't know why not. He should've been home from work an hour ago.

Dad flashes me a harried smile and collects all the papers, stacking them in an orderly pile. "Preconcert ritual to keep the jitters at bay." He gets up and deposits the score on the desk under the window, sweeping the curtain closed at the same time. "We should get some sleep. Did you brush your teeth?"

I groan. I'm eighteen and my dad is still telling me to brush my teeth. "Yes, Dad." I finished my entire bedtime routine in the bathroom, including changing into pj's. I even laid out an extra blanket on the end of his bed in case he gets cold.

"Did you floss, too?"

"Yes."

He nods. "Floss every day, and you'll keep your teeth forever. That's what our health teacher in high school told us. It may have been the only thing I learned in that class."

In my case my health teacher was far more concerned with preaching safe sex than extolling the virtues of flossing. She averaged 3.2 utterly mortifying statements per class, and none of them had to do with teeth.

I slip under the duvet and stare at the ceiling. Without even moving my eyes, I see all four corners of the room. The springs of Dad's mattress constrict and his sheets rustle as he gets into bed. He clicks off the lamp and plunges the room into inky darkness.

"Why didn't Mother come?" I've been thinking about her absence a lot today, sure that it means she still doesn't want to see me, especially because she's never missed one of Dad's premieres before. The absence of light makes me bold enough to pose the question.

"Oh, you know. She had an important embassy function she couldn't miss." Though he tries to keep his tone light, as if it doesn't bother him, there's an undercurrent of strain in his voice. I can just imagine their arguments about me.

"I'm sure." I taste the bitterness on my tongue when I say it.

"Oh, sweet pea, she would have come if she could have." His words lack conviction, only confirming what I already suspected. My mother wants nothing more to do with me after what I did to get my security clearance revoked by the State Department. The official reason was that I misused my diplomatic passport when I entered Myanmar to look for my dad, but I'm sure the fact that I fled the scene of Autumn's murder without calling the police and hacked my way into a free plane ticket contributed to the State Department's decision. I don't answer. There's nothing I can say that hasn't been said already. I've talked to her only twice since, both after my accident.

Dad and I have been in Paris now for a week, our time eaten up by lengthy daily rehearsals. Neil has called every day without fail, except today. This is the longest amount of time we've been apart, with the exception of the days after our car accident when we were both too out of it to even notice. He's become so much a part of me, I hate being this far away. I wonder if this is how my dad once felt about my mother. If he still feels the ache of separation despite their many solo trips throughout their marriage. Does it ever get easier?

"When did you know that you wanted to get married?" I ask.

"Hmmm . . ." Dad thinks aloud. "Well, after we recovered from malaria in Dakar, we went back to our posts in rural Senegal. I had time to bike over to her village once or twice a week, but it was never enough."

I hear the smile in his voice as he recalls his courtship with my mother. I wish I were able to see the side of her that brings my dad such joy.

He goes on. "We talked about what we would do when our peace corps term was up. Evie wanted to get her master's degree in international relations at George Washington University. My Africa stay had gotten me interested in ethnic music, and I was already composing classical pieces that integrated tribal drums. I didn't really have a plan, so I ended up following her and proposing to her because I didn't want to lose her."

"You knew each other for only a year when you got married, right?"

"Well, it was more like eighteen months by the time we planned the wedding."

"Did you ever think you should have waited longer?" I ask tentatively.

"We've had our problems and differences of opinion." He pauses, the weight of his statement clear. "But I've never regretted marrying your mother. Not for a second."

Though I find it hard to believe the woman my dad loves so fiercely is the mother who hates me, I'm happy for my dad that their relationship has stood the test of time. It gives me hope for Neil and me.

He clears his throat. "Why the sudden interest?"

I feel my cheeks grow hot. I don't want to discuss Neil with my dad right now. Not when my insides are churning with so many insecurities about both Neil and the concert. "Oh, no reason. Trying to keep my mind off tomorrow."

"You've been so good in rehearsals. You'll nail it."

"Thanks, Dad."

"Good night, sweet pea."

○ ○ ○

That's where the first memory ends, a bittersweet fragment of my life that reopens the wounds of my mother rejecting me. But my father forgave me, let me back into his life. I wonder what he's doing right now. If the pages of his *Prancing Goat* Symphony score swim before his eyes when he thinks of me.

I stare at the ceiling, a dull pounding pain in my head from where it smacked the floor. Maybe I should go into the next memory from a lower position. I get up on my knees and stretch my arm until my hand comes in contact with the second memory globe. Then I'm pulled under again.

Dad and I sit at a table with Arno, the director of the Metropole Orchestra, and Frederick, the guy who organized the financing for tonight's sold-out performance of the *Prancing Goat* Symphony. They laugh and talk over one another, their eyes still bright with the memory of our standing ovation.

We're in a brasserie in Paris that Arno recommended. He says he loves to come here for both the excellent food and the art nouveau décor. I stare up at the gorgeous stained-glass windows in the ceiling. In the one directly above our table, green and yellow and white glass come together to form an intricate floral mosaic.

The waiter distributes menus. The leather cover of the menu is embossed with the restaurant's name. Julien. Not spelled the same way as that ghost from my past, but an unsettling coincidence all the same. I haven't thought of

Julian much lately. After confiding in Neil about my dark days, Julian pops up on my radar only rarely. I can't help closing my eyes and picturing him as he was the last time I saw him, when he ditched me outside the Irish pub on Halloween. His face is slightly blurry behind the window of the cab, but the sadness in his eyes is clear. Now I swing my head to the right, as if the motion could erase him from my mind, but instead what I see is impossible: Julian behind a steering wheel of a police car—*the* police car—for a split second before glass shatters all around me.

I open my eyes with a start and drop the menu onto the table. Dad looks at me with concern, but our dinner companions either haven't noticed anything or are too caught up in their postconcert euphoria to care.

Flashing Dad a reassuring smile, I open my menu and hide behind it. There's no reason for me to be seeing Julian's face in connection with the car crash. Whenever I try to think of the crash, my mind shuts down. I don't know what happened from the moment Neil swerved to miss the police car until the moment I woke up in the hospital, hooked up to machines and under the influence of pain meds. They told us the driver had miraculously gotten out of the twisted wreckage and fled the scene, that the police car had been reported as stolen, and that they had no leads. They also asked us a bunch of weird questions, like if we'd seen a tornado. I hadn't been back to the crash site, but friends mentioned that the trees and bushes along the side of the road had been flattened.

Julian couldn't have been in that police car. I was definitely angry with him for a long time, but loving Neil has taught me to be more forgiving—both of others and of myself. I'm sure I only had this vision because I'm under so much stress, and the coincidence of reading his name on the menu made my mind invent Julian's presence at the scene of the accident. So why is my whole body tense and shaky?

Dad puts his hand on my arm. "What would you like? I ordered the escargot as a starter."

The waiter poises his pencil above a pad, his eyebrows arched. "The fish," I say, and he nods and writes down my selection.

In an attempt to steady my nerves, I study the patterns of the stained glass. Conversation and laughter whirl around me. Arno and Frederick comment on the excellent sound in the Salle Pleyel and praise the woodwind section in particular for bringing across the haunting atmosphere of the wild Turkish hills. They also compliment Dad for his composition skills and me for playing the piano so well. They don't mention my slew of very minor mistakes, but then, it's possible only Dad and I know the piece well enough to tell. In any case, their attempt to include me in the conversation works. By the time the escargot arrives, with the tiny special fork-like utensils, I'm cheerful and chatty enough that Dad stops throwing me worried glances.

After dinner and a succulent fillet of fish that is a billion times better than ramen noodles from a package, all four of us take the subway back to our hotel in Montparnasse. Dad presses the ornate room key into my hand at the front of the hotel and heads off with Arno and Frederick for a special after-hours tour of the Montparnasse cemetery.

In our room I sit on my twin bed and text Neil that my dad's out, so he can call me. He's six hours behind us, which means it's midafternoon there and he should be finished with his shift soon.

It's pure agony being apart, and from this distance our problems don't seem that big. When I try to imagine a future without Neil, I can't do it. So if I can't live without him, am I willing to make the ultimate commitment? Am I willing to get married?

Eighteen is far too young to get married, but it's legal, so obviously it can't be too wrong an idea. And if we get married, Neil would be okay with us living together. We could finally be totally uninhibited with each other. The thought makes me hot all over.

To distract myself while I wait for his call, I rummage nervously through the drawers of the desk and find brochures for the Tour Montparnasse, one of Europe's tallest skyscrapers, and Les Catacombes. I've been to the fifty-sixth-floor observation deck of the tower before, but I've not dared to go to the catacombs. I was never a fan of morbid curiosities before my brush with death, and I like them even less now.

Soon I've exhausted all the reading material the hotel room has to offer. A glint of silver on my dad's bed catches my eye. He forgot his camera. Dad's the type who only takes pictures of buildings with people in front of them—otherwise he could just buy a postcard, he always says. So our family albums are full of shots of me or my mother or both of us, looking exasperated in front of castles and other landmarks. But as I go through his memory card, I'm horrified to find that not one photo is of me. A stranger scrolling through it wouldn't even know he had a daughter. Do the newest family albums tell the same story? Can I so easily be erased from my parents' lives?

Finally the phone rings.

"Hello?"

"It's so good to hear your voice," Neil says from across the ocean. "Sorry I couldn't call you yesterday. I had to stay late at work."

"Oh, that's okay," I say, even though it wasn't okay.

"I miss you, Felicia."

My heart does a little flip-flop, like it always does when he says my name. "I miss you, too. Only a few more days."

"I don't want you to ever go away for so long again." Neil's voice cracks. "I can't stand it."

I swallow back a sob and try for lightness. "Why don't you come with me next time?"

He doesn't reply for a few seconds, and I kick myself for possibly alienating him so early in our conversation. Every day leading up to this trip I begged him to reconsider coming with me, but he was resolute in his argument that he couldn't afford it. I hold my breath and I hear him sigh. "Where's your dad right now?" he asks.

"Oh, he's visiting Serge Gainsbourg's grave. It's, like, this musical pilgrimage he does every time we come to Paris."

"Is that next to Jim Morrison's grave?"

I laugh. "No, totally different cemetery. Jim's in the Père Lachaise, and Serge is in the Montparnasse."

"They sound like expensive hotels."

"Everything sounds fancy when you say it in French."

"Don't you think it's creepy to visit strangers' graves?"

"Wait, are you saying my dad is creepy?"

"No . . ." Neil tries to backpedal. "I didn't mean . . ."

"Good, because he may well be your dad soon," I say at the same time he says, "But I wouldn't want to do it personally."

"Wait . . . what? Why would your dad be mine? Does he want to adopt me?" I detect a teasing note to his voice, so I know he's understood me.

"Think about it, Neil. I have." I press forward, breathlessly, speaking so fast that my words tumble over one another. I don't want him to interrupt me, or I might never say what I need to say. "It's the right choice for us. I can't imagine anyone ever being a better fit for me than you are. The car accident showed me that we could die at any time. We could die tomorrow. I don't want to miss out on anything. I don't want to miss out on knowing every part of you."

After my impassioned speech, the crackle of our long-distance connection is the only sound I hear. I've rendered Neil speechless twice now. He's silent so long that I start to worry.

"Neil? Are you still there? Do you think I'm totally crazy?"

"No," he says seriously. "I think you're impulsive and wonderful and passionate . . ."

His words make me giddy, and I stand and jump on the bed. The hotel phone cord protests and pulls the receiver out of my hands, causing me to miss the last part of his sentence.

I fly off the bed, grab the receiver, and smash it against my ear in my haste. ". . . when you get back," he says.

I bite my lip. "What was that? Sorry. I dropped the phone."

"I said, I think we shouldn't do this over the phone. We should talk when you get back."

His voice is neutral. I can't tell what he means by talking when we get back. Maybe he means he wants to do this right and propose on bended knee. He's such a gentleman, so I wouldn't put it past him. Or maybe he doesn't think we should get married and he thinks I'll take it better in person. I'm about to ask him when the door creaks open.

"Felicia?" my dad calls in like he doesn't want to disturb me while I'm getting dressed or something.

"Just a sec!" I shout. Crap. I don't want to do this with my dad hanging around. "Can we talk again later? My dad is here. I'll text you when I'm alone again."

"Sure." Neil's voice has a slight edge to it, like he's annoyed. "Love you." And the phone clicks before I can say it back.

"Love you, too," I whisper into the dead line. To my dad I shout, "Come in." I put on my most radiant smile for my dad. I don't want him to ask if something's wrong, because I don't want to think about something being wrong. If I do, I might have a nervous breakdown. I've put myself out there, and I've been left hanging. It scares me more than I could have ever imagined.

The memory cuts out, and I lie stunned on the floor. I can't believe I brought up marriage to Neil. Maybe that's what Neil is missing—a concrete commitment. But I won't know how he reacted to my proposal until I view another memory. I'm dying to find out what happened next.

twenty-four

I PEER UNDER THE SCARF to check for hidden memory globes. But of course there aren't any. I dematerialize the scarf to get rid of the evidence of the Morati's visit.

I reluctantly get up and retrieve my seraphim guard binder. I'll have to be a model student from here on out to justify Furukama's choice of me over Autumn. Why did he choose me, anyway? Autumn has way more experience and respect than I do, so he must think my potential outweighs all that. Sitting in my desk chair, I open the binder to the first page and start reading about meditation.

I practice a few of the exercises, trying to reach the Zen-like state that successful meditation promises. It's surprisingly similar to what I've already practiced—the deep, slow breathing and the one-point concentration that's supposed to drive everything else out of your mind. Despite my perfectly straight posture, I'm feeling incredibly relaxed. There's a sharp knock on the door.

Shaking myself wide-awake, I get up and answer it. It's Neil, his face flushed with excitement.

"Hey," he says. "I left early this morning, and I didn't want to wake you. How was your day?"

Judging from the happiness emanating from Neil, his day went better than mine did. The two memories I viewed are roiling beneath the surface of my skin, begging to be shared with Neil. I want him to know that despite what Nate said about us breaking up on Earth, we did talk about getting married. But I can't let him know that I couldn't help myself. That I gave in to my weakness and didn't report the memory globes like I should have. I can't tell him about Furukama kicking Autumn out of guard training, because that will only lead to questions that have answers Neil won't want to hear. "It was okay." I don't want to keep lying to him, so I figure the less detail, the better. "How was yours?"

"Great! Libby and I made some real breakthroughs today. She's training me in the healing arts, so I can enhance moods without her help. And tons of people came to our music session in the lobby downstairs." He pulls me up out of my chair and drags me across to sit on the edge of the bed with him. "I'm surprised you didn't stop by. You must have seen us."

"I saw you. But Furukama assigned so much homework." I point to the open binder on my desk.

"I'll let you get back to it. I'm meeting Libby to discuss how we can get healer recruits. More than only Keegan." He squeezes my leg in an affectionate way.

I wish that instead of spending so much time with Libby, he would spend time with me. This whole incident with Autumn proves more than ever that I need Neil to keep me good. Without him my moral center has atrophied and I betrayed my best friend again rather than face up to the consequences of my evil deeds. But what can I do? I'm committed to seraphim guard training now.

"So will you come pick me up tomorrow before class?" I ask. "We can walk together."

"I'd like that." Neil gives me a quick kiss on the lips and bounds out of my room. The air tastes stale when he goes, and I let myself fall backward onto the bed. I hate keeping things from him.

I lie on my bed for a few minutes, practicing my meditation breathing before I psych myself up for visiting Julian. Autumn isn't going to help me with memory extraction, so I need Julian to teach me to look into my classmates' memories so that I can identify which are Morati in disguise.

But when I exit my room, Nate is there. I groan and try to step around him, but he blocks my path.

"Hey, hold on now." He grins. "I thought you'd want to go out and celebrate the great job you did today." He lifts his hand like I should give him a high five, but the thought of touching him makes my skin crawl.

"There's no need to gloat."

"Now that you've successfully paid off your debt to me, I've come to offer you a new deal. Another memory for another favor." He looks so sure of himself, I want to smack the arrogance right off his face. Fortunately, with the Morati being so generous, I don't need to make any more deals with Nate.

"No, thanks," I say nonchalantly. "I've put all that behind me." I allow myself a small smile when his eyebrows shoot up in surprise. And this time when I push past him, he lets me go.

"C'mon, don't be mad," he calls after me. "I wouldn't have *really* pushed you down the hellhole. You just needed the right motivation." It's nice of him to admit that after the fact.

When I get to Julian's room, I go in. His condition hasn't improved since yesterday. He lies listlessly on the sofa, on his side, staring off into space. The corners of his mouth lift slightly upward when he notices me.

"How's your headache?" I stay close to the door.

"Much better, thanks to you." He pats the sofa next to him. "Have time to give me another massage? You could use the practice."

I force myself not to blush, stopping the physical reaction in its tracks. I can't let Julian rattle me. "I'm good. I practiced on Neil," I lie.

"So, what's new?" he asks. It seems he doesn't have the energy to pester me much. But that also means he might not be as helpful as I hoped.

"Nate coerced me into getting Furukama to dismiss Autumn because of the favor I owed him. He threatened to push me into the hellhole if I didn't. She's out of the program now. And she hates me." I retrieve the wooden chair from the corner to sit on.

"Wow," Julian says. "That's pretty major. What does Nate get out of that?"

"I don't know. They've never meshed well, so maybe it's a personal vendetta."

"Maybe. What else?"

"They've been watching you closely. They know you haven't left your room."

"Then they know you're consorting with an angel."

"We're friends, aren't we? Friends hang out." I lean on my right elbow and twirl a long strand of hair between the fingers of my left hand.

He raises one eyebrow. "Is Neil aware you're here?"

"Let's not talk about Neil." I shift in the chair, pressing my back against the wooden slats.

"No problem." The intensely serious way he stares at me unsettles me to the core. I have to change the subject, and quickly.

"Can you teach me memory extraction, so I can view what the other trainees are hiding and figure out who is Morati?"

"Angel memories are more difficult to process. If I don't mask their full force, I might overwhelm you. And I don't have the control to mask anything right now. It's too dangerous."

"Remember how I was plugged into the Morati's mainframe? Trillions of memories streamed through me then, and I survived." I lean forward. "I can handle it."

Julian tries to lift himself to a sitting position, wincing as he does. "Care to help me?"

I propel myself out of the chair, hug my arms around his chest, and push him up against the sofa cushions. When I find myself standing over him awkwardly, my lips a mere shadow away from his and my hair brushing his neck, I can't hold back the blush, and it breaks free across my cheeks.

Julian allows himself a small smile, and I realize that he could be pretending to be weaker than he really is. I hop to the side when he reaches out his hand.

"If you want to do this, you have to touch me. That's how it works."

"I know." I scoot the chair close enough to Julian that I can brace my knees against the sofa, and I hold out my palm. "I'm ready."

When our palms connect, I am caught up in a swirl of impressions inside Julian's mind. His memories fly by me at the speed of light, as if I'm careening through a vast universe of stars at warp speed. Each memory hits me like the tiny stab of a pin until I feel like my body will burst apart. This bombardment is similar in scope to what I experienced in the Morati's mainframe, but then I actually experienced the memories of millions of humans as they passed through me, whereas here I catch only snippets that make no sense. I break away and keel over into Julian's lap, my forehead smashing into his thigh. He was right. Trying to view angel memories is not easy.

Very lightly he runs his hand over my hair, making my scalp prickle with a pleasure I don't want to feel. "The more we do this, the easier it'll become," he says. "I can teach you memory extraction. To sort through memories, to judge if they're real or not and to search for specific moments."

I groan and use all my strength to force myself back into my chair. He lets his hand fall heavily onto his knee. I think back to the chapter headings I skimmed through in my seraphim guard training syllabus. "Won't I be learning that sort of thing with Furukama?"

"Furukama has no practice in dealing with angels, since they've never been on this level before. He'll be easily fooled by the Morati. But if you keep coming to me, you'll be able to see through their lies."

"Will I be able to see through yours?" I ask pointedly.

"I hope so!" He laughs, but stops abruptly and squeezes his arms into his sides, contorting his face in the process. "Agh. Hurts to laugh."

"I'd better go."

"Okay. But we have only a couple of months until Ascension Day. We'll have to meet often if we want to catch the Morati before then. One of them might get selected to the seraphim guard."

No one wants to catch the Morati more than I do. "Will the Morati strike again? Would the trainees in the dorms be safer if they crossed the bridges into Areas One and Three?" As the resident expert in Morati psychology, Julian is the best person to consult.

"Furukama asked me that too. I told him if they attack, they'll attack where they can do the most damage. Moving people won't help."

"That's what I thought." It's for the best that Libby and Neil put on their mood enhancement concerts. At least people won't be in a constant state of panic.

"I'll visit again as soon as I can." I stand up and prepare to leave. Now that I have a valid reason to visit Julian, it's probably time to tell Neil. My hand flies guiltily to the skep charm.

As I walk toward the door, an electric current radiates from my heart to my extremities. There's the tinny sound of a metal sign squeaking in the wind, followed by a dull boom. It's happening again. I rush to Julian's window.

"What do you see?" he asks, urgency in his voice.

Since we're on the twelfth floor of the dorms, I have a full view of the east campus. Clouds of dust and debris are rising in the distance, where the eastern bridge crosses into Area Three. "I think . . . I think they blew up the eastern bridge." I squeeze the skep charm tightly between my fingers, praying that Neil was nowhere near there.

I'm knocked to the floor as the dorm rattles and shakes around me. Another blast, much closer this time.

When the building settles, Julian groans. "What do you bet that was Western Bridge? They've cut us off from Areas One and Three."

"Two bombs," I say softly as if in a trance. "And two memory globes."

"What?" Julian pops his head around the side of the sofa to look at me. "What did you say?"

I lean heavily against the wall under the window. There's no doubt of my guilt now. "It's my fault. All this destruction is my fault."

twenty-five

"YOU FAILED TO MENTION that the Morati delivered more memories." The muffled quality of the end of Julian's sentence makes me think he has face-planted onto the sofa out of exhaustion.

"They were there when I got back from class today." I didn't want to believe that my actions were directly related to the bombings, but now I cannot ignore the timing. The Morati have made clear the price of retrieving my lost memories.

Members of the security force are posted at the bridges to make sure only Careers pass back and forth. Did the security force get hit? Am I a killer? Are the deaths of the muse students at the library my fault? What about the healers?

Should I be held responsible for them? And Neil. That first memory I viewed . . . and then Neil almost died. Megan did die. What have I done?

I think back to Nate's accusation that I'm self-absorbed. I've been so single-minded about retrieving my memories that I haven't given enough thought to how my obsession is affecting others. How did I let things get so bad?

Picking myself off the floor, I vow to make this right. To track down the Morati killers not for my own gain but for the good of all of Level Three. Furukama trusts my abilities, and with Julian helping me train, we will find out which of the seraphim guard candidates are Morati in disguise—before it's too late. Maybe I don't have to rely on Neil's influence to be good. Maybe, in spite of my many flaws, I can develop the instinct to help people on my own.

No matter how much they tempt me, I can't view any more memories. Not from the Morati, and not from Nate.

I pass Julian on my way out. He did indeed collapse face-first into the sofa. I pat his shoulder. "See you soon."

The chaos in the hallway makes me want to turn and hide in a dark corner of Julian's room. By the time I reach the stairs, the stairwell is thick with shouting, jostling people desperate to leave the dorm. I'm pulled into the grinding gears of their elbows and knees, and am left hanging on for dear life and gasping for air as I work my way to the exit.

It would be so much worse if they knew it was me who betrayed them. It's not difficult to picture the mob. They would lash out at me, ripping at my clothes and skin and hair with their sharp fingernails and teeth, finally able to give direction to their fear and anger. I'd be torn into a million pieces, scattered into oblivion.

I stare at the cracks in the walls as I'm forced along, trying to read the future of the dorm. The cracks aren't long or deep enough to mean collapse. We emerge into the lobby, and the double doors spit us out onto Western Avenue.

The security force is out in droves, herding us toward Assembly Hill. The mere presence of people who seem to be in charge brings down the level of panic. We settle into an orderly march. A hand grabs my wrist, and I turn to face Moby.

"Did you hear?" Moby releases me and lets out a low whistle. "The bridges were destroyed."

"Was anyone hurt?" I dread the answer.

"There's no official statement yet." He rubs his eyebrow, and we're so close, I can't help but notice the fangs of his snake tattoo peeking out from under the edge of his long sleeve. "But Neil and Libby are putting on a healing concert at Assembly Hill," Moby says.

They organized that incredibly quickly. Is there a way we can help? "We should join them onstage. Me on piano, you on bass?" We don't have any experience at all in healing, but if they can use us somehow to calm everyone down, it's the least I can do.

"I'm down with that."

"Cool." Having a plan of action distracts me from my self-loathing. And for some reason, whenever Moby's around, things seem less dire. I like that about him. "Neil and I were working on a couple of duets for our muse audition. We could do those."

Moby suggests a few rock songs, even humming me the melody to one of his band's hits. When I ask him what year it's from, I'm bummed to learn that it was released after my car accident. Yet another reminder of what the Morati stole from me. I don't even know what year I died or if I would have been around to hear him play or not.

We hear Neil's voice before we see him. It's more beautiful than ever. The ballad he sings hypnotizes and calms the crowd. He has such an ability to connect with others through music. If I went onto the stage with him, would it allow us to reconnect?

Moby nudges me forward. "Let's do this." Because the crowd has relaxed, people are no longer packed so tightly and we're able to approach the crest of the hill with relative ease. Keegan is in the front row, staring up at Neil like Neil is some sort of rock star. Libby is onstage, next to Neil, clapping along. I catch her eye and wiggle my fingers like I'm playing piano, then point at myself and then at the stage. She waves me up.

"Can you sing?" Moby says into my ear as we climb the steps to join Neil, who hasn't noticed us yet because his eyes are closed and he's lost in the moment. When I shake my head, Moby says, "I'll back him up, then."

Moby and I materialize our instruments and position ourselves on either side of Neil. I set the piano at an angle, so that I can see Neil but still register the audience with my peripheral vision. Libby approaches and places her hand firmly on the base of my neck. She presses into the knot of my spine, and an electric current of energy flows into my shoulders, down my arms, and into my fingers. I don't know this song, but I place my hands on the keys and play chords, the music taking a powerful shape around me. Moby finds his way in easily. Neil's forehead creases slightly when he hears our instruments, his eyes fluttering open and taking us both in. But he doesn't miss a single beat.

When Neil hits the final notes and falls silent, he looks at me full on and smiles. I mouth the name of a song we practiced, a midtempo radio hit that Moby said he knew too. Neil nods, and I poise my fingers above the keys. Neil plays the opening chords and Moby catches on immediately, thumbing his strings hard to lay down the backing rhythm. When I start playing, Libby's hand still on me, the notes soar all around, intoxicating, and I soon get caught up in our group dynamic. Moby harmonizes with Neil on the choruses, and his deeper, scratchier voice lends the song an unexpected gravitas.

We all play the last notes together, and the crowd erupts in applause. It's hard to believe these exuberant fans are part of the frightened huddle that accompanied me to the hill not that long ago. Music is truly a healing art.

Letting Neil take the lead, Moby and I join him for a couple more upbeat songs. Then we exit the stage with Libby and watch as Neil sings a closing ballad to send the audience on their way. When our fellow students stream back to the dorms, they huddle in small groups, arms around one another and still singing. Keegan goes with them, hugging his baseball cap to his chest, his face lit up with joy for the first time since Kiara's death.

I'm giddy. There's no greater high than this.

Libby bows before Moby and me. "I'm impressed. You two must consider dropping seraphim guard and joining up with the healers."

She snaps her fingers, and my mind becomes razor-sharp again, the blade sinking in that there wouldn't have been a concert without the horrors that came before.

"Were they bad? The bombings?" I ask.

Libby nods. "I told you before that only celestial beings have the power to fix or destroy certain eternal architecture like the records room. The bridges are like that. We can't repair them without the help of an angel."

"Julian could have fixed them. Before." I mean before he was thrown in the brimstone jail, and she knows it.

"He also might have destroyed them, right?" Moby offers cautiously.

"Except he didn't." I keep my voice low. I don't necessarily want it to carry up to where Neil is still onstage, putting his guitar back into its case.

"No. Not this time." Libby says it diplomatically, but I can tell she hasn't ruled out Julian having some sort of part in the whole mess. "And since Julian is . . . indisposed, and we don't have any other willing angels on hand, we won't be able to cross into Area One or Three for the time being, and the course instructors won't be able to come here. We'll have to rearrange or cancel classes." The heads of the careers, such as Nate and Miss Claypool, stay in the administration building, but the other instructors commute every day.

"But nobody died?" That last word sticks in my throat.

Libby regards me curiously, with slightly narrowed eyes. "No. No reported deaths."

At least I didn't murder anyone today.

Neil comes down the stairs to the stage, holding his guitar case in front of him with both hands. "Great show, guys!"

"Proud to jam with you, bro." Moby claps him on the shoulder. "You have mad skills."

"Thanks." Neil soaks in the compliment. He's still amped, the aftershocks of the concert evident in the way his body trembles.

"We plan to do a concert every evening, three hours before curfew," Libby says. "Both of you are more than welcome to join us whenever you like."

She excuses herself for a meeting with Furukama, and the three of us return to the dorms. Moby's building is farther down than ours, so we part ways with promises of getting together tomorrow to practice more songs.

When Neil and I reach the entrance, he stops and caresses my cheek. "It meant a lot to me. What you did tonight. Thanks."

Little does he know much I did. And I can't tell him either. Not if I want him to keep looking at me the way he is now.

He opens the door for me and then holds my hand as we take the stairs. As we step into our hallway, he comes to an abrupt stop.

"Umm . . . I was thinking," he starts, but then doesn't say anything more.

"Yes?" I prompt.

He puts down his guitar and then pulls at his collar with his free hand. "Do you want to stay with me tonight?"

twenty-six

NEIL'S INVITATION LEAVES me speechless. I have kept him in the dark about so many things. He wouldn't be saying this to me if he knew I was the cause of the bombings and Kiara's death. I have trouble looking him in the eye.

When I don't answer, Neil bites his lip. "Of course, I understand if you have too much homework."

"No . . . I mean . . . I'm surprised, that's all. Are you sure?"

"When I saw you onstage tonight, it made me realize how hard you're trying to see things from my point of view. I don't want you to think that I'm not trying to see things from yours." He looks so sincere, it breaks my heart a little.

"Thank you." I can't trust myself to say more, or the

whole chain of events leading up to this moment might spill out.

"So is that a yes?" Neil asks with a tentative smile.

I nod, my mind going numb. My throat constricts as he leads me by the hand into his room. Neil and I both kick off our shoes, facing each other. I lie down on top of his covers at the very edge of his bed.

Neil gets in beside me and presses himself against my back, nuzzling my neck. When he snakes his arm around me, hitching up my shirt and running his fingertips lightly right below my breastbone, every muscle in my body freezes even as every nerve ignites.

I curl my toes in as he explores my curves under my clothes, touching me in places he has never dared to before. When I can't stand the intensity of it any longer, I buck against his fingers. I turn into his waiting arms and find his mouth, kiss him with the pent-up need of hundreds of nights of waiting, thrust my fingers up the back of his neck and thread them through his hair.

He shifts his weight, and all at once he's kneeling between my legs, and my hands are on his hips. His trusting eyes meet mine, and guilt crushes my chest.

I push him backward, rolling off the bed and into a crouch. I look up. His mouth forms a perfect *O* of surprise. "Are you okay?" he asks.

"I can't do this." But when his face registers hurt, I cover my real feelings with a lie. "It just hit me. I forgot about this super-important assignment for Furukama. If I don't do it, he'll kick me out. I might have to pull an all-nighter even."

Neil forces a smile as he sits up. "If he kicks you out, there's always a place for you with the healers."

I stand and back away a few steps, reaching for my shoes and pulling them on quickly. I can't keep my hands from fidgeting, and my feet are itching to run. "Thanks. But I have to see this through. If I can somehow stop the Morati plot, I have to try."

"It seems we both have our jobs, then."

He makes a move to get up, but I break for the door. "Okay, I better get started. See you tomorrow."

Before he can answer, I'm out of there. I fly down the hall, down the stairs, through the lobby, out the doors, and onto Western Avenue. It's the semidark of twilight now, so curfew is in effect. But I don't care. I run as fast as I can down the road, until I'm past all the university buildings, all except the seemingly endless row of dorms. Most of these sit empty, waiting for more trainees to ascend from Level Two.

I pass Assembly Hill and I'm into the sports fields. I dash across a football field, then a soccer field, and finally a baseball diamond. I collapse onto home plate, exhausted from trying not to think about the scene with Neil.

A rustling sound comes from the dugout, then a girlish giggle. Two people sit entwined, and when the girl turns slightly, I recognize Autumn. How strange that she's all the way out here with some guy.

Then the guy turns his face. It's Cash, which I don't get. They're together a lot, it's true, since they're both on the security force. And Cash does seem to really admire Autumn. But I never detected any sparks between them. In any case, I'm glad she is happy.

Autumn and Cash are so much in their own world, and I don't want to startle them, so I start to tiptoe away as quietly as I can.

"Felicia. It's always Felicia," Autumn says, and I freeze, thinking she's spotted me. "Everyone chooses her over me. Even Furukama."

Cash mumbles something. I sneak closer to the dugout, but at an angle, to keep out of their line of sight.

"I wish, just once, someone would see me," Autumn says with the petulant tone that defines my memories of her. "And not her."

"Someone besides me?" Cash asks. He sounds vaguely annoyed. But then he laughs. "Isn't my love enough for you?" From my vantage point next to the bleachers, I see him knock his shoulder into hers.

"She showed me a memory of us when we were kids. I wrote a play and we performed it for the neighbors. And guess what?" She pauses.

Silence. "What?" Cash finally asks.

"Every single one of them fawned over Felicia and ignored me. Even my own parents. Maybe it was my fault, because I idolized her too. I wanted her to have the starring role." I choke up thinking about how lucky I was to have her as a friend, and how I blew it not once, not twice, but apparently many times over.

But then her voice hardens. "Felicia soaked it all up, like it was her right. She has always been like that." Did people really ignore her? How could I have not noticed that?

Cash whispers something into her ear, and she giggles again, shoving him playfully. They start to wrestle, which turns into kissing, and I leave while they're occupied.

The running helped me calm down a little bit, but I still don't want to go back to my room.

I walk somewhat aimlessly back in the direction I came, and I find myself turning right between two of the dorm buildings, onto the main thoroughfare to the bridge that leads to Area One. Or rather, the former bridge.

Picking my way through shards of ancient stone, I approach the bridge slowly. The bridge bottomed out in the middle, but the stone edges that protrude from both sides of the chasm are remarkably smooth, with a gentle concave slope marred by the circular grooves made by the pulse bomb. I get as close as I dare, peering down into the canyon the bridge once spanned.

I place my hand lightly on one of the stones of what's left of the bridge, my fingers tracing the deep cracks etched into its surface. I wish I could somehow fix it. The gray color shimmers silver for a moment, and the stone appears less damaged somehow. But that's impossible. Stress is making me see things that aren't there.

Hugging my arms to my chest, I proceed south along the gorge until I find a bench facing out. The outline of buildings in Area One is so much like Earth that homesickness creeps up on me. I lie down on the bench and rest my chin on my folded hands.

I try to practice the meditation drills Furukama assigned for tomorrow, but it's no use. I'm too distracted—by the twin memory globes that revealed I asked Neil to marry me. By the twin bridge explosions that revealed my guilt. And by having to run away from Neil because I'm keeping too many secrets from him.

I stew for what seems like hours, until the sunrise begins to paint the sky gold over the gorge. I go back to my room to pick up my binder before class.

The morning bells ring as I open the door to my room. Neil will check on me soon, I'm sure. I rush across the room to grab my binder, and my shoes crunch on broken glass. The framed photo Neil gave me of him in his Scout uniform lies facedown on the floor. It must have fallen during the bridge bombing, but I don't have time to clean up the mess now. I turn to leave, glancing at the Morati's small table as I do. Another memory globe hangs suspended on a wire hanger with a circular base, like a shiny Christmas ornament for sale in a store.

twenty-seven

I FREEZE IN TERROR. I cannot touch this globe, or who knows what else the Morati will destroy. But if Neil sees it, he'll make us go straight to Libby with it, and I'll never know if Neil said yes to my marriage proposal. Obviously I can't view the memory now, but if I wait it out, keep patient until the Morati are caught, then I can view it without consequences.

A knock on the door springs me into action. I leap across the room, drop the binder, and pick up the hanger by its base, careful not to let the memory globe swing into contact with my skin. "One second," I call loudly as I sink to the floor to shove the whole thing under my bed. I materialize a silvery bed skirt to hide the globe from prying eyes.

Neil opens the door and peeks in as I'm bending down to retrieve the binder from the floor in front of the small table. "You ready?" he asks.

Keegan is beside him, something that is becoming increasingly common these days. "Good morning, Miss Felicia," he says in a way that makes me feel ancient. I'm only five years older than him, not fifty.

"As ready as I'll ever be." Binder in hand, I join them in the hallway, and we start walking.

"So did you finish your big project?" Neil asks. Keegan hums and thumps a notebook against his leg.

"Oh, man, it took me forever." Lies beget even more lies. He won't bring up last night with Keegan around. Instead we chat about Libby's plan to test more healer recruits.

We part ways like nothing awkward happened last night, with a quick kiss and a wave. I'm impressed with Neil's poker face in regards to my abrupt departure. He has the enviable ability to go on as though everything's fine, even when it most certainly isn't. I guess that does make him a great candidate for the healing profession.

When I get to the gym, Cash is standing at the door, keeping it open. His black combat boot rests atop the poor rubber duck. "I'm glad you decided to continue with the class after all. You can leave your binder on the table here and pick it up later. We don't need it today."

No mention of Autumn's expulsion or my part in it? I examine him for any signs of his late-night rendezvous with her, but he's no more or less cheerful than usual. "Have a good study session last night?" I ask, a hint of suggestion in my tone.

He looks at me, slightly puzzled. "Furukama-Sensei assigns a lot of work, doesn't he? But he's only hard on us because he wants to toughen us up."

Cash's poker face is as good as Neil's today.

Inside the gym, people talk about Autumn's absence. There are various rumors going around as to why she is missing. Some say it's because she had a fight with Furukama. Some say it's because she answered a call to become a healer. When my classmates see me, however, they look at me suspiciously. "I thought you wanted to quit," Wolf grunts. I shrug and walk over to join Brady. We sit down together next to Cash and Moby.

Furukama is seated at the front with his legs crossed, his arms outstretched and resting on his knees, and his eyes closed. He silences the chatter with a deep, vibrato hum. "Seraphim reign supreme," he says. We run though some meditation drills. Then he stands and asks us to pair up.

Once we do, Furukama begins to lecture us on what he calls mind blocking and mind stunning, two of the most important skills a seraphim guard can possess. Mind blocking involves protecting your own mind from foreign invasion. It is essential in battle because opponents may try to plant thoughts or try to compel you to do things you normally wouldn't. It's how he suspects the Morati were able to convince the healers and William the librarian that they were dying. Mind blocking would also keep others from extracting memories, the latter a skill the Morati already possess.

Mind stunning allows you to incapacitate someone, since the mind controls the functions of the body. It is a more difficult skill to master.

"Class begins with meditation," Furukama says. "Then we spar." He scans the room, nodding slightly when he sees me. "Wolf. Come help me demonstrate."

Wolf looks all too pleased to be Furukama's first choice now that Autumn is gone. He bounds to the front of the gym and stands next to Furukama, pulling at the hem of his black jacket to straighten it.

"First mind blocking and its opposite, mind mining." Furukama squares his body so that he is facing Wolf, and offers up his palm. "While Wolf attempts to mine my mind and extract a memory, I create a force field in my mind to protect my memories."

As we watch, Wolf connects his palm to Furukama's and they circle each other, almost like they're dancing. "Tell me what you see," Furukama demands of Wolf.

"A great wall." Wolf wheezes with effort. "Like the one in China. Trying to climb it, but it's too slippery. Can't get a foothold."

How can Wolf speak so coherently while his palm is connected? I am always immediately sucked in, and have no outside awareness of what goes on around me. Wolf's ability must come from practice.

"Good," Furukama says. "Now you try to keep me out."

Wolf closes his eyes, and his forehead furrows in concentration. "Okay. Ready."

Furukama purses his lips almost imperceptibly. "A heavy steel wall." He doesn't say anything for about thirty seconds, and then, "A small breach in your fortress. I rip it open. I am inside. In your memory you sing in the shower."

Everyone laughs. Wolf pulls his palm away and ducks his head in shame. He starts to walk back toward his partner, but Furukama stops him. "Now we demonstrate mind stunning."

Wolf reluctantly returns to his former position facing Furukama. He's no longer excited about being Furukama's demonstration partner.

Furukama reaches out his arm so that his palm is only inches from Wolf's forehead. "I strike." As we watch, Furukama slams his palm toward Wolf but stops just short of touching him. Nevertheless, Wolf reacts by falling to his knees and then collapsing into a heap at Furukama's feet. "Wolf cannot move. I focused my energy on Wolf's frontal lobe. That was a soft blow, and Wolf will be fine after a minute."

The silence in the gym is complete. Then Wolf gasps and sits up. He reaches for his ridiculous samurai topknot, as if to check that it's still there, and then skulks back to his seat.

"Now you practice with your partners," Furukama says. "To start, if you are the attacker, your objective is to find an embarrassing memory. If you are the defender, your objective is to protect your memories. The practical applications of psychological warfare are many. If you are privy to secret fears, you have ammunition to use in battle."

Brady and I face off. He stands with his thumbs hooked into his belt loops. "Want to go first? Think you can do better than the poser?" he asks.

"Who couldn't?" I say with false bravado.

"Furukama makes it seem easy, but then, he's been at it for five hundred years. Go on. Give it your best."

I steady myself. The gorge dividing us from Area One seemed pretty insurmountable. I can use that as a moat around my memories so that Brady will have to scale the sheer cliffs to get to them. Once I form the image, I lift my palm to indicate that Brady can start.

When he connects, I don't rush to access his memories like I would in a normal memory transfer situation. Instead I concentrate on keeping him out while trying to stay moderately aware of my physical body—like a split consciousness. With one half of my mind I picture my moat, and with the other half I draw the outline of my body in the physical space of the gym.

On the inside, I build the cliffs higher and higher to counter Brady's attack. On the outside, I can see Moby and Cash, the student pair closest to us, in a fuzzy blur.

I put up a decent fight, but Brady breaks through at about a minute and a half and forces us into a partial memory of me waking up on a transatlantic flight, rubbing my eyes and wiping drool from the corners of my mouth.

I pull my palm away. "Uh . . . no one else needs to see that."

Brady punches me lightly in the arm. "Hey, I went awfully easy on you. I reckon you've got more embarrassing moments than that."

It was gentlemanly of him to not peek in on me while I was in the shower. "So you did a specific search?"

"That's right," Brady confirms. "It's easier to get past somebody's block if you mine for something specific. In your case I searched for a memory of you buckled into a plane seat. First you lock on to that image, and then you force your way in. Now you try."

I take a moment to come up with a specific image. It has to be something common enough that he would have done it, but unusual enough that I can easily pinpoint it in his memories. For some reason I choose tetherball. Brady and I touch palms again, and I conduct a search attack, picturing a schoolyard, a pole, and the plump white ball hanging from it by a rope.

But I don't get far. Brady's mind is boarded up with an endless amount of DO NOT ENTER signs. I poke and prod at it, looking for weaknesses, but before long Brady pushes me out completely and I'm staring at his face even though our palms are still connected.

"What did you look for?" He grins and then lets his hand fall.

"You playing tetherball."

"There's your mistake. I was homeschooled out in the sticks. Never got the chance to play it."

"I'll get you next time," I tease.

"Sure, sure," he jokes back. "Your nose twitches when you concentrate real hard. Like a bunny. It's awfully cute."

"Well, you have a vein that throbs in your forehead," I shoot back.

"Let's try it again, Twitchy." He nods encouragingly, and we go through the drill again. By the time we switch partners, he's seen me drinking orange juice straight from the container, using my finger to brush my teeth, and ripping a page out of a library book. I've seen Brady scrubbing potatoes and playing hopscotch with his sister—hardly as embarrassing as the memories he's found of me.

Brady rubs my shoulder. "You have to get the hang of finding the good stuff. But it's quite a feat that you saw anything at all today. It's awfully rare for the first class."

"You think so?" I need to excel to meet Furukama's expectations, and to stay on track to eventually expose the Morati.

Furukama assigns us new partners. A willowy girl introduces herself as Emilia. Her white-blond hair is plaited in a single thick braid that reaches her midback, and her loose silk pants and camisole look more like pajamas than workout gear. Her relaxed posture and sleepy eyes peg her as an easy target. As soon as we begin to spar, she is alert, and she doesn't allow me in a single time. She seems content, though, to view drab memories of mine—moments when

I'm washing dishes or standing in line at the supermarket.

At the end of class we line up to leave. Furukama didn't even check on me once. Maybe he's already regretting choosing me over Autumn. Then again, if Autumn was going to find the Morati, you would think she would have done it already. Furukama, too, for that matter. They've both practiced memory extraction a ton, after all.

Of course Julian was probably right when he claimed that they didn't have the advantage of practicing with an actual angel. My sessions with Julian should give me a steep learning curve.

With that in mind I head back to the dorms to seek out Julian. I knock twice to announce my arrival, and then enter his room. But it's empty. Julian is gone.

twenty-eight

I CLOSE MY EYES and concentrate on homing in on Julian's signal. I reach out across the campus and find him in the administration building. My guess is that either Libby or Furukama has brought him in.

Before I go to Julian, I pass by my room to drop off my binder.

Outside Neil's room there is a cluster of students, mainly girls. One of them, a short olive-skinned girl wearing a light green headscarf, approaches me nervously. "Aren't you the girl from Neil's band? The piano player?"

Flustered by this unexpected attention, I can only gape at her. "Uh . . . yeah. That's me."

"Oh! Neil's so dreamy!" she squeals, and the others in her group join in the fangirling.

"That he is." I open the door to my room.

"Omigod! You live across the hall from him?" One of them shrieks as I tuck myself inside. "You're soooo lucky!"

I shut the door firmly behind me, muting the excited chattering of the girls in the hall.

I chuck my binder onto my desk and take a quick peek under the bed to check on the memory globe. It glows even brighter, calling to me to touch it. I turn away quickly; the less I look at it, the better.

As I exit my room, the cluster of girls observes me with bright eyes and huge expectant grins. I raise my hand in a half wave, and they start squealing again. How loud will they scream when Neil finally appears? At least they have the decency to not enter his room and roll around on his bed. But then, everyone respects the unspoken but inviolate rule of room privacy here, with the exception of the Morati, obviously.

I follow Julian's signal and arrive at the administration building. I admire the bell tower before climbing up the wide stone steps to the entrance. The small wooden door stands in contrast to the ivory grandeur of the rest of the building. It's like they're showing off how great they are, but they don't want you to come in.

Inside, the impression is similarly grand. The entryway could be a replica of the main hall of Grand Central

Terminal in New York City, complete with an information desk in the center, manned by a yellow-uniformed girl with the shiniest blue-black hair I've ever seen.

According to my scan Julian is in a room on the right-hand side of the great hall. All the heads of careers have their offices and quarters here, including Nate. I approach the information desk. The girl flips through a glossy fashion magazine. It must be frustrating, knowing that she can never wear anything featured on its pages unless she touched the actual fabric on Earth. Not that most of the featured fashion is anything real people actually bought.

"Excuse me. Which way to Furukama's office?"

The girl looks up from her reading. "Down that hallway," she says in an Indian lilt, pointing to the left.

"Thanks." So it must be Libby who has Julian in her office. "Is Nate around? Or did he get stuck in Area Three?"

"Nate is here." The girl frowns and slides her magazine into a drawer. "Please do not tell him I was reading."

"Trust me, I won't."

I turn to the right, expecting the information desk girl to correct my mistake. But she doesn't say a word.

I continue to follow the signal of Julian's brain waves. He's very close. In fact, he must be a few rooms down from where the door stands open to reveal Libby inside, sitting at a desk, writing something on a pad of paper. She's leaning forward toward Neil, who sits across from her, his back facing me. Their heads are close together, engrossed in discussion. Keegan is slumped on a small sofa, his head resting on his shoulder, and the brim of his cap pulled all the way to his chin.

Before I can sneak past, Libby looks up. "Felicia!" she calls cheerfully. "Are you here to join the healers?" Neil turns at the sound of my name. He gives me a restrained smile, no dimples in sight, and my heart sinks. He's not going to call me out in public about fleeing his room last night, but I can tell he's bothered by it. He'll like me even less when he finds out why I'm here.

I take a deep breath. "Uh, not exactly. I'm here to visit Julian."

As I expected, Neil frowns.

"Julian is in my custody now," Libby says. "We need to better monitor who has access to him. That's why I'm keeping him here."

I don't want to do this in front of Neil, but since he's attached to Libby at the hip now, it can't be helped. "I'll need access to him every day. As part of my training for seraphim guard."

"I assume this is Furukama-Sensei's suggestion."

There's not another chair in Libby's office, so I sit on the sofa with Keegan. He straightens up, lifts his cap, and gives me a terse nod of his head.

"No, it's Julian's."

"You've been to visit him?" Neil's posture goes rigid. His eyebrows press so close together, they almost touch.

"I had to visit him, to make sure he was okay," I say. Neil nods, and his eyebrows relax slightly. He may not be thrilled about my visit, but he understands compassion. "Julian thinks if I do extra training with an angel, it will be easier for me to find the Morati posing as humans."

Libby considers this. "Perhaps someone further along in the program than you would be more ideal for such training."

"The thing is, I don't think Julian is so keen to cooperate with anyone but me," I say.

Libby looks at Neil, and he shrugs. She twists her hair and puts it up with her pencil, biting her lip. "Let's discuss with Furukama-Sensei if we can find candidates to train with Julian in addition to you."

"That's really up to Julian, isn't it?" Anyone who could take on the Morati would be in the seraphim guard class, and that's precisely where Julian thinks the Morati are hiding out in disguise. Not to mention if anyone else finds the Morati first, I won't be able to get my memories out of them. I need to be the one who uncovers and confronts them.

Libby narrows her eyes. She doesn't like being challenged. "If he won't comply, perhaps a little more brimstone exposure will convince him," she says hotly.

"Great idea. Throw away our one advantage again—"

"Let Felicia do it," Neil interrupts. "Look what she achieved in Level Two. She won't let us down." Is he defending me because he's on my side? I want to think so. Maybe he hasn't forgiven me for last night, or for so many other things, but I'm relieved that he still has faith in me.

"Fine." Libby straightens her red scarf. "We'll all go visit him together."

Keegan gets up to join us, but Libby waves him away. "Not you, Keegan."

"Aw, man! I miss all the good stuff." Keegan juts out his lower lip.

Neil bops him on the head affectionately. "We'll be back in a minute."

Libby, Neil, and I walk down the hallway past three more offices until we reach one with a burly member of the security force standing at attention outside the door.

Julian's new room is not much different from his old one—smaller maybe, but as bare. The trusty eggplant-colored sofa is still the central attraction, and he has added a small folding table, like the one Grammy always had me pull out for her so she could eat her evening snack of tinned peaches while watching the evening news.

When we enter, he looks up from his game of solitaire. "Oh, good." Julian gathers up the cards and shuffles them. "Now we have enough players for a game of hearts."

If his behavior is any indication, he's made quite the recovery since yesterday.

"I'm glad you're feeling better," Neil tells him, not at all unkindly. "And that you're willing to help Felicia catch the Morati."

Neil and Julian size each other up, and I realize that they've not had much contact. In fact, this is probably only their third meeting after Julian's retrieval of Neil in Level

Two and Neil being present for Julian's arrest.

"It's my pleasure. I do enjoy spending time with her." Julian lifts up his palm like he's offering it to me already for training. "Touching her."

"As long as it's only her palm you're touching." Neil steps forward to lace his fingers through mine, clearly drawing a line but remaining outwardly calm. In that moment I know that Neil is worth at least ten of Julian. And that he believes I'm worth a second chance.

There's a period of silence as we all let this awkward conversation sink in, and then Libby clears her throat and begins to lay the ground rules for our visits. We won't be continuously supervised, but the person guarding Julian has permission to come in at any time, so we won't have complete privacy either. That's more than fine with me.

"You can start now if you want," Libby says as she leaves.

Both Neil and Julian wait for my decision. I don't want to let go of Neil's hand, not after the way I ran from him last night. "Tomorrow," I tell Julian. "I'll be back tomorrow."

Libby dismisses Neil from their meeting, explaining that she wants to talk to Keegan alone. She's doing it as a favor to us, and I'm grateful.

Neil and I walk back to the dorms together. He suggests we take the time to practice a few more songs today, and I tell him about his new fan base. But we don't discuss Julian or the fact that I'm going to be spending a lot of time with him over the coming weeks.

Despite my forewarning, when we reach our hallway,

Neil shakes his head. A group of maybe thirty fans stands around his door, chatting excitedly. As we approach, they swarm us and call out names of songs they want to hear tonight. Neil materializes a Sharpie and writes their requests down on his hand and forearm until there is no skin left to write on. When their frenzy dies down a bit, he turns and whispers into my ear, "I don't think it would make a good impression if we practiced in either of our rooms. Let's go somewhere else."

I'm not surprised. He might have recently invited me into his room, but it was when no one was around to see it. He wants to be a good role model for his fans.

I suggest the lovely spot near the gorge where I spent last night, and Neil agrees. At the gorge we try out some of the song requests, testing out how much of them we remember. We decide that seven of the forty-odd requests are doable, but we'll have to ask Moby about some of the others since either we're not very familiar with them or we haven't heard of them at all.

Soon it's time for us to head to Assembly Hill to meet up with Moby for a brief sound check before the next concert.

"Before we go, I want to tell you something," Neil says.

My breath catches in my throat. This sounds serious.

He takes both of my hands in his and looks me in the eye. "I meant what I said today in there with Libby. I believe that you'll fight to find the Morati with everything you have."

It's all I can do not to shrink away. We're both hiding so

much from each other, and it seems impossible right now to bridge this gap between us.

I want to be worthy of the trust he has in me, to go ahead right now and confess everything. The deal with Nate that led to my second betrayal of Autumn. Finding out that viewing my memories is the catalyst for the Morati's destruction. And that I have a memory globe right now under my bed. After all, it's the tried and true template for our relationship—that I bare my soul and he listens and forgives. But I want more. I want give-and-take. I want him to bare his soul to me. Until he does that, I can't confide in him.

"What's really going on with you?" I say in an attempt to get him to open up. "You can tell me anything."

His gaze falters, and he zones in on my left ear. "I'm fine. Keegan has been on my mind a lot. I've been working with him to convert his rage about Kiara's murder into something constructive. He's practicing the drums. It would be great for him to get to play with us one day."

I want to hear about Neil, not Keegan, but it's clear that's not likely to happen. If I press him, we'll end up fighting.

"Yeah, that sounds cool." I nod with fake enthusiasm, but my eyes prickle with tears.

He touches my cheek. "It's scary to go up against the Morati again, but we'll get through this."

"I hope you're right," I say.

twenty-nine

THE NEXT DAY during seraphim guard class, we work on mind stunning. While I'm doing drills with Emilia, Furukama taps me on the arm and asks me to stay after.

"Oooh, you're in trouble," Emilia says in a singsong voice before hitting me with a mind stun.

When I come to, Emilia is smirking down at me. I wasn't concentrating hard enough, and Emilia sensed her opportunity to knock me down.

I get up and face her again. She tosses her long braid over her shoulder and crouches down slightly, back into a fighting stance. We spar twice more, and both times I end up on the floor.

Next Furukama has us do physical drills such as

punching and kicking. He explains that such physical training can gain you the edge in hand-to-hand combat situations. The more you land blows, the more your opponent loses energy and mind control.

We switch partners. Brady is gentler with me, but by the time Furukama dismisses us, my whole body is sore. Today is not my day.

"See ya, Twitchy." Brady slaps me on the back. "Stay tough." He files out with the rest of my classmates, leaving me to face Furukama. Does my dismal performance today mean he'll kick me out?

Furukama retrieves his black binder from his table at the front of the gym. "My office is more private." He gestures for me to follow him.

We walk from the gym to the administration building. On our way everyone either lowers their eyes in respect or looks at Furukama in unadulterated awe. He's a legend around here.

When we enter the administration building, the girl at the information desk salutes us. Furukama leads me to the left wing, and we enter a narrow hallway. At the end of the hall he slides open a Japanese-style screen door painted with cherry blossoms, and we enter a room with tatami flooring. At the center there is a low table with two steaming cups of green tea. The walls are bare except for paintings of coiled green snakes near the baseboards—the only aspect that seems out of place with the traditional Japanese décor.

"Please. Sit." Furukama removes his sword and sets it gently between the two ceramic cups and then sits cross-legged in front of the table. "Drink."

I kneel and then take a sip. The tea is the bitter, frothy brew used in tea ceremonies. I try my best not to gag, but Furukama smiles wanly when he sees my mouth curled in disgust.

"How do you rate your skills at this moment?" Furukama asks. Here it comes. He wants me to justify why I should stay when Autumn had to go.

"I'll get better. I'm training with Julian starting today."

"Bold approach." Furukama doesn't go near his tea, but he rubs the gold plating on the hilt of his sword in continuous tiny circles. "I must choose the strongest candidates to move on to the guard. You have much potential."

Getting selected to the guard is not my goal. "Why don't you go? You're the best of all of us."

He sighs, and his shoulders droop, showing unexpected vulnerability. He looks at me in a kind of wonder, as if no has ever dared ask him about himself before. I've always thought of him as older because of his position of authority, but seeing him unguarded like this makes me realize how young he appears. He was probably younger than I was when he died back on Earth.

"The unknown," he says quietly. "I cannot abide it."

And then I understand. Furukama clings to all this artifice, his strong, silent samurai persona, because it's all he's dared to imagine for himself. He watches as countless students move on, but he stays. Underneath he's as scared as the rest of us.

"It's okay. I can't abide it either." Which is true, and the reason I want my memories of what happened between Neil and me so badly. If you know what the future holds, you can prepare for it.

He laughs, tilting his head back and letting out what must be centuries of bottled-up mirth. He stands up, still shaking, and begins dancing the twist. It's so un-samurai-like and jarring. Is he drunk?

Something is definitely off about Furukama.

As I watch him, I become surer of it. Isn't the twist from the 1960s? He could have picked it up from the former residents of Level Three, those from decades ago. They moved on, but maybe they left the twist behind.

But it isn't only his dancing that bothers me. It is his nationality. Are there more sections of Level Three somewhere? There have to be, because this one seems to be the American default. Yes, there is some diversity in races, spoken languages, and nationalities, but based on my admittedly small sampling, everyone here died on United States soil. Except, presumably Furukama, because why would a Japanese samurai from hundreds of years ago be in North America?

What if Furukama is a samurai poser?

He stops gyrating his hips and arms and sits with a thud. He wipes his brow. "I haven't danced in a long time."

"You're not from the thirteenth century, are you?"

As an answer Furukama offers me his palm. "Take a look for yourself. If you can," he challenges.

I lift my palm to his, and before I connect, I decide to look for blue jeans. Those were definitely not around in ancient Japan. When our palms meet, I'm sucked into the same vast white space that I encountered the last time I was in Furukama's head, at my seraphim guard processing. I run in my bare feet on the slick surface, but I don't seem to get anywhere. I concentrate harder, imagining the grainy texture of denim under my fingers.

A trapdoor opens up below me, and I fall into a bedroom, onto green shag carpeting. My hand, or rather Furukama's hand, is resting on his knee. Furukama wears jeans, the twist plays on the record player, and a yellow rubber duck with an orange beak stares down from his desk.

I exit the memory with the suspicion that Furukama wanted me to view this. Otherwise, how could it have been so easy?

"And so you now know my secret," Furukama says. "I died in 1961 at the age of nineteen. My father was a scholar of the samurai period. We traveled and lived in Japan for two years before moving back to San Francisco."

"Why not show people the real you?"

Furukama gives me a conspiratorial smile. "When I reached Level Three, I reinvented myself. I became a samurai, and I left my small suburban life behind. The real me is the me I decide to be. Do you understand?"

"Don't worry." I push the still-steaming cup of tea across the table. "I'll keep your secret."

He rises and bows deeply. "Thank you for coming." He transforms into his statue state, which is my signal to go.

I retreat down the hallway and prepare myself mentally for my first official session with Julian.

I pass Libby's office. Inside, Libby and Neil sit in a semicircle of chairs with seven others—all blushing girls except for Keegan. Did they recruit part of Neil's fan club to be healers?

Julian lies facedown on his sofa again, and he doesn't look up when I lightly rap on his door to get his attention. The burly guard snorts. "He hasn't moved since yesterday that I can tell."

I shut the door between the guard and me. "I'm ready for our session," I say.

Julian sits up slowly, swiping the back of his hand across his forehead and then stretching as if he's awoken from a long, satisfying nap. And maybe he has.

"What shall we do today?" he asks with his trademark smirk. After my meeting with Furukama, I want to see if Julian has anything underneath his slick exterior.

"Show me something true." I sit next to him and hold out my palm.

Julian hesitates. I think he's going to refuse, or make a joke out of it. But instead he looks at me searchingly, letting his fingertips barely graze mine. "All you had to do was ask."

Then he presses his full palm against mine, and I'm

jolted into Julian's memory. It takes me a second to get my bearings, because this is a memory of the two of us. It's much less fractured than last time, easier to hold on to. Does this mean he's more in control now? Because this was pre-accident, I remember this day. My own point of view is so strong, I experience the memory as myself.

Julian and I ride bicycles. It's warm, but the leaves are already changing color. We race along the Nidda River, much farther out than I have ever been before, and much farther than anyone I know would ever venture.

Watching the wind ruffle Julian's hair, I feel free. He pedals fast, so I pump my legs to keep up with him. By the time we reach the dunes, I'm breathing heavily. "Let's stop here," I shout.

Julian slows, allowing me to catch up with him. We jump off our bikes and lay them on the boardwalk. The vegetation is different here; we could be at the Mediterranean Sea. Julian sits down under a stubby pine tree, and I arrange myself so that my head is in his lap. I stare up at him. The early afternoon sun forms a halo above his head, and I shield my eyes with my hand.

Despite squinting, my eyes fill with water, so I close them. I wiggle around to get more comfortable. A heaviness settles in my limbs. I haven't slept well in weeks, but now, lying here with Julian's hands in my hair, I'm only a few breaths away from peace.

"I could stay here all day," I mumble as sleep overtakes me.

○ ○ ○

At this point I feel myself drifting out of the memory, but then something grabs hold, and I find myself snapped into Julian's point of view. I'm inside his head now, in this memory. It's such a vast space that I hear an echo in his thoughts. I see through his eyes—he's gazing down at me sleeping in his lap—but it's a level removed, almost as if I peer through frosted glass.

"I could stay here forever," Julian whispers. He brushes loose strands of Felicia's long hair away from her forehead, taking a few pieces to weave together into a braid. He is fully immersed in this scene, fully grounded by the closeness of her skin and the sound of her breathing. He knows how easily moments evaporate into the mist. In the future he'll look back on this day and it will seem like a dream within a dream, but for now it belongs to him.

By the time Felicia starts to stir, he has woven all her hair into tiny braids and then unraveled them again. Her hair lies in a crinkled fan around her face. If only he could tell her how much he cares about her. But he can't. She'd never understand the depth of his feelings, or how they could even develop. She might even think it creepy if she knew how he looked for excuses to view her through the Morati's portal in the palace—that he followed her life on Earth every chance he got. She was like a splash of bright color in his otherwise dull, white world.

It would be even worse if the Morati council knew of

his affection. They would ruthlessly use it against him. No. He'll have to carry this through, hide his love behind a veil of indifference. In order to keep Felicia safe, he will do anything. No matter how much it hurts.

The memory changes again then, zooming out of Julian's point of view and spinning back into mine.

A fat droplet of water plops onto my cheek and brings me back to consciousness. I open my eyes when Julian shifts under me. "It's starting to rain," he says softly. "We should go."

The sky is gray and threatening above me. How could the weather change so rapidly? How long was I asleep? I sprint for my bike. "We're never going to make it. We're more than an hour away from home."

"We have to try." Julian races around me and mounts his bike first. "That's all we can ever do."

We ride against the rapidly rising wind, and grains of sand pelt my face and bare arms. Twenty minutes into our journey, the rain trickles down, and soon enough we're caught in a downpour. We take cover in a copse of trees. I shiver, and Julian pulls me tightly against his chest. Water rushes down his face and neck in rivulets, and his wet lips part in a sigh. I have the urge to tell him that I love him. But I beat it down, because he would think I was crazy. I barely know him.

So I slip my hands under the drenched fabric of his T-shirt and let my fingertips run over the smooth planes of his back. He strips off his shirt, and it lands in a damp puddle at our feet. Then he kisses me, and the force of it makes me stumble back into the rough bark of the tree. I let him guide me down to a patch of shiny grass, lost in the delicious swirls of summer wine that pool in every part of my body.

"You have a twig in your hair," Julian teases me between kisses. I reach up and tap my head until I find it. I fling it away. I catch sight of my watch and the late hour. "Oh crap!" I use Julian as ballast to push myself up. "My mother will kill me if she sees me like this. We have to go."

The rain has let up a bit, but it's still a slog to get back home. Because I'm in such a hurry, I have time to give Julian only a quick cheek kiss at the corner before heading to my house.

I emerge from the memory to find my head in Julian's lap. It hits me with such a strong dose of déjà vu, I gasp.

The side of my scalp feels tight, and when I reach up and touch a braid there, the thoughts Julian had in his memory rush into my mind. Were they real? Did he show me his true self? Or is it another invention? I can't think straight with Julian looking at me like he is, like he wants a chance to reenact that day right now.

My instinct is to flee this scene, but I close my eyes and find my strength. It wouldn't be fair for me to run away, no matter how uncomfortable this is for me. Not when Julian finally seems to be making an effort to be genuine.

Julian carefully lifts my head from his lap and shifts his body to lie next to me. It's an awkward dance to get comfortable, and a tight fit for both of us, but Julian keeps his hand on my hip, so I won't fall.

I don't need to open my eyes to feel the weight of his stare. "I should go."

"You could stay," Julian says, his voice hitching. His lips brush my cheek, featherlight. The tangle of feelings for him I've been holding back—fascination, fear, frustration, desire—come loose inside me.

"Don't," I say, though it comes out strangled. Too weak. Still, I force myself to meet his gaze. His face is just inches from mine. "I can't do this. I need to be good." If I cross this line, not only will Neil be lost to me forever, but I'll be lost to myself.

"You are good," Julian whispers. "Too good."

I don't agree, and I don't think anyone else would either, but I know what he means. Despite everything Julian and I are to each other, and how easy it would be to close this distance between us, I won't cheat on Neil. Sighing, I place my hand over his on my hip. In his memory, when I was asleep, he thought about how he needed to feign indifference so that the Morati wouldn't hurt me. "So the things you've done, all the lies you've told, were to keep me safe?"

"Yes. Always." I believe him. I understand now where he's coming from, even if I still find it difficult to forgive.

"Why do I feel so close to you? You've lied to me time after time, but I can't seem to be able to let you go."

"I'd like to think it's because you love me," Julian says.

Love. The word buzzes around in my head. Do I love Julian? If I do, it's not in the way I love Neil. When I'm with Neil, I want to be a better version of myself. When I'm with Julian, I want to be reckless and selfish. I hate that he brings out my bad side.

I sit up, my back to him and my feet firmly on the floor. "Oh, Julian." I pour all my regret and longing into the utterance of his name.

He stands and walks to the window and presses his palm against the glass pane. "But you want to know the truth?"

"That's all I've ever wanted."

"The truth is, you feel so close to me because you *are* me."

"What the hell are you talking about?" My stomach lurches. If the truth is this crazy, maybe I don't want it after all.

He lets his arm drop to his side and turns slowly to face me. "You are part angel, Felicia. And that part came from me."

thirty

"THE NIGHT YOU WERE MUGGED in Kenya, the day before your thirteenth birthday, I stood in front of the window to Earth in the Morati's palace and just happened to see you. And then suddenly, inconceivably, your thirteen-year-old self stood in front of me, in Level Two." Julian shakes his head and looks toward the ceiling. "You were there only for an instant, but I was irrevocably changed, and so were you."

I remember seeing Julian in my nightmares—nightmares that turned out to be a memory of my brief first visit to Level Two.

"But how can that be?" I fly to my feet, stride across to the window where Julian stands. "I don't feel like an angel." If anything, I feel more like a demon.

"I don't know how or why, but our shadow DNA

transferred to each other during the fissure. You have eight percent of my DNA. And the eight percent DNA that you lost?" He puts his hand over his heart. "It's here. In me."

Is this why Julian and I have always had this strange, overpowering connection? Because we are literally part of each other? My knees buckle, but Julian catches me before I can faint. He scoops me up in his arms and sets me gently back on the sofa. I tuck my legs underneath me and squeeze my arms across my chest.

"Angels have DNA?"

"Angels don't have mortal DNA, but we have shadow DNA. A human's mortal DNA is connected to their immortal shadow DNA. When a human dies, the shadow DNA is what's left. Some call it a soul. It's the part of you that moves on." Julian runs a hand through his artfully disheveled hair. "We exchanged shadow DNA, and it made you stronger. Superhuman."

My being part angel does explain some mysteries. Why I never got sick as a teen and why I recovered so much more quickly than Neil after our car accident. Why I was able to wean myself off the Lethe drugs in Level Two faster than others, and why I got headaches and felt weak in the brimstone jail. And the incident at Western Bridge, where I thought I repaired a tiny part of it, even though that's something only angels can do. Maybe I wasn't hallucinating it. "Why didn't you tell me this before?" I ask.

He sits on the opposite side of the sofa, like he doesn't dare to touch me. "I should have. I guess I had this foolish notion that you could love me for me." He looks at me slightly askew, his features soft and vulnerable. My heart leaps with yearning, but I don't trust it. Because as much as I want to believe Julian is essentially good, if a bit misguided, he is Morati, after all.

And that makes me eight percent Morati. Eight percent evil.

"The Morati haven't killed me. What do they want?" I ask.

"If I knew . . ." His pupils flick away just for a second, but that tiny movement reveals everything. He might have told me about my hybrid nature, but he's still hiding things from me for my own good.

"Never mind." I hastily untangle the braid Julian put in my hair and smooth the crinkled strands between my shaking fingers.

"I'm on your side. I always will be," he says.

I can't stand to look at him anymore. "One hundred percent on my side? Or only eight percent?"

"Felicia!"

"See you tomorrow, Julian." I speed for the door.

"The Morati are dangerous," he warns as I leave. As if I needed to be reminded. I slam the door on my way out.

Libby's office is empty. Neil must be at sound check already. Yesterday's concert went well, if you judge by the crowd's reaction.

I rush over to Assembly Hill, burning with even more secrets that I won't tell Neil. That I'm part Morati. That every time he looks at me, he's looking his greatest enemy in the face. That I'm evil, and somehow I've always known it. I have to push through the crowd to get to the front. It's later than I thought, and people are restless for the music to start.

Keegan is new onstage, his small frame dwarfed by an enormous drum set. He grips his drumsticks with such force that his knuckles are white. Neil probably put him up here to build up his confidence, but the panic in Keegan's eyes tells me it's going to backfire. I don't protest. It might humiliate him even more to kick him out at this point.

Libby waits behind my piano bench. Neil plays the opening notes of a song, and I slide into place, running my fingertips over the keys. I steady myself and turn my head to take in our audience. It's like viewing a giant, undulating patchwork quilt, with all the career groups sticking together in vast swatches of color. There's a tiny speck of red right up at the front—the superfans that Neil has recruited to be healers—and black around the edges of the crowd, where the security team stands just in case.

Normally when you play with a drummer, the drummer sets the tempo for the rest of the band. But Keegan is inexperienced, so he follows the beat put down by Moby on the bass. Keegan is a fraction of a second off, playing rolls on the snare drum that lag behind the rest of us. The music feels heavy, like playing in a sea of molasses.

Moby tries to adjust for Keegan's ineptitude by slowing to his speed, but Keegan gets frustrated and bangs on the high hat, snare, and bass drum willy-nilly. A pressure builds in my head every time he hits the cymbals, which is at least every four beats. I throttle my floor pedal, and my teeth grind together as I pound out the notes. Libby's hand on my back digs into my spine, and the energy she pumps into me congeals and clogs in my veins.

Dark thoughts gather at the base of my skull. I want to scream at Keegan to stop his god-awful racket. I want to rage at Neil for misjudging putting Keegan onstage as a kindness. I want Libby to back off, to stop breathing down my neck. The darkness presses up against the energy within me, pushing it slowly down the length of my arms.

Keegan kicks over the cymbal, and it lands with a crash between Moby and Neil. The dark energy surges into my fingertips and into my piano keys. Libby backs away from me, and Moby and Neil stop playing. I continue like a woman possessed, and the music hovers over the crowd like a black cloud. The purple spirit trappers punch the yellow demon hunters, and the white guardian angels hurl insults at the green caretakers.

My hands are jerked off the keys, and the music stops on a high, keening note that echoes over Assembly Hill. The crowd stands frozen in place, their mouths gaping open as they stare up at me. I'm a public menace, and now everyone knows it.

Neil lets go of my arms, and they drop to my thighs. Keegan huddles behind his drum set, and Moby tries to coax him out.

Libby directs Neil to play a ballad, something to calm

the crowd. "What were you thinking?" she whispers harshly into my ear.

Neil begins to sing, his rich, warm voice soaring over the crowd, filling their ears with promises of safety, love, and happiness. I can almost believe the message is for me. But it's not, and it never will be.

I bolt, tripping over my bench as I go. Without looking back at the stage, I run.

Sometime later there's a soft knock on my door. I lie facedown on my bed. My foot throbs to the rhythm of the memory globe underneath the bed.

The door creaks open.

"There's glass in your foot," Neil says. I stepped on a shard of his picture frame when I tore off my shoes and threw them at the wall. I thought I'd cleaned up all the pieces when I'd hung the photo of him back up, but apparently I didn't do a very good job of it.

"Don't I deserve the pain?" I mumble into my bedspread. "Isn't it clear enough now that I'm a horrible person?"

"You didn't mean to agitate the crowd like that." The bed shifts as Neil sits down. He takes my foot into his lap and extracts the shard. The throbbing recedes into a dull ache. Did I mean it, though? Deep down? Because if I didn't, why did it happen?

I turn over onto my side to face Neil. He recoils with a gasp. "What happened to your eyes?" he asks.

I'm sure my eyes are puffy and red, but do I really look

that bad? "I'm sorry," I moan. I've been saying that a lot lately.

"It's okay. We calmed everyone down. But, Felicia . . ." He pauses. "We took a vote, and you're out of the band. I mean, for the time being. Maybe once things have settled down, in a few weeks, Libby will reconsider."

As if the fallout from tonight's concert weren't bad enough already, now I've lost my last real link to Neil. We don't room together, we don't train together, and now we won't play music together. I'll never see him. He's slipping away, and there's nothing I can do. I want to ask him if he voted in favor of me, but I'm too scared of the answer. At least he hasn't broken up with me, but can that be far behind?

I reach out my hand to him, but he backs away. "Keegan's waiting for me. He needs more practice, so I gotta go. But I'll pick you up for class tomorrow?" He gives me a half wave and scrambles out the door, like he's afraid of me. Like he knows what is festering inside me.

I turn, and twin black smudges shimmer up at me from the bedspread. It looks like makeup. I materialize a mirror, and it's immediately clear why Neil freaked out. My eyes are painted with black eye shadow nearly up to my eyebrows, and my eyelashes are coated with heavy mascara. I don't know how it got there, but I want it gone.

Frantically I wipe at the eye shadow with the edge of my sheet, but no matter how much I rub, I only succeed in dirtying my sheet. The eye shadow doesn't come off. It's like a physical manifestation of the Morati—a permanent reminder written on my eyelids that my soul is stained with black.

thirty-one

WHEN I ENTER THE GYM the next day, I'm frustrated and angry and ready to knock someone over. Neil left without me. He's avoiding me after my meltdown onstage. Not that I blame him. I'd avoid me too, if I could.

Moby approaches me, his balled-up fists gripping the frayed sleeves of his black shirt. "I dig the eyes. Totally badass."

"Thanks." I tilt up my chin. If I can't remove the eye shadow, I'll have to own it.

"I voted to keep you in the band. Keegan's the problem, not you." Musically speaking, Moby's right. But if the main purpose of the band is to enhance people's moods, then I'm the problem.

"That's sweet of you. But maybe this a good thing. Now I won't have any distractions from training."

Moby nods, even though it's a weak attempt to look on the bright side. "Let's spar?"

As an answer I throw a punch from my right shoulder, keeping my arm straight and aiming for his ear. He blocks it with his left forearm, bringing his right arm in at a diagonal to push it down with his hand. He then throws a punch from his right shoulder, and my left arm comes up to block it. We continue this chain of punches and blocks, faster and faster, until both of us are panting.

He spins out of my reach, doubles over, and rests his hands on his knees. "Damn, girl, what has gotten into you?"

If only he knew.

I switch to training roundhouse kicks and arm blocks with Emilia. Furukama comes over to demonstrate how it is done, helping me position my arms so that the right one is turned and reaching toward my left hip, while the left one is bent toward my shoulder with the knuckles facing out. When Emilia's leg comes up, I launch my knuckle toward her neck to block and then bring up my right fist in an overhead punch that glances off her cheek. Then I kick and she blocks. She's more flexible, so her kicks go higher, but I'm laser focused, landing all my kicks and punches until she, too, bows out.

For the remainder of the training, Furukama demonstrates a new fighting technique, and we alternate partners. By the end of the session, my legs and arms groan. I don't know how I'll lift them tomorrow. But even more concerning is how I'll face Julian in our private training.

I have no doubt he'll be turning on the charm. What scares me is that he'll eventually wear me down. And if that happens, I can't be alone with him. If I give in to Julian, I'll kill my last shred of a chance with Neil, and maybe the last shred of my humanity too. I can't risk it. I need someone to train with us.

The most likely candidate is Brady. First because he genuinely seems to enjoy my company, and second because he often spends nights guarding the brimstone jail, which strongly suggests he can't be Morati.

I corner him as he's leaving.

"Howdy, Twitchy." He still hasn't dropped his nickname for me. "Fixin' to go back to the dorms?" Neither he nor the other recruits in my class are aware that I'm training with Julian on the side.

We step over the rubber duck—Furukama's ridiculous rubber duck—as we exit, and head toward Eastern Avenue. Once we're out of hearing range of our classmates, I stop him. "You're ambitious." He's one of the best in our class, and he's determined to get selected this rotation. "Why is the seraphim guard so important to you?"

"Cancer took over my life. I couldn't escape the treatments, the hospital visits, the looks of pity." Brady faces me, conviction lighting up his face. "But in Level Two I joined the fight against the Morati, and for the first time in forever, I felt strong. Seraphim guards are the toughest, and I don't ever want to be weak again."

I hug him. I can't take away what he went through, but I can offer my support. "Do you want to improve your odds for Ascension Day?"

Brady runs a hand through his wavy hair. "How?"

"Julian. I train with him after class."

"I reckon that's why you were on fire today?" That was less about training with Julian than it was about me being part of Julian.

"We could train with him together."

Brady answers with a loud whoop and then covers his mouth when he sees people staring at him. He whispers, "Let's do it."

We go to Julian's new room in the administration building. When I enter with Brady, Julian scowls and says nothing.

"When you met Brady, it wasn't under the best circumstances. But I trust him, and it would be good to have someone on my side. Are you willing to train Brady, too?"

Julian stares at me and then at Brady. He shrugs. "Sure, why not?" He rises slowly, holding his lower back like an invalid, and pushes his tray table to the side with his foot. "Sit," he instructs. I materialize my trusty wooden chair and set it in front of Julian's sofa. Brady sits next to Julian.

We explain to Julian what Furukama has taught us so far, including the mind stuns, mind blocks, and the physical drills. Julian proposes that we concentrate on two critical skills: sifting through memories to uncover ones more deeply hidden, and distress calls.

Both Brady and I have practiced memory extraction before, of course, so we start with distress calls.

"Felicia, you know how you always find me by searching for my brain waves?" Julian asks. "Distress calls start out the same way. Once you find their signature, you open up a channel to them, and then you can communicate telepathically. It's how I kept in touch with the other rebels in Level Two."

"I've never even tried something like that before," Brady says.

"It's not easy. The other person has to be open to it. Most people block access to themselves by default, as a privacy measure." Julian stands, now more steady on his feet, and offers me his seat. "It's better if you face each other to start."

Brady and I arrange ourselves so that we're sitting cross-legged on the sofa, with our knees loosely touching. Julian instructs us to examine each other carefully and then note three remarkable features of the other out loud.

By now I'm pretty familiar with Brady, but I've never stopped and openly stared at him before. He has brown wavy hair, wide-set amber eyes, a strong jaw lined with stubble, and a friendly face. His skin is the color of caramel, like he's been in the sun a lot, and he has a mole right above his left eyebrow. He wears a black button-down shirt with pearl snaps, black jeans, black cowboy boots, and a bronco belt buckle. He doesn't have his sword with him, since he wears it only when he's on jail duty. "Silver belt buckle, beer-colored eyes, and pearl snaps," I say.

"Nose twitch, elegant fingers, and too much eye makeup," Brady says about me.

Julian snorts. "These are the things you'll picture when seeking out the other. Hold them in your mind, get a good picture of the person, and then reach out. Once you find them, concentrate on opening a dialogue and send your message."

Brady goes first. I close my eyes and focus on letting him in, but I don't feel a thing.

After a few attempts Brady gives up. "I can't find you, and you're right in front of me."

When I try, I can faintly make out the shape of him. I send out a signal and wait.

"It tickles," Brady says. "In the back of my head."

It's something. Not enough, but with steady practice I might be able to call for him one day.

Over the next few weeks I fall into a regular, punishing schedule: class, training with Julian and Brady, and then deep meditation.

I see Neil most mornings. He picks me up and we walk as far as the administration building, where he meets for healer training. Though he's a sweet, steady anchor to my days, we never have the chance to have any meaningful discussions, because of the constant interruptions from fans. Officially we're still a couple. He still holds my hand, still gives me a good-bye peck on the cheek. Unofficially I dread the inevitable day when he decides we've drifted too far apart to stay together.

But instead of dwelling on it, I throw myself into training, going through mental and physical drills with a ruthlessness that surprises my fellow trainees. They don't know the darkness that drives me, and the slim hope that if I face down the Morati, I might once again see the light.

I'm careful to never be alone with Julian. I arrive at his room with Brady and leave with Brady. When it's my turn to touch Julian's palm to sift through his memories, he sometimes teases me with images of our kisses, but I become adept at skimming over them, of avoiding getting pulled in.

Sometimes I go to Neil's concerts. I stand in the back so he doesn't see me and so I won't accidentally infect the crowd with my bad moods. Sometimes I linger in our hallway in the evening, hoping for a glimpse of him, wishing he would smile at me the way he used to. Sometimes I miss him so much, it aches.

Usually I go straight to bed after my sessions with Julian. Nights are for meditating my way to a sleeplike state. A time when I do my best to ignore the memory globe swinging on its wire hanger, thumping against the bed skirt like Poe's tell-tale heart.

Just when I am beginning to grudgingly accept my Spartan existence of training and mediation, Furukama makes an announcement in class.

"Attention please." He claps his hands together. "Today we put your skills to the test. Each of you will participate in a double elimination tournament. If you lose two matches, you will be in danger of immediate expulsion."

All thirty-nine of us gasp. Only a fraction of us will be chosen to join the guard on Ascension Day, but to be kicked out entirely? It is unexpected and unprecedented.

I'm especially freaked out. I'm so close to a breakthrough. Every day more power unlocks inside me. I might even expose the Morati tomorrow, but I won't be able to if Furukama bars me from further training. If I lose my two matches, I might lose everything.

Furukama instructs us to line up single file around the gym. He draws names from a hat to pair us up. The object of the spar is to be the first to extract the image from your opponent. Furukama goes down the line, starting with Brady, and inserts images into our minds. When he reaches me, he lifts his hand to my forehead and inserts an image of an apple.

Solemnly Furukama calls the first two names. "Felicia and Wolf. You may begin."

Wolf tries unsuccessfully to mask his displeasure at having to fight me. We've sparred in training, and nine times out of ten I've beaten him. But in a tournament like this, it takes only one slipup. I rub my hands on my pants.

Planting his feet in front of me, Wolf lifts out his palm to connect with mine. He chooses his default defense—the steel wall he used with Furukama during their demonstration, and something I've now torn down numerous times in the past few weeks. While I work on breaching his wall, he pokes around, looking for weaknesses in my force field. When I get through the first layer of steel, I find that Wolf has erected a brick wall behind that. Clever. Within a minute, though, I break through that, too, and grab the image of a katana sword.

I shout, "Katana." Furukama declares me the winner as Wolf curses. Furukama directs me to the opposite side of the gym to wait for the next winner, and directs Wolf to stay put to wait for the next loser.

Next up are Brady and Zhu Mao. They circle each other as they engage in their mental battle. Brady extracts Zhu Mao's bamboo tree image and joins me in the winner line.

Furukama continues with the pairings until all of us are either in the winner or loser line. Then he goes down the loser line and gives them each a new image to spar with.

My first fight in the winners bracket is with Brady.

"Ready, Twitchy?" he asks. I nod, though I'm dreading this fight.

He lifts his palm to mine, and we spar. Brady is inventive with his defenses. He creates a densely wooded forest, and as I try to pass, branches scratch at my face and arms. I concentrate so much of my energy trying to protect myself while on the offensive that I leave my force field vulnerable. Brady snatches the apple image, lifts his hand to his mouth, and makes a crunching sound as he snaps his jaw, as if he's taking a big bite of the piece of fruit. "Apple," he says loudly enough for Furukama to hear.

"Well played." I slink over to the first-time loser line. At the end of this series of fights, there are three lines: the winner line, consisting of those who have won both fights; the first-time loser line, consisting on those who have lost only one fight; and the second-time loser line, consisting of those who have now lost two fights. The two-time losers sit on the floor.

Furukama goes down the first-time loser line and gives us each a new image. Mine is of a cherry blossom tree in full pink bloom. I wouldn't mind sitting under one of those with a bento box instead of having to spar.

My next match is against Zhu Mao. I can't lose this, or I'm probably out. She extends her palm languidly, but as soon as I connect, her arm goes rigid. I'm shaky at first, but I manage to get through her walls and extract her image of a cat. She pouts as she joins the rest of the two-time losers on the floor.

I have one match left. When I face off against Emilia, I bundle up my cherry blossom tree and set a barrier of fire around it. When our palms connect, I'm blinded by the whiteness of a blizzard. I dig deeper and deeper, shivering all the way, until I find myself trapped inside the Morati's mainframe again.

The point of view switches, and I'm looking at myself trapped inside the mainframe. I raise my eyes until I'm staring at Emilia's face reflected in the shiny surface of the mainframe, her glowing alabaster skin framed by silver hair. Libby was right when she said I could be the one to expose the Morati posing as humans.

Because Emilia is Morati.

thirty-two

I TEAR MY PALM AWAY and shout, “Morati.”

Emilia’s eyes grow wide at the same time mine do. I squeeze my hands into fists and wince as my fingernails cut into my palms. I did it. I exposed one of the Morati. Her pupils dart back and forth, as if she’s looking for an escape route. But then she laughs. “No. That’s not the image Furukama gave me.” She shakes her head like my accusation is crazy. Like I’m crazy.

I’ve seen into her hidden memories, seen her in Morati form, and I’m certain she’s one of them.

Quicker than a heartbeat, Brady is at my side, issuing commands. “Wolf! Moby! Help me pin her down.” The tournament is forgotten. It is no longer top priority now that a suspect has been identified.

Wolf and Moby spring into action immediately, grabbing Emilia by the arms to immobilize her. She struggles against them. Furukama strides over to where we're standing, Emilia still protesting that she has no idea what I'm talking about. "Test me yourself," she cries to Furukama. "She's wrong!"

"Everyone outside except these five." Furukama indicates me, Brady, Wolf, Moby, and Emilia.

The trainees don't need to be told twice. They rush out of the gym like it's on fire.

"I trust Felicia," Furukama says. "A stay in the brimstone jail should clear this up."

Grunting, Emilia kicks at Furukama, but he glides out of the way before her foot can connect.

We arrive at the entrance of the jail, Emilia fighting us the whole time. The two daytime guards open the heavy stone door for us. Furukama dismisses Moby and me, and enters with Wolf and Brady. Furukama can handle Emilia's interrogation, but I wish I could be there. I wish I could do more to help. If I had the chance, I would ask Emilia so many questions. Who are the other Morati? Where are the rest of my memories? Why did they take them? What is their plan for me?

Moby excuses himself, claiming he left something back at the gym. I walk back to the dorms in a sort of daze. Is it my imagination, or has the low constant hum of the Morati's presence grown louder and more insistent within me? Now that I have exposed Emilia, the other Morati may strike to protect themselves.

When I reach my hallway, Neil leans against his door, waiting. He's alone; there's not a single fan in sight for the first time since the night I fled from his bed. He gives me a tentative smile, like he doesn't know what to expect from me, and all at once I'm done with this distance between us. He's here and I'm here, and a storm might be brewing outside and everything could change tomorrow or in fifteen minutes, but I have right now. And right now I want Neil. I push him up against the door in a desperate kiss.

He turns the knob behind him, and we stumble backward into his room. I kick the door closed. We fall onto his bed, our hands all over each other and our mouths unable to get enough.

I pull at the buttons on his shirt. To be close to Neil is all I've ever wanted, and with our bodies entwined, I can't fathom what kept us apart.

My lips find his earlobe, and my teeth can't resist biting down. He shudders under me, and his muscles go taut. I kiss him at the base of his jaw, which is his Achilles heel, and he jerks his neck. "Wait." He pushes against my shoulders, gently, and sits up. "Before we do this, I have to tell you something about me."

Neil's words bring me back to reality, to the secrets between us, to all the broken promises I want to forget. I swing my legs over the side of the bed so that they dangle next to Neil's. "What?"

"Every day I wrestle with myself. Every day I say, 'Today will be the day I tell the truth.'" He stares at the door. "But then I chicken out, and I go back to living this lie." He sniffles and then beats a fist on the bed.

I put my arm around him gingerly. "You're the most generous, good-hearted person I know. How can that be a lie?" *Too good for me, for sure.*

Neil wipes at his wet cheeks with the back of his hands. "That's just it." His voice trembles. "I'm not good. Not at all."

"What—" I start to ask, but he cuts me off.

"Don't." He draws in a shuddering breath and then crawls back onto his bed and curls into himself. "Can you . . . please . . . I need . . ."

I stare at his shaking body. What does he need? For me to leave or for me to comfort him? All I know is what I need. I lie down next to him and hold him as tightly as I can.

What could Neil have possibly done that he thinks is so bad? He's not like me—easily corruptible. He'd never have kept all the memory globes to himself. He'd have turned them all in. He certainly wouldn't have one under his bed right now, taunting him, whispering to him. But whatever he has done, it must be a big deal if he's so upset about it that he's crying.

After a while Neil shifts to face me. "Thanks for staying. I've missed you lately."

"I've missed you, too."

"Would you mind sharing a sleep memory with me? One of our naps back on Earth?" He holds up his palm tentatively, as if I might refuse him.

"Of course not." Should I tell him about Emilia? No, not now. Not when we're finally connecting again. I won't ruin this moment with talk of the Morati. The Morati have already ruined enough.

We slip under the blanket, and then I reach up so our palms can connect.

I let him choose and we end up in one of my favorite memories—an abnormally chilly late spring day after school when we huddled together under the down comforter in his bed.

"Did you like the strawberries?" Neil whispers into my ear, his warm breath sending tingles down my spine.

"Yum." My lips find the hollow right below his ear where his jaw meets his neck, and he jolts, like every time I kiss him there. I want to explore his entire landscape and find the other sensitive spots on his body, but I've been barred from most of the regions under his clothes.

"We could go get more." He shifts beside me, moving the blanket and letting cold air in between us.

"Are you crazy?" I push the comforter up over our heads so that we're buried under it, all traces of chill gone. I unbutton his shirt and press my cheek against his chest, so that I can listen to the thump of his heart. I swirl my fingertips down the bare skin of his sides and stomach, and his heartbeat speeds up, and dances erratically.

My own heartbeat thunders in my ears as I inch myself lower, tasting the ridges and planes of his body as I go. Until I come to the hard copper button of his jeans. I start to undo the button, but he laces his fingers through mine and pulls me up again.

"Felicia," he says, his voice cracking. "Look at me." His eyes are intense, his curls cling to his forehead, and his bottom lip is stained red from the strawberries. My breath catches in my throat. The way he squeezes my hand tells me that his self-control might not last too much longer. Maybe I'm not as ready as I think I am.

I kiss his forehead, and he closes his eyes. Our heads emerge from the blanket.

All that's left of the fire are embers, but for now they're enough. Because Neil settles behind me and rests his arms around my waist, tucks his legs in behind mine, and tickles the wisps of hair at the base of my neck with his soft exhales of breath. I love the contrast between the cozy heat under the comforter and the cold air of the room on my face. It reminds me of being outside in the winter, immersed in a hot spring in Japan, catching the swirls of snow with my tongue while my body toasted in the hot spring.

My eyelids grow heavier, and I slowly lose consciousness and start to dream.

Memory me is sleeping, and most of the me reliving the memory is too. Only a tiny sliver, like a pilot light, stays alert.

○ ○ ○

In the dream I have during that after-school nap, I stand on a highway in the searing sun, and the asphalt melts around me, causing me to sink like I'm in quicksand. But before I'm buried alive, the scene changes.

I'm in Neil's bed, inside his dream, and the bed is slightly blurred around the edges. I am looking out from Neil's naked body, which is entwined with someone else's, his fingers running through long dark hair. He opens his eyes, but he's not looking at me. He's looking at some other girl.

I'm dumped out of the memory, a memory of a time when Neil had a racy dream. And I was somehow able to hijack that dream during our viewing of the memory. Neil backs away from me, and I can tell by his horrified expression that he knows what I saw.

"Felicia, why are you invading my dreams? I trusted you!"

As upset as I am about the content of Neil's dream, his accusation forces me to go on the defensive. "I didn't mean to! It just happened. I swear . . . I'd never . . . I didn't even know I could do that."

"I can't believe it." Neil gets up and paces the room. He shakes his head and wrings his hands, and he looks everywhere but at me. "Here I was, working up the courage to tell you. But you couldn't wait. You had to poke around my mind and take it from me."

Neil's words slap me out of my stupor, and I sit up, wriggling out from under the blanket. The fact that he's freaking out this much confirms my suspicions that he has been hiding something big from me. And now I really, really need to know what it is. "Neil, calm down. I'm sorry, okay? I wasn't trying to pry."

He stops and twists in my direction, glaring down at me between heavy lids. And for the first time I'm seeing flashes of a Neil who doesn't want to be with me anymore. This recognition is the scariest and most heartbreaking I've ever had.

"Anyway, it doesn't matter. It was only a dream, and you have no control over what you dream." I say it as much to convince myself as I do to convince him. And then, because I can't help myself, I say, "Was that Gracie?"

"Yes. That was Gracie."

His admission stabs me in the chest. Why was he dreaming of Gracie when he was sleeping next to me? A deadly cocktail of anger and mortification flows through me, and I jump up, run through the door, cross the hall, and push into my own room so that I can hurl myself onto my bed.

"Wait!" Neil calls behind me. Chasing me.

"Get out of my room!" Reaching my bed, I whirl around to face Neil, and as I do, my foot catches on something underneath. I kick my leg to free it and accidentally catapult the metal wire and the memory globe it holds straight at Neil. I reach out my arm to deflect it at the same time Neil does, and after a brutal squishing sound, I realize with absolute horror we've both touched it. And then we're sucked in.

thirty-three

AS I EXIT THE AIRPLANE and walk though the terminal, my palms sweat and my heart races. What if Neil didn't get my text message with my new flight information? What if he did and he decided he didn't want to come pick me up? We haven't talked since the phone call in Paris when I practically proposed to him. And his few texts back to me have been short and generic. Maybe I scared him.

When I enter baggage claim, my eyes lock on to Neil. It's almost like slow motion—the way we run toward each other, the way he hugs me so tightly that he lifts me off the ground.

"I'm so happy you're back." He sets me down. His cheeks are flushed and his whole body shakes in excitement.

He grips my hand tightly, interlacing our fingers, and as

we wait for my bag to come out on the carousel, he pumps me for details about my trip. When I point out my suitcase, he grabs it with his free hand, pulling me with him. He doesn't want to break off our contact for a second.

Even in the car he keeps only one hand on the steering wheel. The other rests on my thigh except when he has to shift gears. When we get to my apartment, I thank him for taking a half day off from work to come pick me up.

He looks at me as though I've lost my mind. "Of course I came. But I didn't take off. I went in early." He deposits my suitcase next to my closest in my room.

"You must be exhausted." I strip off my sweater and my shoes and hop into bed. "Come take a nap with me."

We lie side by side facing each other. I take a deep breath and plunge right in with my most burning question. "So, remember our last phone conversation? What do you think about us getting married? I mean, obviously it doesn't have to be now or anything. But it would solve so much, wouldn't it? We could live together."

"Uh . . . do we have to talk about this now?" Neil avoids my gaze.

My heart plummets. I'm starting to think that as clear as it is that he loves me, Neil doesn't think I'm marriage material and doesn't want to have to tell me yet. Or maybe he thinks eighteen is too young—it is too young—and that there are infinite women in his future who are better for him than I am. Maybe I have to be much more convincing, even when I'm not all that convinced myself.

I push him onto his back and straddle him, lifting his arms over his head and pinning them down. "Yes. You're my prisoner, and I have ways of making you talk."

Neil goes totally still and squeezes his eyes shut. Then his body starts to shudder under me. He's crying.

Neil has never broken down in front of me like this. Ever. I don't know how to react. "Neil . . . what's wrong?"

"I—I'm not good enough for you. You don't want to marry me. Trust me."

My head spins. He can't be serious. "Are you crazy? If anyone's not good enough, it's me."

"I'm not a virgin," he blurts. His cheeks blaze crimson.

Those words are the last ones I ever expected to hear come out of his mouth, and for a long, terrible moment time stands still.

But then it sinks in, and I roll off him, jump up, and press myself against my bedroom wall. "What do you mean you're not a virgin?" I screech. My eyes must bug out of my head. My pulse is racing and I might faint. I can't believe it. All those rules he made about keeping our clothes on. All that bullshit he said about signing the virginity pledge. All that self-control that I hated but admired. He was my example of purity. He's the one who made me want to be good. But it was based on a lie.

"This is why I didn't want to tell you. I was ashamed, and I knew you wouldn't understand."

"You're right. I don't understand. Because you gave me a reason to be happy again. You've seen everything I am, and you still love me. But you couldn't do the same for me and show me who you really are. I never needed you to be perfect. I needed you to be real." I'm so angry, I could punch a hole in a wall.

Neil's eyes are rimmed in red, but his tears have given way to righteous fury. He gets up and stands opposite me. "Well, now you know the real me. I'm no saint. I'm nobody's savior. I'm just as fucked up as anyone else."

I fall back onto my bed. Curl into myself. Close my eyes. "Was it Gracie?" I say in a small voice.

"Yes." That one word has the power to crush my heart in its fist.

My head and heart are heavy with the weight of the thought of Neil and Gracie having sex. It's so unimaginable. And I can't explain it, but for some reason it makes me feel dirty. Like everything he and I did together was a lie.

The room is silent and as cold as winter. As the minutes tick by without either of us daring to speak, I envision snow falling swiftly and burying me alive.

The bed shifts under me. Neil reaches out and brushes my hair behind my ear, but I won't look at him.

"I'm naked," he says. And my eyes can't help to fly open and rove over his body when I hear that. The sheet is strategically placed so I can't see everything, but I can tell by the bare skin of his hip that he's telling the truth. "I remember you once thought you had to be naked in order to bare your soul." His tone is wistful, and my heart hammers in my chest, remembering the day I confessed my sins to him.

"So how did it happen?" I ask grudgingly.

"After Gracie and Nate broke up, the church gossip was that Gracie must have had sex with him and that's why she didn't come to services anymore. At school, when she was there, we only saw her alone. The day she came to see me at my house, it was the day after she told Nate she missed her period and she thought she might be pregnant. She didn't tell me that, though. Nate told me later. She was hysterical and crying, and I couldn't understand a word she was saying. When she finally calmed down, she asked if we could go to my bedroom. No one else was home at the time, but she wanted privacy. She insisted. And I was still so in awe of her. Even when she closed the door behind us, I didn't protest. I didn't think about it. I was consumed by the improbable fact that Gracie Logan, this older girl, this gorgeous girl, was in my room." Neil shakes his head at the memory.

He goes on. "She told me that she hated Nate. Everything with him had been a mistake. She had been in love with me all along but hadn't realized it. I had never felt so dizzy in my life."

I cough. I'm not sure I want to hear the rest of this story, but I don't want him to stop telling me either.

He inhales deeply. "She said—and I'll never forget this—she said 'Look at me, Neil. I want you to look at me like you always do in church. When you think I'm not watching.' I was so overwhelmed, but she didn't seem to care. She pushed me against the wall and kissed me, and I . . ." He stops, the last words mangled by emotion.

He covers his mouth with his fist and squeezes his eyes shut. "I don't really even know how it happened. One minute we were standing, and the next we were on my bed and . . ."

I hold my breath, bracing myself for the awful details.

"And then it was over. She kissed me and put her clothes back on and left."

I let out my breath.

"I felt terrible. I mean, it was magical. It was. But it was also wrong. I didn't know how wrong until the next day. Gracie called me and told me to meet her at the bridge over the creek on Route 4, the one where all the couples go to park. I took my bike. I had to, because I was too young to drive. I wanted so desperately to see her again. I wanted to apologize to her for being so weak. I wanted to ask her to be my girlfriend, as if that would make it less of a sin."

He's shaking now, and there are goose bumps on his exposed skin. "When I got there, she was standing on the outside of the guardrail. She was kind of swaying, and I remember thinking that if she weren't careful, she'd lose her balance. There'd been a lot of rain that spring, so the creek was pretty full, but still, it wasn't that deep. I was only about twenty yards away from her when she saw me. She opened her mouth and whispered something I couldn't hear, and then . . . she let herself fall. I screamed and ran toward her, but it was too late."

"But she didn't die." I remember Nate saying that she had come back to town.

"No. When she hit the water, I panicked." Neil exhales loudly through his nose. "But then she surfaced, and she was laughing. She begged me to jump in too. But I couldn't. When she waded over to the bank and toweled off, she said that meant I was scared of commitment. Like Nate. The bridge was a test, and I failed. She never did come back to church, and she refused to answer my phone calls. I saw her at school, but we were never alone again. And after she graduated, she went to college in New York. I always wondered if she used me to get back at Nate. But I really loved her."

I'm so conflicted. My heart goes out to Neil for what he went through, but I can't reconcile it with the way he always took the moral high ground. "There was nothing wrong with you loving Gracie," I tell him. "And you shouldn't feel guilty for having sex with her. It doesn't make you a bad person."

He raises his eyebrows slightly, and waits for me to say more.

"What I can't understand is all your talk about the importance of virginity and waiting until marriage. Is it something you said so they wouldn't judge you at church?" I'm curious how he'll answer. "I mean, how can you even sign that pledge if you're not actually a virgin?"

"I rededicated my virginity."

"I don't know what that means. How do you 'rededicate' your virginity?"

"I heard a speaker at one of our youth conferences talk about it once." Neil's tone is defensive. "And it made sense to me."

"Okaaaay, so they encourage you to rededicate your virginity?"

"I wouldn't say they encourage it. It's not a 'get out of jail free' card or anything." He manages a self-deprecating laugh. "But it's an option for those of us who messed up. Giving into the sin once doesn't mean you have to continue to do it."

"Are you saying that even if Gracie had become your girlfriend, you would have made this rededication pledge? Or did you make it because if you couldn't have sex with Gracie anymore, then you didn't want to have sex with anyone?" Every muscle in my body tenses, waiting for his answer.

"It wasn't like that."

"I bet you're still in love with her. I bet that's the real reason you don't want to marry me. I'm just a poor substitute for Gracie."

"I never said I didn't want to marry you," he protests. "I said you wouldn't want to marry me. And look—I was right, wasn't I?"

"I don't know, Neil. I really don't. This is too much for me to process right now. Because guess what? Lying is a sin too." I turn my back to him and close my eyes. "I think it would be better if you went home."

"But—"

"Please," I say wildly. "I need some time alone."

Neil gathers his clothes, gets dressed, and puts his shoes on. His retreating footsteps are followed by the slamming of my front door. Only then do I allow myself to cry.

thirty-four

THE MEMORY ENDS. When I come back to myself, I'm lying half on top of Neil, half on the floor. I'm too stunned to speak, and for a minute Neil must be too. The next Morati strike can't be far off. But then Neil pushes me away. Roughly.

"Where the hell did that come from?" He glances from my face to the ruffled bed skirt, and his eyes widen. "You were hiding that memory globe under your bed, weren't you?"

"I'm not the only one good at hiding things. I confessed all my sins to you, but you kept secrets from me." Well, not my most recent sins, but that's a technicality.

"You put the rest of us in danger so you could keep viewing memories. How could you keep evidence to yourself? You might as well be in league with the Morati."

"You're wrong. In fact, today I caught one of the Morati. I saw into her true memories, and she's in custody."

Neil gets up and paces the room. "But what about the rest of the Morati? You don't want them to be caught—not when they are supplying you with your memories."

"That's not true. I want them to be brought to justice as much as you do." Even if I am one of them.

Neil laughs bitterly. "Right." He stalks over to the table the Morati put there. Its intricate filigree makes it stand out from the rest of the furniture in the room. "I think it's pretty telling that you kept their table."

"They stole our memories. I just wanted to know what happened between us." I may not like that Neil lied to me or that he had sex with Gracie, but at least it's out in the open now. In reality his actual confession hurts less than the fact that he didn't feel like he could confide in me. Trust is the basis of any relationship. Maybe we grew apart because he wouldn't trust me and I somehow picked up on it on an unconscious level. Maybe that's what has been driving me to regain my memories to find out the truth.

"It looks like Nate was right about us breaking up. Does that make you happy?" Neil asks.

"We don't know that for sure." I finally stand. "We need to view more." Once we have the whole picture, we can heal our relationship. We can close the gap between us and truly be together.

Neil shakes his head. "When will it end? When will

you understand that what matters is not what happened then but what is happening right now?"

But he tried to hide what happened then. If we hadn't viewed that memory, then he might never have told me. "Were you ever planning to tell me about Gracie?"

"I can't talk to you when you're like this," Neil says. "I'm going outside for a walk."

His non-answer is one blow too many. And it fills me with rage. I pull the skep charm out of my shirt with such force, the chain breaks. My whole body buzzes, and I hurl the charm at the wall, aiming for his photo at the center of my collage. The charm falls with a soft thud onto the carpet, but at the same time there's a metallic scraping sound as a ripple of energy the size of a Frisbee opens up, obliterating Neil's photo in a bright light and melting the other photos it touches.

As we watch, the ripple expands outward, the circle of light growing larger, consuming nearly all of my collage.

I gasp and drop my arm. The circle flickers and fades, and then it's gone. I sprint to the now almost bare wall, run my hands over the surface. It's hot to the touch, and the ripples have left a circular pattern of grooves, like the ones found at all the Morati's later bombing sites. My knees wobble and threaten to give out as I try to recall the chain of events that led up to the other bombings after I viewed memories. Each time electricity ran through me right before the energy blasts.

"What the hell was that?" Neil chokes out. He looks at me as if I've grown horns and a forked tail, and for all I know, maybe I have.

"Did an electric current hit you just now? Or before? When the other bombs hit?" Before the library bombing, he bent over and clutched his stomach. I'm sure of it.

"No. Why?"

If I am the only one feeling the electricity, then maybe it's coming from me. Maybe *I* am the bomb. But I wasn't anywhere near the other bombing sites, so I don't know how it's possible.

"I—I don't know." The ripples of energy appeared when I threw the skep charm at the wall. I pick it up off the floor and examine it closely. It's an ordinary metal charm on an ordinary gold chain. It must be a coincidence. Unless it's not. When Autumn saw my charm, she thought it was an obol. Megan said obols are what Careers use to travel between levels, and I found out later that they have to use the regulated portals in Areas One and Three. But what if this particular obol can open portals anywhere? If that's the case, why wasn't Nate opening portals anywhere he pleased? Or was he? I am so confused.

"Is that your skep charm?" Neil asks, reaching out his hand for it.

I snatch my arm out of his reach and tuck the charm into the pocket of my capris. If it holds such power, I have to keep it safe. "Yes. Not that you care," I snipe at him.

"Where did it come from?" He's mystified, and wary.

We sit next to each other on the end of my bed, and the fight goes out of me. It's time to tell him the whole story. No more lies. I explain that Nate dropped it in the brimstone jail while dumping a demon into the hellhole, and that I was there visiting Julian. He tries to interrupt me, to ask me questions, but I barrel on, needing the momentum to carry me through. I theorize that it could have been me who caused what we thought were bombings, but that might actually have been unstable portals that opened via some mystical combination of viewing the memory globes and touching the skep charm, though I have no idea how this happened or why. I admit that it sounds far-fetched, and that I could be totally misreading the situation. I stress that probably only the Morati know the truth and that's why we need to talk to them. But I don't tell him what Julian told me, about my being eight percent angel. How could he handle that, when I can't come to terms with it myself?

When I stop talking, he doesn't reply for several minutes. He's so still, I almost think he's somehow perfected Furukama's trick of turning into a statue. Finally he tilts his face toward me.

"Maybe we should break up," he says, and the words I dread the most in the world are out in the open.

I'm so light-headed, I might float straight out the window. "You don't really mean that, do you?" I ask, my voice shriveled. Oh God, I shouldn't have told him what I did. I'm such an idiot. Of course he doesn't want to stay with someone as evil as I am.

"Yes. I do." He sighs. "There's something off about you."

So that's it, then. We're broken up. I'm utterly numb.

"I'm still me," I squeak.

"Are you?" Neil turns to face me full on, his features hard, though his eyes are still kind. "I sensed a change in you after you viewed that first memory globe. And now it's like you're possessed. You have this singular obsession with your memories, and you don't care about anything or anyone else."

"I care about the memories *because* I care about you."

Neil shakes his head. "Why did you have that memory globe under your bed when you had the suspicion it might cause more destruction and endanger more lives?"

"Why didn't you turn me in after the first memory globe?" I counter. "I think on some level you wanted me to view them."

"I trusted you to do the right thing."

"Trust?" I almost laugh. "You want to talk about trust? You didn't trust *me* with your secrets, but you trusted the Felicia who existed in that memory."

Neil walks over to the far corner of the room and plucks one of the few remaining photos from the collage wall. It's the one of Autumn and me in Iceland, and it bubbles and curls up on one side, where it was scorched. "That Felicia is a myth. She always has been. The Felicia you are now is the only one who counts. She's the one holding all the power."

If that's true, why do I feel so powerless?

He doesn't get that I'd give anything to be that myth, because she's the one who knows what really happened to us. And knowledge is the real power. I flop backward onto the bed. "You're wrong."

"Felicia, listen. Because I want you to understand this." He returns to my side and takes my hand in his. He lightly traces the love line on my palm, sending calming vibes up my arm. "I wasn't hiding that memory from you because of Gracie. I was hiding it because of *me*."

"What do you mean?" I sit up.

"I'm questioning everything, because nothing's like what I thought it would be. I've lost my compass, and I don't know which way is north, or if I should be headed that way." He draws in a shaky breath. "Your faith in me was the only thing keeping me going. It was wrong of me, but I didn't want you to stop thinking of me as a good person. And I thought that if you saw that memory, you would. I'm sorry."

He looks up at me warily, as if bracing for my condemnation. But he's right that my expectations of him were unrealistic. By sticking to my highlight reel in Level Two, I curated a Neil memory museum, framed him as a masterpiece. Now, confronted with the real boy next to me, I realize he's just as much a work in progress as I am.

I squeeze his hand. It was enormously difficult for him to lay bare his soul like this. All at once I understand what Neil has been trying to tell me. Goodness is a series of choices, every day, not a static character trait. But if he thinks a single choice in his past defines his worth, then we both need to change our concept of what "good" is. "I'm sorry too. And for the record, you're more than good enough for me."

He smiles sadly. "You're good enough for me too."

"Maybe not yet. But I want to be." I stand up. "First I have to tell Furukama about this energy blast I created. And about its possible connection to the obol and the memory globes.

Maybe he'll know what's going on, or at least what we should do about it."

"Right now?"

"I've already waited far too long." I bet that Furukama is still in the brimstone jail, interrogating Emilia. We can add this to his line of questioning.

He stands up beside me. "I can go with you. If you want."

"You'd do that? Even though we're broken up?"

He draws me into a hug. "No matter what happens, I'll never stop caring about you."

"Thanks, but Furukama would probably prefer that I come on my own. He's a very private person."

Neil nods. "Good luck."

To avoid any Morati who may be out looking for me, I keep in the shadows on the way to the jail. Like I did the night when I went to visit Julian there, I rush from tree to tree, hiding myself behind their trunks. When I pass the Forgetting Tree, I wonder again what Neil wrote on his scrap of paper, but laugh when I realize that I simply don't care that much anymore. It's so liberating that he finally confided in me, like a giant weight has been lifted from my shoulders. Is it possible to rebuild our relationship? I want to believe it is.

When I reach the tall stone doors to the jail, they are open and unguarded. Alarm bells go off in my head. Maybe Furukama had an emergency and called the guards down to him. If so, I need to help out. I pause long enough to send a mental SOS to Brady just in case. I think about his silver belt buckle and lock on to his signal. He's in the dorm, so he must not have been on guard duty tonight.

I enter the jail and tiptoe down the stairs, my senses on high alert. On my last visit I got a headache, thanks to my fraction of angel DNA. I'll have to make this quick, if I can.

When I reach the base of the stairs, I duck behind a column and scan my surroundings. Emilia stands inside the bars of Julian's former cell, but she's not with Furukama. Instead it's Autumn who jiggles a key in the lock of the cell door, unlocking it with a clang. What is she doing? And where are Furukama and the guards?

Emilia rushes the door and exits with a smile on her face. She is slow, stumbling over her own feet like a drunk, but as she nears my hiding place, I prepare to stop her from getting away.

Just as I stick out my foot to trip Emilia, Autumn grabs Emilia's arms and twists them behind her back. As Autumn drags her toward the hellhole, Emilia struggles against her. She looks up and sees me staring. "Help me, Felicia! Autumn has gone mad!"

If she knows me still, Emilia's not as far gone as Julian was, but Autumn has her completely overpowered. Her long hair is plastered to her sweaty skin, and she grimaces in pain.

"Shut up." Autumn curses, but then smiles at me. Her pupils are huge and crazed, like when Furukama kicked her out of training. "It's fine. I'm taking out the trash."

"I won't say a word. I swear," Emilia pleads.

I step forward, my hands stretched out beseechingly.

"Don't do it. Furukama can't have authorized this."

Autumn laughs. "Who cares about Furukama? She's going into the hole." She smashes the bottom of her palm against Emilia's forehead, knocking her out. She really means to throw her in.

If she's not here under Furukama's orders, she must have gotten rid of the guards. It could be a personal vendetta against Furukama, but it could be something more sinister.

Autumn drops into a crouch behind Emilia and shoves her arms under Emilia's armpits. I can't let her do this. I close the distance between us, smashing into her just as she pivots to heave Emilia into the pit.

The force of my tackle knocks them both to the ground. The key flies up, ricochets off the inside edge of the safety railing, and falls into the pit. Emilia's limp body somersaults and then lands with a crash against the brimstone bars of the last jail cell.

Autumn squirms away, but I straddle her back and clamp her arms down at the wrists with her palms facing up. "If you won't tell me the truth, I'll force it out of you."

She bucks beneath me, trying to throw me off. I hit her between her shoulder blades, and she collapses, clenching her hands into fists. I force one open and connect my palm.

I sift through her memories, an automatic response now that I've been practicing with Julian. It's almost like flipping through an old family photo album, as I recognize familiar faces of friends and parents and siblings gathered at barbeques and pool parties and trips to quaint European villages.

But there's someone I never expected to find in Autumn's memories. Cash. I had no idea she knew him on Earth. I jump into that memory to investigate.

"You're dressed up," Cash says to Autumn, his gaze raking over her body in a way that sets her on fire. He tucks his hands between her gold belt and white gown and pulls her in for a kiss. "What's the occasion?"

"Halloween party at the field house." She snuggles up to him. Then she reaches for the gold halo headband she bought today to complete her costume. She holds it up. "I'm going as an angel."

"One day you'll be one for real," Cash says fiercely. "And then we can be together forever."

"I know." She looks up into his pale blue eyes and sees the promises shimmering there. She's never been lucky when it comes to love. And when Julian showed up at the sushi restaurant that day, she thought everything had changed for her. That someone might actually prefer her company to Felicia's. But it became increasingly hard to ignore the way he was always sneaking glances at her best friend and mooning over her like a lovesick ape.

Then Cash came and swept Autumn off her feet. After she confided to him that she was envious of Felicia, after they made love, after she found out that Cash and Julian are real-life angels from heaven, Cash insisted that his being here should remain a secret from Felicia. Autumn is more than happy to oblige. Felicia still presumes that Autumn is dating Julian—making Felicia believe that she's going behind Autumn's back with Julian was also Cash's idea—and Autumn thinks it's hilarious that Felicia is so racked with guilt. It serves her right to have to suffer once in a while.

The doorbell rings. That must be Julian now. On her way to let him in, she pops a peppermint into her mouth and crunches down on it with her teeth.

At the door Julian barely masks his contempt for her, but once they're in the living room with Cash and seated around the coffee table, he's all respect and compliments. Autumn admires Cash for having that kind of power over Julian.

"Why is this job taking you so long?" Cash asks, cutting through Julian's fawning.

Julian leans back in his chair. "Cassius," he says, addressing Cash by his real name. "This kind of job takes finesse. If there's a problem—"

"The problem is that you're not following the plan," Cash says. "You're supposed to be driving Felicia to suicide, not falling in love with her."

Suicide? Cash didn't tell Autumn about the suicide angle. She may be fed up with Felicia getting all the attention, but she doesn't want her to get hurt or to *die*. A chill comes over her. What has she gotten herself into?

"I need time to put all the pieces in place, that's all," Julian insists, flustered.

Autumn's head spins. "Cash, why are you talking about suicide? That's not what I agreed to." She only wanted to teach Felicia a lesson.

Cash turns to her, puts his hand on her knee. His blue eyes are like deep pools, and she gets lost in them. The room blurs. Everything slows down. Her heartbeat. Her breathing. Her thoughts. Cash loves her and only wants the best for her. She has to listen to him. "Sometimes we have to make small sacrifices for the greater good," he says.

"Yes, you're right. The greater good."

Julian snorts with disgust. "Why don't you compel Felicia to commit suicide, since you obviously have no problem compelling Autumn to hate her." Autumn's mind is fuzzy, but she knows Cash is on her side. Felicia doesn't care about anyone but herself, and she deserves what's coming to her.

"I wish. But unfortunately, we can only bring desires to the surface that are already there, however small. In any case, I'm taking over from here on out," Cash says to Julian. "You failed. You're being recalled to Level Two and you can forget living on Earth."

Julian shakes his head. "We have a plan for tonight. Right, Autumn?"

Autumn smiles, anticipating the look on Felicia's face when she tells her that she and Julian kissed. Never mind that they didn't. "We do." She scoots closer to Cash on the sofa and runs her fingers lightly over his collarbone. "Give Julian another chance. It will be awesome."

Cash puts his arm around her. "If you say so. But, Julian—dump Felicia tonight and then get out of town. Can you do that?"

Julian nods. "Of course."

"Good." Cash gives him an authoritative stare as Julian slinks out.

"I'll see you later," Autumn calls behind him. "Ten o'clock!"

The door slamming is his only response. "I don't like him." Autumn curls her lip and reaches for her flask of vodka. She takes a gulp, and some of it runs down her chin. Cash licks it off her face and then kisses her hard. It makes her feel the right amount of reckless.

"Nobody likes him," Cash says. "He has been Earth-obsessed ever since the fissure and watching Felicia get mugged. He thinks he's clever about hiding it, but he's not."

"Will you let him stay?"

"If he's successful. But let's not waste time discussing him," Cash says with a devilishly seductive smile right before he bites her earlobe. "We have better things to do."

Her phone vibrates on the table. It's a text from Felicia that she has arrived at the field house. "Ooooh!" Autumn jumps up. "I'm so ready for my fight scene."

"You'll be great." Cash follows her to her room, where she picks up her chiffon wrap and lets him drape it around her shoulders. "And don't forget your halo."

I exit Autumn's memory and stare at her, openmouthed. Cash and Julian and my best friend were conspiring against me. I may have betrayed Autumn, but she betrayed me, too.

thirty-five

DENIAL AND ANGER weigh down my chest. This cannot be the same girl who wrote stories with me, who baked sugar cookies with me, and who gave me a charm bracelet and called me her best friend. "Why did you do it?" I scoot forward, readjusting my position so that my leg presses down on her spine and my knee immobilizes her neck. I push down on her shoulders, grinding her cheek into the stone floor.

The chamber fills with Autumn's frenetic laughter. She twists violently under me, flipping onto her back and throwing me off balance. I fall onto my side, banging my knee. Before I can get up, she lunges forward and grabs my neck with both hands. "I did it for love."

"You think Cash loves you?" I choke out. "He's a Morati. He has bigger plans than you!"

"He's all I ever wanted. He sees *me*. He told me it's *my* time to shine. Everyone treats you like you're some special snowflake. But you're not."

"You're right. I'm not a snowflake." I put my palms together, like I'm praying. I thrust them upward and slam my arms apart in a *V*, tearing her arms off my neck and making her stumble onto her butt. "I'm a snowstorm."

I place my palm against her forehead and focus my energy on her frontal lobe like Furukama taught me, so I can mind stun and incapacitate her, but she slaps my hand away and laughs. "You keep forgetting I've been here longer than you. And you're not the only one who had an angel to train with. Cash will be here soon."

Brady appears in my field of vision. He got my message. "Yeah, well you keep forgetting who your real friends are," I say. Brady slides in next to me, and we both slam our hands against her forehead at the same time.

With both of us focusing our energy on her frontal lobe, Autumn's resistance crumbles and she loses consciousness.

"What the heck is going on down here? Where's the key to the cells?" He pats Autumn down but doesn't find it. If we had it, we could lock Autumn in while we look for Furukama.

"It fell into the pit. Autumn tried to throw Emilia down it too."

"I don't believe it." He rises slowly.

"I read her memories. She's working with the Morati. Cash is one of them."

"Cash? Aw, hell."

"How'd you know she had a key?" I ask.

"It's the only way to open the cells. And only Furukama has got a key."

"There's no way he gave it to her willingly."

We both know what that means. Somehow Autumn incapacitated Furukama to get the key. She took out two guards. There's no way to restrain her. She'll wake up soon, and she said Cash was on his way, probably with the Morati cavalry in tow. We are screwed.

Emilia coughs and groans, lifting her head with effort.

"Did Furukama interrogate her?" I point at Emilia.

Brady shakes his head. "No, he wanted her to weaken first."

I skirt around Autumn's limp body and offer my hand to Emilia. She takes my wrist, and I help her sit up. She slumps backward into the brimstone bars. Not ideal, but I don't have time to move her. I pull the skep charm out of my pocket and dangle it in front of her face. "Do you know what this is?"

"An obol," she answers. Her gaze darts back and forth between Autumn and me. She's scared. "To travel to Earth and back using the regulated portals from Areas One and Three."

I shove the obol back into my pocket. "Can it open other portals?"

"What other portals? Those are the only two back to Earth." Her pained, panicked expression doesn't change. It's possible that my dorm room has a portal that no one is aware of. Maybe it also leads back to Earth. Or maybe that burst of energy I created is something else entirely. It doesn't seem as though Emilia knows. Either that or she's too frightened to tell me.

Brady cuts in. "We're all alone down here. We have to fetch help or get out."

"If the Morati come after us, it's to our advantage to fight them here."

"But two against . . ." He trails off. We don't know how many Morati there are.

We need backup. But who? We can't call Julian to come down here into the brimstone, and besides, after the revelation of Autumn's memory, I don't know what to think about him anymore. He was working with Cash to drive me mad enough to commit suicide, but he claimed everything he did was to protect me. Anyone in our seraphim guard class could be Morati. That leaves Neil and Libby. But what can they do? Enhance our mood while the Morati slaughter us? "Who do you trust?"

"You."

"Sweet, but not helping."

"Nate."

My eyes bug out. "Nate? Are you serious?" After his threat to throw Neil and me down the hellhole, even though he claimed later it wasn't serious, he's the last person I'd trust. "Though, I guess he does hate Autumn."

He shrugs. He's at as much of a loss as I am.

"Okay, go," I say.

Brady dashes for the stairs, and his feet pound into the stone as he ascends. He pauses long enough to yell, "Good luck."

Autumn is still out, but I don't turn my back to her. I crouch next to Emilia, ready to defend her from Autumn.

Emilia's eyes are closed and crusted with yellow. I slap her cheek, and she looks over at me in a stupor.

"Who else in our seraphim guard training is Morati?"

"What?" She doubles over and vomits yellow onto her shirt, barely missing my shoes.

Damn it. It's too late. She won't even be able to crawl out of here now. I pound my fist into the floor, and my hand screams in pain.

Autumn laughs. She's awake. I spring up, positioning myself halfway between her and Emilia, my knees slightly bent. I will kick her ass if I have to.

"I was eavesdropping on you when you thought I was unconscious." She lifts herself casually onto her elbows. "You know why Nate hates me?"

Like I care about that now.

"Because I was the captain of the seraphim guard team that beat the crap out of the demon hunter team in last year's softball tournament," Autumn says. "What a petty idiot."

So that's why Nate threatened to kill Neil and me. To get back at Autumn for a freaking softball tournament.

Unbelievable. But Nate is not my top concern.

"You're a traitor." I'm still trying to fathom how I could have been wrong about her all this time. And how she was able to trick everyone else for so long, even Furukama.

"Speaking of traitors"—Autumn stands up and inches closer to me—"it was Julian's idea to kill me in your bed. I had to be killed to come straight to Level Three and prepare everything here for Cash, for when he came through the mainframe."

I don't believe Julian would do that. But then, I can't believe Autumn is standing in front of me now with a murderous gleam in her eye either. "Why would you let yourself be killed?"

"I'd do anything for Cash. Because Cash would do anything for me. Everyone thought it was over when you crashed the system in Level Two, but it was only a distraction so that the Morati could come through. Soon the war will really begin."

Even though she's obviously demented, she might have some of the answers I seek too. If I can keep her talking until Brady gets back, I might have a chance to beat her. My temple throbs. The brimstone headache is coming on.

"Why did the Morati steal my memories?" I ask. "And why did they return some of them?"

"To manipulate you. And it worked, didn't it? You would do anything for those globes I delivered to your room. It's truly pathetic how weak you are."

I can't stop the shame from exploding red across my

face. I let my obsession color all my decisions and played right into whatever the Morati's plans are for me—and they must have a plan, because otherwise they would have disposed of me right away. I was so blind. "But they're not manipulating you, right?"

Autumn only smirks knowingly. "You don't want to face the truth about how selfish you are. I don't blame you."

Like Eli taught me to do in Level Two, I summon all my rage and frustration and concentrate it into a blast of energy that I hurl straight at her chest. *That's for lying to me.*

She flies across the room and pounds into the opposite wall. I charge at her and swing my fist into her stomach. *That's for conspiring against me.*

When she doubles over, I bring my knee up, catching her in the chin. *That's for taunting me.*

The force of impact throws her head back, and her feet slide out from under her. She falls onto her back with a moan.

As I prepare to kick her in the side, her moan fills me with guilt. Maybe I'm enjoying this too much. My foot connects with her rib cage, but she grabs on to my ankle and hurls me into the corner. I hit the wall shoulder-first, the impact reverberating though my body.

Before I can react, she comes at me and punches me in the abdomen, making me double over. While I'm clutching my stomach, she decks me in the mouth and then the bridge of my nose, snapping the cartilage. "Oh, look. You still believe you can bleed. How sad."

The pain is excruciating, and I concentrate everything

I have into shutting it down. I reach up and touch my split lip, healing it as I do. My nose continues to gush blood until I clamp it with my thumb and forefinger.

She slams into me, knocking me to the floor. I throw out my arm to break my fall, and my bone crunches. I scream, letting go of my nose to cradle my elbow.

Autumn bends over me. "It's too bad Neil will never know what happened to you."

I'm desperate enough now to call Julian. I reach out for Julian's brain waves and try to send an SOS. But my signal is fuzzy. The brimstone must be causing interference.

"Getting some static?" Autumn raises her eyebrows. "I've blocked all your signals." She digs her fingernails into my biceps and begins to pull me toward the pit. Emilia groans loudly, and Autumn turns at the sound.

While Autumn's distracted, I pull together my energy again to form a concentrated blast, and aim for her torso. Her nails scrape my skin as she's blown back. I make a break for the stairs and put out another call to Julian.

Autumn crashes past me, throwing me off balance and into the bars of Julian's former cell. "You're not going anywhere but down," she screams. She turns and lunges at me, her hands forming claws in front of her, but I jump to the side and she bangs into the bars chin-first and her eyes roll wildly in her sockets.

As I continue to retreat toward the stairs, I shoot more energy blasts at her, but they hardly faze her. I'm getting weaker. It wasn't such a good idea to stay down here after all. She darts around me and blocks my exit.

"Wait," I say. I'm almost completely tapped out, and I need time to recover my strength. "I want to ask you something."

Autumn shakes her head. "No questions." She places her hand almost tenderly on my forehead. "Should I stun you before I throw you into the pit? That would be the best-friend thing to do."

I step out of her reach and try to run around her, but she catches me easily and carts me over to the hole.

Autumn yanks me up by my shirt. "But then again, you were a sucky best friend." She prepares to pitch me over the railing, and I scream.

"Don't," a male voice commands. I perk up, hoping against all hopes that someone—anyone—has come to my rescue.

As the new arrival nears, I deflate completely. It's Cash, and he's grinning ear to ear. "Thanks, Autumn, dear. Let me do the honors, won't you?"

thirty-six

CASH SAUNTERS OVER to us, flanked by the twins from seraphim guard class, Ira and Ian. They are all dressed in dark suits with white oxford shirts and pale pink ties, like groomsmen at a wedding. As usual Cash's hair is slicked back and his teeth are so white, they practically glow. In fact, now that they no longer need to hide their Morati essence from me, their bodies shine with an otherworldly light that brightens every corner of the dank chamber.

"She's all yours." Autumn shoves me over to him.

As soon as I'm out of her grasp, I break into a run. If I can get up the steps, I have a chance. But I haven't made it five feet before the twins block my path like a brick wall.

"Leaving so soon?" Cash asks.

I turn toward Cash and Autumn, pressing my back against the twins. I expect Cash and Autumn to come for me, to stalk me like predators after prey. Instead both are facing the pit, peering into it. Cash has his arm around Autumn, and they stand as though they could be tourists enjoying the view.

Cash runs his hand down Autumn's spine. He whispers something into her ear, and she smiles. Then he calmly reaches out and backhands her. She falls, and as her cheekbone smashes into his foot, her pupils contract and the hazel of her irises reappears. The crazed look is gone, replaced by confusion.

Cash kicks her off his foot. "Hey, Autumn. I think it's time we broke up."

She lies still for three beats, and then rage ignites her face. She springs up and slaps Cash so hard that he stumbles back onto the railing. "Break up?" she shouts hysterically. "I let you murder me for *this*?"

Cash calmly reaches out and mind stuns her. She shakes like she's been hit with high voltage, and Cash catches her in his arms. He carries her over to Emilia and dumps her onto the ground, as if he doesn't have use for either of them any longer.

Cash approaches me, offering his hand. I take it automatically, as if compelled, and he gently pulls me toward him, like he's asking me to dance. "I'm sorry about that. I got here as quickly as I could."

"W-why?" He stunned Autumn, but he didn't kill her, or she would've disappeared.

"You know why." Cash's voice is low. Hypnotizing. "You've felt the truth inside you for some time now. You're one of us. You can join us."

"Because I'm part angel?"

"So Julian told you." Cash chuckles. "At least he's good for something."

"Autumn said you kept me alive only because you wanted to use me."

Cash's face darkens. "Autumn is a fool. Her envy stunted her reasoning skills and made her easy to control. You are worth ten thousand of her."

I raise my eyebrow. "I saw her memory. You wanted me to commit suicide! Don't pretend that you're my friend now."

He reaches for the knot of his tie and loosens it. Tiny pearls of golden sweat form at his hairline and trickle down his face. "Your suicide would have brought you to Level Two much sooner, but you weren't very cooperative. Everything we did then was for a reason. As is everything we've done now."

I take a step back. "Like bombing innocent people."

"Only the first bombing, the one that took out the records room, was operationally imperative. The second bombing and killing the healers were meant to destabilize Level Three. The rest of the destruction was your handiwork, wasn't it? We laced your memories with water from the Styx, the river that flows between all levels, in the hopes that you would open portals when you viewed them."

"But how could viewing memories cause destruction or open portals?"

Cash sighs, like he's disappointed that he has to spell it out for me. "We think you are the first ever human-Morati hybrid. And somehow that gives you the power to open portals to other levels. The obol that you wear around your neck is the catalyst for you to be able to use your ability. At first the portals you opened were so unstable that they caused isolated destruction of whatever place you last spoke about. But your seraphim guard training taught you control and concentration so that you can open stable portals."

Unease creeps up my spine. "How do you know all this?"

"We're connected, you and I. Even more so after your residence in our Level Two mainframe."

"In your pursuit of opening portals, you stood back and let all those people die." Good and bad may have shades of gray, but it's clear that this is evil. "And because you hoped I would open a portal for you, you stole my memories?" If my memories were important enough for the Morati to steal and to dole out to me like a trail of breadcrumbs, then those memories must have some greater purpose. They must contain some greater truth.

"Join our fight against the injustice we Morati were dealt, and you can know everything."

I take another step back. "I will never join you. Never."

Cash makes a fist, and for a moment I think he's going to punch me. But then he twists his arm so that his palm is facing upward. As he opens his hand, a white memory globe grows until it's the size of the ones I viewed in my room. It's breathtakingly beautiful, and there's nothing I want more than this.

My arm rises unbidden, and my fingers stretch toward it with yearning.

But I snatch my arm back. I won't give in.

Cash extends the memory globe farther in my direction. "This one globe holds the key to restoring all your memories and to getting the answers you seek."

The only way to discover the full extent of the Morati's plan for me is to agree to become a part of that plan. I can't do it. No amount of knowledge is worth giving up my soul and selling out mankind.

"No," I say. But my voice wavers, and Cash grins.

"No?" He steps back and throws the globe high in the air. As it soars, it breaks into hundreds of lighted globes that float all around me, suspended by the force of his will. It is the most stunning sight I've ever witnessed. "Do me a small favor, then. You have the obol, yes? Take it out."

My hand reaches for my pocket, and I slide the skep charm out into my palm.

"Excellent. Now all you have to do is view a memory. Any memory at all. You'll open a portal, and we'll all walk through it to Level Four so that we'll be one level closer to our goal. Nothing could be easier."

As I stare into Cash's eyes, the globes reflect in his dark pupils like a universe of stars waiting to be discovered. The ice blue of his irises melts into the inviting turquoise of a tropical ocean. A whisper tickles the back of my mind, faint at first and then growing steadily into a thrumming chorus, serenading me from all sides. "Know yourself," it says.

My angel DNA surges through my veins, assuring me that I'm better than human. I could be perfect. I could be divine.

Dimly aware that he's using his power of compulsion, I squeeze my eyelids shut and shake my head violently, trying to force him out.

"Go on. Touch a globe to restore all your memories. Know yourself. Know how you lived. Know how you really died."

I can't help myself. I reach for the closest globe. It wouldn't be so bad to join the Morati. Why have I been so against them all this time? I try to come up with reasons, but they seem so inconsequential. They pale in comparison to the gifts Cash offers me.

"Felicia!"

Neil's voice breaks through the spell Cash has on me. I jerk my arm down to my side, dropping the charm. It clatters to the floor. I spin. Neil runs toward me.

Cash curses, and the memory globes start to swarm, swirling around him until they converge into one globe. Then he closes his fist and it's gone. The twins tackle Neil before he can reach me, and wrestle him to the ground. Nate comes up behind them and jumps on one of their backs until the four of them become a great ball of tangled, kicking limbs.

Before I can join the fray, Cash rushes at me and launches himself at me with a flying kick. My arms go to the block position I've practiced so much in class, and as his foot nears my ear, I protect myself with a knuckle to his cheek and jab with my right fist into his neck. But unlike in class, Cash reacts with a sweep of my standing leg, sending me careening backward. I grab Cash's knee, and he falls on top of me. He scrambles for the skep charm and then clamps down on my wrist, tying the chain around my forearm.

He lets go of me and springs up. "Let's try this again, shall we?"

Cash opens his hand, and the memory globe blooms once more. He lifts his arm like he's going to throw a baseball, and I realize he means to pelt me with it in order to open up a portal. I leap to the side at the same time that Autumn crashes against Cash, pressing his lower back against the railing of the hellhole. "Don't hurt her," she cries.

He pushes her away roughly, coughing. Yellow spittle dots his chin. "Call her off, Felicia." He thrusts his arm out, leaning his side over the railing and dangling the memory globe over the pit.

Autumn lunges at Cash again, and he loses his balance, pinwheeling his arms. He catches hold of Autumn's hair, and the momentum propels them both over the railing. As Autumn latches on to the steel bar with her right hand, I sprint toward the hellhole and reach for her. "Take my hand," I yell at Autumn.

Cash swings from Autumn's hair, drops the globe, and grabs on to my left wrist. The globe splatters against the side of the pit. The force of his swing causes Autumn's grip to slip from the metal. I catch her with my right hand. "Help me up," Cash demands. "Or your memories die with me."

Scuffling and cursing continue in the background as Nate

and Neil keep the twins occupied. I can't keep holding both Cash and Autumn. My shoulders bellow with the strain of their weight. I have to let go of either my memories or my best friend. Either way I lose.

As I look into Autumn's petrified eyes, I realize how I have been investing all my time and energy in the Morati's narrative version of my life, letting them shape me via my memories. I spent my time chasing before, trying to find myself in my past, when all along I held the power to create myself in my present. It is time to take my life back. To be the best version of myself that I can be.

I shake my left arm violently, and Cash digs his fingernails into my flesh. He's not going to go easily. My feet begin to slide. If I can't get Cash loose, he'll pull me in too.

"Help! Neil! Nate! I'm slipping!"

Autumn takes a deep breath. "I'm so sorry, Felicia. I let envy control me. I deserve this."

Tears well in my eyes. "Don't say that. We've both made mistakes. But the future is a clean slate. We can be friends again. Best friends." My knees buckle. My strength is gone. We'll both go down together.

She shakes her head. "It's too late for me. But not for you."

She twists her arm within my grasp, forcing my fingers open. "No! Don't let go!" I shout. I clutch at her, but I can't reach her.

She throws herself around Cash's waist. Cash's fingernails tear down the length of my hand, and his screams send chills down my spine.

As both Cash and Autumn fall into the abyss, I sink onto the floor and curl into myself, too horrified to even cry. My best friend. Gone. My memories. Gone.

I'm dimly aware of movement above me. Three bodies are thrown into the pit. The twins and Emilia? Shrieks, high-pitched and close, pierce my eardrums and then become quieter and quieter until they are nothing at all.

Nate gets in my face. "Are you okay, Felicia?"

I open my eyes. Nate and Keegan stand over me. Keegan must have arrived recently. I sit up with a start. "Where's Neil?"

Nate harrumphs. "What? No thank-yous?" He pulls Keegan with him. "Come on. Let's clean up the mess up top and leave the two lovebirds alone."

Considering we broke up, "lovebirds" probably isn't the most accurate description. Maybe it will be again soon. But even if it won't be, I have to make sure Neil's okay. I'll never stop wanting the best for him. Ever.

"Nate!" Neil calls out. He's by the stairs, lying in the fetal position, his arms clutched over his chest. Nate stops, leans over, and offers Neil his wrist to help him up, but Neil refuses it with a grimace.

Hurt registers on Nate's face until Neil says, "I think my ribs are broken."

"That's nothing compared to the shape the other guys are in." Nate chuckles morbidly.

"Yeah. Thank you for being here for me," Neil says. "I appreciate it." As I begin to crawl toward them, Neil lifts his knuckles for a conciliatory fist bump.

Nate crouches down and knocks his knuckles against Neil's. "No one messes with my little brother but me."

Neil smiles. Then he turns his gaze toward Keegan. "I told you to stay outside!" he admonishes. "You could've gotten hurt."

"You guys needed me," Keegan says defiantly. "And I kicked some Morati butt."

"That you did." Nate claps Keegan on the shoulder. "Now let's go." He nods at me and leads Keegan back up to the surface.

As soon as I reach Neil, I cross my legs and pull his head into my lap. I stroke his hair, mourning everything I lost today, but marveling, too. I am sitting here, despite all the odds, with this beautiful boy by my side. Even if we have only this moment, it's up to me to make the most of it. That's all I can do. "I could sing to you. I hear music really helps the healing process."

He grins at me, rewarding me with the first dimple I've seen in ages. "Yes, please."

I'd sing "Blessed Be the Tie That Binds"—it is kind of our song, after all—but it now reminds me too much of how I'm forever bound to the Morati, and there is nothing blessed about that. Instead I make up some lyrics to the *Prancing Goat* Symphony on the spot.

Neil covers his ears in mock distress. "Okay, okay—you can stop singing now."

"Why? Because you feel better? Or because I'm torturing you?"

"Both?" We laugh. It's no secret my singing voice is atrocious.

He sits up. "I like you better without all that black eye shadow." I touch my eyelid with my finger, and it comes away clean. The eye shadow is finally gone.

"How did you find me down here?" I'm lucky Neil came and called my name when he did. "Can you stand?"

He nods, and we both rise to our feet.

"Julian got your distress call. He found Nate and me and told us where you were. He's waiting outside." Neil pulls at his collar. "He wanted to help . . ."

But he couldn't because of the brimstone exposure.

". . . but I begged him not to," Neil finishes. "He can't lose any more power. He has to get stronger so he can rebuild the bridges and the portal. Level Three needs him."

Even when Neil is rushing to my rescue, putting his own life at risk, he still has the presence of mind to be concerned about everyone else's well-being. It's so typically Neil to put others before himself.

"What about Brady? Furukama? Are they up there too?"

"I didn't see them," he says.

I fill Neil in on what happened before he came, including what I saw in Autumn's memory. When we return to the surface, Neil steps between the waiting Julian and me, in full-on protective mode.

"I was so worried!" Julian says.

"Were you? Then why were you plotting my demise in

Autumn's memory of your meeting before the Halloween party?"

Julian gulps. "You saw that?"

"I did."

Julian puts his hand out to me beseechingly. "I've done some things I'm not proud of. But I stopped working with the Morati a long time ago."

I won't let Julian emotionally manipulate me anymore. And I want answers. "You knew Cash was here. You knew Autumn was involved. Why didn't you warn me?"

"They were watching me on Earth, in Level Two, and here, and they threatened to hurt you if I told you about them. I couldn't let that happen."

From what I saw in Autumn's memory, I know he's telling the truth about the Earth part, and the rest is plausible, though frustrating. "Okay," I say warily.

"They already punished me for contacting you at all. Autumn was the one who sent the anonymous tip and got me put in jail. She even bragged about it to me. They didn't want to torture me, just teach me a lesson, so Autumn convinced Furukama to let me out after one night."

"In your memory of our bike ride together, you claimed you'd do anything to protect me," I say as calmly as I can. "And yet you sent Neil down to face Cash instead."

Julian's so wrecked, I'd swear there are tears in his eyes. "I *would* do anything to protect you. If you don't believe anything else, believe that." He steps closer. "You have no idea how close I came to rushing down those stairs."

"That's true," Neil confirms.

Julian blinks, and a tear escapes. "But I realized that what you most needed was an antidote against Cash's false promises, someone who represented goodness to you, and only Neil could provide that."

I try to imagine how it might have gone if Julian had come instead of Neil, but I can't. He was right that Neil was the exact person who could break through to me at the moment of my compulsion. "Julian, I—"

"Don't." Julian's lower lip trembles. "It's okay. I'll be fine." And then he turns and walks away.

Neil slips his hand into mine, and that simple act breaks me. I pull him in and we hold each other. I let my tears flow as the thoughts of recent events all flood into my mind at the same time.

I always thought the universe demanded reasons, that by viewing my memories, somehow the story of my life would make perfect sense. But I've learned the hard way that reality is messier than fiction, and no matter how much you want to, you can't sneak a look at the last page to see if everything turns out okay.

Neil leads me back to his room. We don't talk. We simply lie in his bed, foreheads and knees touching, hands clasped, breathing each other in. And right now that's all I can ask for.

thirty-seven

THE BELLS RING, marking the start of a new day. I untangle myself from Neil's sheets and lean over him to stroke his cheek. His eyelashes flutter, but he doesn't open his eyes. He smiles and then says, "You were right. It is nicer to wake up next to you."

I laugh and snuggle back in next to him. "I could stay here all day." Especially considering I don't want to yet face any of the fallout from last night.

"Stay as long as you want." He sits up, the sheet sliding down to reveal his bare chest, and gives me a searching look.

"Are you sure? You're really okay with us sharing a room?"

Neil blushes, but he doesn't bow his head. "Yeah, I think

I am. Level Three is different from what I was taught to expect from the afterlife. I didn't know the rules of this place, and I automatically assumed that the rules I learned on Earth carried over. But they don't. I get that now."

This is a giant step for Neil, especially after yesterday, when we basically broke up. "What changed your mind?"

"Seeing you fight down there, I remembered why I fell in love with you in the first place. You've always been strong. But you don't realize it sometimes."

"Strong?"

"You are who you are, and you don't pretend to be someone you're not." He turns his head away. "Not like me."

I catch his chin so that he has to look at me again. "No regrets," I say. "But no more secrets either, okay?"

He nods. "No more secrets."

That means I have to tell him about my Morati DNA. I don't really know how to say it after all this time, so I start casually. "So guess what I found out?"

"What?"

"Since my thirteenth birthday I've been eight percent angel."

Neil sits up straighter. "How is that even possible?"

"I don't know, but Julian said it happened when the fissure opened between Level Two and Earth."

"And you believe him?"

"He doesn't lie *all* the time." I scoot over to sit next to him against the headboard.

Neil shakes his head as if it's too much to take in.

"Amazing! I mean, that's a good thing, isn't it?"

"Well . . ." I hesitate. Neil might hate me when I tell him the truth. "Not really. Because I'm eight percent Morati, I think it gives me a tendency to become obsessed. You told me yesterday you thought something was off about me." I lower my head so that my hair falls over my eyes.

Neil puts his arm around me and pulls me to him. "No. Some of the Morati chose to rebel, like Mira and Eli. And even Julian. They fought against evil. And so do you."

I'd like to think I wouldn't be drawn into the Morati's schemes again. I still feel their presence here, but I can't be sure if it's only Julian or if there are more, lying low, waiting for another chance to ascend to the next level somehow.

"That reminds me. I have a present for you," Neil says.

"One of my birthday presents?"

"No." He takes my wrist and unties the chain that still holds the obol, letting the charm slide off and fall onto the bed. "This skep here, it's a part of another story."

I rub my wrist, glad to have the charm and its destructive power gone. But I still don't know how Neil managed to obtain something on Earth that originated in the heavens. "Can I ask where you got the skep?"

"I found it on my desk at home," Neil says. "With a typewritten note that said 'Felicia might like this.' I thought one of my parents left it there. But now that I know what it really is, that doesn't seem very likely."

"No, it doesn't."

Neil hands me a small white box. "Open it."

I remove the lid and poke around under the cotton inside until I uncover a charm in the shape of the infinity symbol.

"This is the start of our new story." Neil threads the charm onto the chain. "And we'll write it as we go. No promises that can be broken, just infinite possibilities."

"I love it. Thank you."

We stay like this for several minutes, letting everything sink in. There's so much uncertainty right now. The one thing I can be sure of is that Neil is squarely on my side. But if Neil and I should break up someday, we break up. It won't be the end of the universe. My afterlife will go on.

Then Neil lifts the sheet, a seductive glint in his eye. "How shall we start chapter one?"

"I might have a few suggestions," I say, pouncing on him. He throws the sheet over our heads, and for the first time we join together without a single reservation.

Two days later, when we finally emerge from Neil's room and venture outside onto the green, we discover a new, more peaceful Level Three. Julian has rebuilt both bridges, so full classes can resume. Julian's next task will be to try to repair the files in the records room, so we can find any Morati who may be flying under the radar, but he needs to regain his strength first.

Furukama is fine after his shock of being mind stunned by four of his trainees—Autumn, Cash, Ira, and Ian—in his office. Brady tells us that it was Cash who knocked him out on his way back from finding Nate. Furukama and the career council reprimand Nate and Keegan for throwing Emilia and the twins into the pit when they could have been interrogated. Keegan claims he did it as payback for Kiara's murder.

I fill in Furukama on everything that happened with Autumn and Cash—even that I had a part in the explosions by viewing Cash's memory globe gifts instead of turning them in. Maybe in part because I know about his reinvention and he wants me to keep his secret, Furukama lets me off lightly—he dismisses me from seraphim guard training. But he also hugs me, so on the whole I think he's grateful for my contribution to exposing the Morati.

If Furukama, the security team, and most of Level Three are surprised that Autumn was working with the Morati, Nate is not. "I always knew there was something off about her," he boasts to whoever will listen. I remake my former room into a shrine of sorts for her, though. In the end she was my friend, and she sacrificed herself so that I could live. Despite everything else she did, I honor her for that.

The weeks fly by, and soon Ascension Day is upon us.

As I make my way to Assembly Hill, I run into Julian. Since he repaired the bridges, he is being celebrated as a hero, and Libby allowed him to join the muse program with us as a reward. We haven't had the chance to talk, because his entourage usually surrounds him, but today he is alone in front of the rebuilt Muse Collection Library.

"So it all worked out for you, didn't it?" I ask him. "You've been found innocent of the bombings, you're popular with the people, and you're going back to Earth as a muse. You got everything you ever wanted."

He reaches out and lightly grazes my cheek with his knuckles. "Not everything," he says sadly.

I deflect the emotionally charged moment by asking a question that's been tumbling around in my mind. "How did Cash know that, as a hybrid, I could open portals?"

"I'll show you," Julian says. "Even though this memory doesn't paint me in the best light. Okay?"

When I nod, he materializes the eggplant sofa right out here on the lawn. We sit down together, like old times, and we connect our palms.

Julian drives the stolen police car, pumping the gas pedal. He's on the lookout for Neil's car, because Cash has ordered him to hit it head-on and take Felicia's life. Julian doesn't know why vehicular homicide is not considered murder, but it isn't. In any case, Julian doesn't want to go through with it. He has a plan. He'll have to crash into them, or Cash will become suspicious, but he can do it so that Felicia has a maximum chance of survival.

Julian turns on the sirens as a warning. He switches lanes as he rounds the bend, and Neil's car speeds straight toward him. At the last second he swerves, but Neil swerves too and the cars collide, metal grinding and glass shattering. As they spin together, Julian locks eyes with Felicia.

The cars screech to a halt in the middle of the road. Julian exits the police car from the passenger side and rushes over just before a second police car comes barreling at Felicia, who is still trapped in the wreckage. He recognizes the driver, Octavia. Cash must have sent a backup Morati assassin. Felicia throws her arm out in front of her face in a protective gesture, through the broken window, a metal charm glinting in her palm. A blast of light flies out of her fingers. It steamrolls toward the oncoming car, flattening grass and shrubbery alongside the road before it entirely encompasses the car and zaps it into oblivion.

Julian stops in his tracks, utterly stunned and terrified. Somehow Felicia made an entire car and its driver disappear. It's impossible, and yet he witnessed it with his own eyes.

Julian approaches Felicia with caution, dialing 911 on his cell phone.

"Nine one one. State your emergency," the dispatch says calmly.

"There's been a car accident. Two people are hurt."

"Where are you? Why are there sirens?"

"I don't know what it's called, but it's the old country road off Route 4. Hurry!"

He hangs up. "Are you hurt?" he asks Felicia, his whole being on high alert.

She stares straight ahead, like she's in shock. "I—I can't get out." Her long hair is stuck in the twisted frame of the car. "Please help Neil!"

Julian rips Felicia's door off the hinges and throws it to the pavement. He leans over her and gently extracts an unconscious Neil from his seat belt, keeping Neil's neck straight as he pulls him over Felicia and lays him in a patch of grass. Julian administers CPR and makes sure Neil is breathing normally before he turns to Felicia in anguish.

"I have to go before the ambulance arrives." He kisses her on the forehead and wipes a tear from her cheek. "I'm so, so sorry. I hope you can forgive me someday."

Felicia doesn't say anything, and Julian knows he doesn't deserve an answer anyway. He's a coward, and he proves it by racing off across the field as fast as his feet can carry him.

We exit the memory, and Julian flinches like I might punch him.

"I made a car disappear?" I ask incredulously.

"That's why Cash didn't want you to have that memory. He was scared of you. He theorized that as a hybrid you might be able to destroy angels. He thought if you knew, you would eventually use your power against him and the other Morati."

"Why didn't you show me this before?" I ask.

"Honestly? Because I thought you would smite me, first chance you got."

"You think I have it in me to smite you?"

"You look like you want to smite me right now."

I laugh. "I do a little."

"Told you."

"Fair enough," I say. "But the water from the Styx wasn't involved in the car crash. I thought the three main ingredients were a hybrid, the Styx, and an obol."

"Cash said you probably blacked out when you were thrown from the car and maybe partially crossed over, which would mean going through the Styx."

"Okay, but how did Cash go from theorizing that I could kill Morati to theorizing that I could open portals?"

Julian wipes his hands on his jeans. "Later, once you were already in Level Two, Cash found Octavia, the assassin he thought you destroyed. She was hiding out in a hive, afraid that Cash would punish her for her failure. That's when he knew that what you actually did was open an unstable portal to a higher level. But he didn't tell me that until recently."

"But you're a hybrid too. Can't you open portals? Why didn't Cash just use you instead of setting up this elaborate scheme with me?"

"I can open them, but only to lower levels. We're linked, and so our powers are balanced out that way. I bet you can open them only to higher levels."

It's not a theory I want to test out anytime soon, that's for sure.

Back in Level Two, when I relived the memory of my supposed death, the shock of Julian's betrayal left a deep scar in my psyche. But now I understand that he was manipulated as much as Autumn and I were. That doesn't make it right, but it gives me a reason to forgive. "After the crash you stayed to make sure I was okay. You helped Neil. That counts for something."

"I ran away. I left you there." He groans and punches the arm of the sofa with his fist. "If I had stood my ground right then and there against the Morati, if I had stayed and protected you every day of your life, maybe you'd still be alive."

So many maybes. So many ways for things to have gone differently. So many versions of the story that will never be told.

I touch his arm, and his fist relaxes.

"It's okay. We'll be fine." I can't be sure whether he's finally telling me the whole truth or merely his understanding of the truth, but in the end I don't care. I can accept Julian for who he is, bad and good and everything crazy in between. "Friends?" I ask. It's the most that I can offer.

"Friends," he says.

Julian and I walk together to Assembly Hill, where a crowd has already gathered. There's an air of celebration as Area Two prepares to send off the twelve chosen candidates for the seraphim guard, including Brady and Moby. Over in Area Three they are bidding farewell to the retiring Careers and the people older than sixty-five, who get an automatic pass to Level Four.

There's a barrier put up between the ascension site, where the graduates stand, and the rest of us. I join Neil in the front row. Brady comes up and hugs me. "Bye, Twitchy," Brady says. "I don't know where in creation I'm going, but I reckon it'll be exciting."

"Aww! I'll miss you," I tell him, "but I won't miss that nickname." We both laugh.

The portal opens. It's a door leading to a staircase, one that looks more like it goes up to a dusty attic than the heavens. Furukama and Libby stand to the side and bow to each graduate as they ascend. Both Moby and Brady turn and wave at us as they pass through, and my eyes fill with happy tears.

The last graduate walks through the portal, and it closes behind her. Libby throws her arms up, and confetti and glitter rain from the sky. She twirls and twirls, laughing, until she bumps into Neil and me. I've never seen her so unburdened. She winks at us. "I used to be fun, you know," she says.

She continues dancing through the crowd, and all at once I imagine I see my mother the way my dad used to see her. I wait for the sting of rejection to pierce my heart like it usually does when I think of her sending me away, but it doesn't come. And that's when I realize I've finally forgiven her.

After the ceremony Neil and I go to the Forgetting Tree.

I've thought about this moment a lot over the past few weeks. If memories make you who you are, then the Morati killed a version of me by stealing them. I'll never know how I actually died. I'll never know if Neil and I stayed together on Earth or not. I may never know the fates of my family and friends. But maybe my best memories are just waiting for me to make them. Whatever is in store for me, I can't stop it. I'll take the days of my afterlife as they come.

I materialize a scrap of paper and a pen and then write "My stolen memories" on it. Neil stands close by as I pin the paper to the tree. And then he takes hold of my hand.

Now I understand what letting go means. It means not allowing anyone else to define you, and that includes past versions of yourself. It's not about throwing away keepsakes, or distancing yourself from the people who matter, but about accepting that you're a person who's going to make mistakes sometimes, and that's okay. Mistakes don't define you. It's what you learn from them that does.

We don't erase the past. Our triumphs, our failures, our loves, our betrayals—they all provide the clarifying context that makes life more meaningful. Without our roots we might be carried off by the first wayward wind.

But we also need to realize we can fly.